# THE LAND OF
# BLOOD
# AND
# BULLETS

# THE LAND OF BLOOD AND BULLETS

## THE THIRD ADDISON J. FREEMAN STORY

## J. J. ZERR

Primix Publishing
East Brunswick Office Evolution
1 Tower Center Boulevard, Ste 1510
East Brunswick, NJ 08816
www.primixpublishing.com
Phone: 1-800-538-5788



Published by Primix Publishing: 12/18/2025

ISBN: 979-8-89194-607-1(sc)
ISBN: 979-8-89194-609-5(hc)
ISBN: 979-8-89194-608-8(e)

Library of Congress Control Number: 2025927337

I dedicated my first novel to: Those who served

This is dedicated to the spouses of those who served

It is one thing to fight for your country

And another to make your country worth fighting for

Spouses of those who served, thank you for your great service

# 1861

# 1.

The church bell clanged and jolted Addison Freeman upright in bed with his heart thumping.

His wife, Mariah, beside him, also sat up. She didn't say anything. She listened.

Addison expected, they both expected the ringing to stop, and then either one, two, three, or four distinct gongs to signal danger from either north, south, east, or west. But the clanging went on, and on, and on. The only other time such clanging had occurred had been to announce that Kansas had been admitted to the Union as a Free State. Great, good, wonderful news!

"It's pitch dark out," Mariah said.

He knew they both thought: Good news would have waited until sunup.

Little bare feet pitter-patted on the wooden floor. "I scah wote!"

Dim light spilled into the bedroom from the wick-set-low lamp in the kitchen.

"I'm scared, too, Sweetheart." Mariah swung her feet over the side of the bed and lifted her two-year-old daughter to her lap.

"Mariah!" Addison said.

"I'm pregnant! Not crippled! Put your pants on and find out what happened."

Pregnant! Mariah the healer, the closest thing to a doctor in Brotherton, tossed that make-you-blush term around as casually as "Hello. It's a lovely day, isn't it?"

Put your pants on! she said. During much of 1858, he'd slept with his pants on. Members of Found Grace Church had uprooted themselves from Illinois and traveled by wagon train to Kansas to vote that Kansas would not enter the Union as another state sanctioning the abomination of slavery. The members of Found Grace Church had transformed themselves from farmers to crusaders, Holy Crusaders. The trip had transformed Addison from a young man squirming under his father's oppressive thumb to a self-sufficient, reliable scout for the wagonloads of families trusting him to find ways to avoid or warn of trouble along their journey. He'd slept with his pants on through much of the Crusade.

After arriving in Kansas, the members of Found Grace Church had established New Found Grace Church and built the town of Brotherton. During the next year, 1859, pro-slavery factions from Kansas and Missouri mounted several attacks bent on exterminating the Illinois transplants. Round the clock and round the compass vigilance marked that year, and Addison again spent many of his nights sleeping with his pants on.

In 1860, Brotherton had finally been blessed with a respite from the fighting, and that year, most nights, he slept with his pants on the chair beside their bed.

<u>Put your pants on!</u> Her command had sent his mind on a meander over the last couple of years. The meander had taken about five ticks and four tocks. Now, the command came back. It spurred him to act and follow his wife's orders.

In his own way.

Socks, pants, boots, shirt, hat, belt gun. Then, though it was a short hike to the Meeting House, he saddled Outlaw and took a long gun as well. A few extra minutes here could save a bunch of them later.

Second Street was packed with people, mostly men. They all wore pants. Some of the women wore them as well.

Actually, they wore Eunice Skirts. Early in the Holy Crusade, the Found Grace Church wagon train came to Thompson Township, Illinois, a town filled with rabid anti-abolitionist sentiment. Joshua Reedley, the wagon master, had judged the townsmen as having itchy trigger fingers, but he thought they would be reluctant to cut loose on a gaggle of women. He asked a handful of the wives and daughters to lead the wagon train into the town.

Reedley got more than enough volunteers and picked four to ride in front of the wagons. One of the four, Eunice Carlson, was a good seamstress, and she taught the other women how to split a skirt and sew it back together to create baggy-legged pants. The women sewed, then rode astride, not sidesaddle, ahead of the wagons to meet gunmen blocking the road. The wagon master had been right. The men of the town had not wanted to shoot women. But the mounted women made it clear they'd shoot the men if they did not clear out of the way.

The men and women crusaders, and now, citizens of Brotherton, had learned to keep their pants ready to hand. If they didn't sleep in them.

The bell in the tower of New Found Grace Church, located on Second Street, stopped clanging. The men, and the few women, jamming Second Street and flowing toward the Meeting House stopped also, but when no further clangs sounded, the crowd set off again, their mumbled voices buzzing above them like a cloud of "No see 'em" insects.

Even in the predawn darkness, and responding to the church bell summons, it was amazing to see this mass of people and realize how Brotherton had grown in just … three years.

In 1858, the Holy Crusade traveled three days into Kansas from Atchison before selecting the spot for their new home. Otto Vogelsang sketched out a map of a town on a scrap of lumber. Main, Second, and Third Streets accommodated the Found Grace Church families, and a handful of Illinois families who'd joined the wagon train as it passed through their towns.

In addition, the Emigrant Aid Society had funded the movement of east coast abolitionist voters to Kansas for the same purpose that drove Found Grace Church to the spot: become Kansas residents and cast ballots so the state entered the Union as free, not sanctioning the abomination of slavery. Preacher Cromwell's congregation, an east coast version of Found Grace Church, accepted the Emigrant Aid Society's invitation, and funding, and swelled the population of Brotherton such that the new preacher's church was built on Sixth Street.

As amazing as the growth of the town had been, the transformation of its citizens during their fight for survival was equally astounding. After the citizens of Brotherton fought off a number of pro-slavery raids against the settlement, Preacher Cromwell, a dyed-in-the-wool anti-violence advocate and practitioner, had decided he could not let other people do his fighting for his well-being and took up a rifle. Equally flabbergasting, Mariah had as well.

And now the church bell summoned them to meet another emergency.

Lord, be with us.

Addison climbed aboard Outlaw and directed him around his house to Main Street, which was clear of people, though the boardwalk was full of pedestrians. Outlaw cantered them to the center of town, where Addison put his horse in the pen behind his mother's house.

At the main entrance to the Meeting House, a jam of people funneled inside. Addison walked around the crowd and along the C Street side of the building and entered through the kitchen.

Outside, the talking had been a buzz. Inside the hall, with a roof to corral the voices, the buzz had become a roar.

"Hey! Hold it down," Mayor Gallant Argyl shouted from the raised platform centered on the wall opposite the kitchen.

The people froze in place. They stopped talking. For a moment.

Then, the flow of bodies recommenced as did the jibber-jabber, beginning as that buzz again, but growing rapidly.

"Shut up!" the mayor hollered. "Shut. Up! Anybody who keeps talking will be shoved outside, and you won't be let back in."

The Meeting House was set up for a communal dinner, with rows and rows of tables. The crowd filed down the center aisle and around the tables at the center of the space, near the speaker platform.

Addison hurried across the room and sidled down the side of the hall to where the mayor stood with Preachers Larrimer and Cromwell, and Ziggy Hostetler.

Ziggy ran freight wagons from Atchison to the center of the state. He was also the best source of news for Brotherton. Riverboats conveyed goods and people—and news—to the Kansas border, as did railroad lines that terminated at the Missouri River. Sometimes, the information Ziggy's wagons carted was worth more than the supplies. This, obviously, was one of those times.

Addison reached the speaker's platform. "Mayor, you need any errands run?"

"No. Joshua Reedley and Marshal McTavish are notifying the lookouts of the news."

Since the Holy Crusade first arrived, they had manned, and womaned, four lookout posts at the corners of what became Brotherton. During the first two years, those lookouts had saved Brotherton time and time again. Now, though, after a year of no anti-abolitionist attacks every couple of months, someone proposed eliminating the posts. Joshua Reedley always insisted, "The pro-slavers didn't attack us the past twelve months, but they still hate us. This is no time to relax our vigilance."

The town council had always, to this point, heeded his advice.

The mayor had turned back to Ziggy.

Deputy Town Marshal Addison Freeman hoped he might get the news early. He sighed and worked his way to the rear of the hall. There, he found Jibway Jim seated at one of the tables.

Jibway was a member of the Ojibway tribe. He and Addison had become blood brothers while scouting for Ziggy Hostetler's wagon trains.

Addison sat next to him and nodded a "Good morning."

The Indian had gone to a missionary school in his youth. He spoke better English than most of those around him, yet occasionally, he reverted to speech according to "The way white man think I should talk." He said, "How."

Addison always shook his head at such tomfoolery. Especially since Jibway did it quite often in the midst of a tense situation.

"Is Maybell feeling better?" Addison asked.

His blood brother's head twitched. Addison knew that meant "No."

Jibway's wife, Maybell, was with child. She was a Negro and formerly the slave of a sheriff with an office in Prairietown, located halfway between Brotherton and Lawrence. The sheriff had sent raiders against Brotherton soon after the Holy Crusade started building the town. The raiders had been repulsed, and the men of New Found Grace Church girded their loins for battle and attacked the sheriff. In the fight, the sheriff was killed and his slaves, including Maybell, were emancipated.

Maybell was a slip of a woman, standing five feet tall and weighing about one hundred pounds soaking wet. Yet, she had proved herself to be the toughest woman in Brotherton.

One of Jibway's pigtails had slipped over his shoulder, and he nudged it back. "The wife, it's funny. She always handled whatever life threw at her, but now she carries a baby, and this tiny little person has beat her into submission."

Addison admired his blood brother, and he admired Maybell. He was happy they'd found each other. Both were aliens, of a sort, in a white man's world. Both had stood up to the prejudice and refused to cower to those attitudes.

Addison continued, "Mariah suffered some stomach upset, but it didn't last long. Please, God, Maybell gets over it soon."

The mayor banged on a chunk of wood atop the speaker podium with a hammer. "Preacher Larrimer, would you lead us in a prayer?"

Larrimer, the preacher of Found Grace Church, had launched the Holy Crusade. He rose from his chair. Even at this ungodly hour, the man of God wore his dark suit and blazing white shirt. He raised his eyes toward the ceiling. "God of heaven, God of earth, be with us, Lord, as You have been through our journey to Brotherton, through our battles against the abomination of slavery. Abide with us as we face our future. In Your holy name, we pray."

"Amen!"

The mayor said, "Ziggy, tell them why we rang the bell so early in the morning."

About dad-burned time, Addison thought.

Hostetler rose from his chair against the wall. He rubbed a hand over his bald head, then swiped it down over his bushy beard. The look on his face appeared to Addison as: Oh! That's whar my har's got to. Then, Ziggy's dark eyes flashed a bolt of rage, like it did as he reached for his whip to administer encouragement to the haunch of a lazy mule pulling his wagon.

Ziggy sucked in a lungful and let it out. "Some southren states have pulled out'ta the Union. They attacked a Union fort. That means we're in a war!"

# 2.

Ziggy, in his raise-the-roof voice, declared, "We're in a war! Have been in one fer two weeks now."

Hear-a-pin-drop silence lasted a tick and a tock; then pandemonium cut loose.

War? Vote to have Kansas enter the Union as a free state. That was supposed to be the end of it. And for the last year, it seemed like that might be the case. But, "We're in a war!" Ziggy said. Now, half the nation was at war with the other half. It was hard to contemplate how much worse this war would be compared to fighting packs of pro-slavery gunmen for two years. "We're in a war!" And it took two weeks for the news to reach Brotherton!

Addison's eyes moved to Mayor Gallant Argyl. He stood behind Ziggy. The mayor's head nodded ever so slightly, at about a head dip a second. After perhaps ten of those tiny nods, he moved Ziggy aside, picked up the hammer, and beat on the chunk of wood resting atop the podium.

Throughout the hall, men began to "Shush!" others. The pandemonium ebbed to a roar, which ebbed to a buzz and finally snuffed. Till only the hammer whanged; then it stopped.

"Sit down!" the mayor barked.

Everyone sat. Except Sylvan Waverly.

Sylvan had been a deacon in Found Grace Church. When Preacher Larrimer launched the Holy Crusade with half the congregation, Waverly had been left in charge of the stay-behinds. One of his responsibilities had been to arrange for the sale of the farms of the entire congregation, and then, when summoned, bring the proceeds of the sale and the rest of the families to the new settlement in Kansas. Waverly, though he'd never voiced opposition, or even disagreement, with Preacher Larrimer's crusade, saw opportunity in the departure of the crusaders. If the stay-behinds stayed behind forever, in effect, each of them would see the size of their farms doubled. Including his own.

The mayor roared, "Sit down, Waverly!"

The man stayed on his feet. His wife, Adele, on the chair next to his empty one, pulled on his arm. He jerked it free. "I have something to say, and I'm saying it. Then, I'll sit down."

The former deacon's behavior surprised Addison.

Early in the Crusade, when the wagon train came to Thompson Township, and after the Crusaders had subdued the anti-abolitionists, word of Waverly's treachery back at Found Grace Church reached the wagon train. Joshua Reedley took Addison with him, and they rode back to the starting point. There, they removed Waverly from his position, installed a new deacon, and brought Waverly with them to rejoin the wagon train. Since that time, Sylvan Waverly had been quiet, subdued. Reedley's son Maurice, also called Maurice the Wiseacre, said of him, "Waverly's so quiet, he wouldn't utter a peep if he was a chicken and the biggest, hungriest hawk in the world was diving right for him."

Until Maurice said that of the man, Addison had considered Waverly as almost invisible. Perhaps, he thought, forgettable is the better word. He was quiet, always in the background, never in front. Forgettable.

"All right, Waverly, say your piece," the mayor growled, "but make it quick."

"To get here," Forgettable said, "we had to fight our way across Illinois, Missouri, and half of Kansas."

*We? You didn't lift a finger to help us fight for our lives!*

"Then we had to fight for a year and a half to stay here. And that was not in a time of war. All we had to do was defend ourselves against bands of ruffians, not an army. Brotherton is out here in the middle of nowhere. With nobody close enough to help us."

"Waverly!" the mayor bellowed. "Sit. Down!"

"I'm not done—"

"You are done. Deputy Marshal Freeman. Take Waverly to jail and lock him in a cell. Maurice Reedley, help the deputy, and stay there with the prisoner. Freeman, you come back as soon as you lock him up."

All the way to the jail on Sixth Street, Waverly continued to rant that Missouri was pro-slavery and hated us because the Emigrant Aid Society sent a lot of settlers into Kansas to vote for the state entering the Union as free. And that had happened, but most of the other Aid Society pilgrims had been spread around the state. "But Brotherton," Waverly shouted, "is the only town that is one hundred percent Emigrant Aid Society. Missouri will think it's our fault the state went anti-slavery."

Waverly was wrong about that. Establishing Brotherton had been all Preacher Larrimer's idea. Furthermore, Lawrence, Kansas, was founded and settled by anti-slavery east coast pilgrims before Found Grace Church launched its Crusade. But Addison acknowledged that where hate is involved, a thing didn't have to make sense before bullets started flying.

Addison also knew pockets of abolitionists and of pro-slavery zealots dotted Kansas. That Missouri would single out Brotherton and send an army against it, so far from the border, rather than attack other closer targets seemed a bit far-fetched. But then he thought further about it.

From the end of 1858 through most of '59, was it far-fetched to think there'd be one rich, rabid anti-prohibitionist in western

Missouri who'd spend his fortune paying gang after gang of gunmen to wipe out Brotherton? As objectively as he could make himself think about it, the idea did seem far-fetched. But that is exactly what had happened. Once the Brotherton folks discovered and eliminated that rich, rabid apostle of the pro-slavery religion, peace visited their town.

Waverly may not have been one hundred percent right, but what he said merited some consideration.

Still, Addison was relieved to depart the jail, consign Waverly to being invisible again, and head back to the Meeting House. As he walked, he thought about Brotherton.

Brotherton citizens all owned plots of farmland, but the farms were outside the town to the west, north, and east. None of the plots had a house on them. Everyone lived in town for mutual protection. Likewise, all the horses and cows were corralled together in communal pens and a large barn north of Eighth Street. That had been Otto Vogelsang's idea. Then he laid out a compact and orderly town. Main, Second, Third, Fourth, Fifth, Sixth, Seventh, and Eighth Streets ran east/west. A and D Streets formed the east and west boundaries of the settlement. Preacher Larrimer's New Found Grace Church sat at the center of Main Street. Preacher Cromwell's church sat on Sixth Street. B and C streets ran down the sides of the churches.

Orderly and compact. That was Brotherton, and the layout had served them well their first two years in Kansas. Now, however, "We're in a war!" Ziggy had said.

War meant armies. Armies had cannons. In that realization, the compact and orderly arrangement of their new home seemed tailor-made for total destruction by cannon fire.

Addison's mind revisited Thompson Township again. There, he'd had to shoot and kill three men. He'd had to, to save others. Joshua Reedley had helped him find a way to carry that burden. Now, war, cannons, the taking of lives by … the dozen, who was there to help find a way to carry that kind of burden?

Preacher Larrimer's prayer: "Abide with us as we face our future." Yeah, verily, Lord!

Addison entered The Meeting House through the kitchen.

"Deputy," the mayor said. "Just in time."

Reedley and Sheriff McTavish stood on the platform against the wall. Addison remained where he was.

"We're going to discuss security measures for Brotherton," the mayor said. He seemed to be organizing his thoughts. For a moment. "Neighboring Missouri is officially committed to the Union, but we know many of its citizens heavily favor the South, including the governor of the state. Kansas is calling for volunteers to serve in militia and cavalry units. Before I ask if anyone wants to volunteer—"

Orson Seiling cut the mayor off and jumped to his feet. "I'm the first Kansas Militia Volunteer from Brotherton. Who's with me?"

Eight other young men stood with: "I'll go;" "Me, too;" "Count me in."

Addison stayed rooted and silent. He glanced at Jibway. His blood brother sat statue still.

Orson stood next to the center aisle, a couple of rows in from the front doors. He faced Addison. "You're not volunteering? Maybe you're afraid."

Orson sneered at Addison, like a school bully. "Fraidy cat, fraidy cat!"

The standing volunteers snickered.

Orson Seiling!

Before the Crusade, Addison had been in love with Lizbeth Waverly. Orson had married her, though. Then, Orson had traveled with the first half of Found Grace Church to Kansas while Lizbeth remained behind. As the Crusade crossed Illinois, additional families joined the wagon train. One of the families was Mariah's. Addison had been attracted to her. She, however, had been attracted to Orson, and they began a clandestine relationship that lasted until the crusaders began building their new town. Then Orson got Mariah in the family way. He couldn't marry her because he was already married. So, Addison convinced Mariah that she should marry him.

"I love you enough for the two of us," he'd told her.

She had appreciated that he had saved her and the baby from shame, but also came to appreciate that she loved her husband so much more deeply than the surface affection she'd experienced with Orson Seiling.

During all the fighting in Brotherton's first year of existence, Orson had matured, had come around. During that year, Lizbeth had died of consumption, and Orson had remarried. He'd wed Lorelei Belmont from Preacher Cromwell's congregation. The battle for Brotherton's survival had begun maturing Orson, the aggravating juvenile. Matrimony finished the job.

So Addison had thought.

Orson Seiling!

Addison remembered something Jibway had told him: "Maturity in some has the lifespan of a butterfly."

Orson said, "Still afraid to volunteer, Addison?"

Addison looked down at the floor for a moment, raised his head again, put on a smile, and headed down the center aisle for his antagonist, boot heels clunking on the hardwood floor.

Orson's sneer melted.

Addison stopped close in front of Orson and stared at him.

Orson frowned, then looked around, as if wondering if his fellow volunteers would come to help him.

Orson leaned back and raised his hands in front of his face.

Addison brushed the hands aside and gently patted Orson on the cheek. "You nailed me, Orson. I am a fraidy cat, and for sure, I am not a brave patriot such as you proved to be since the start of the Holy Crusade."

Addison continued down the aisle and out the door onto Second Street. As he retrieved Outlaw, Jibway rode up on his big black.

"Why don't you see if Maybell is well enough to come for lunch?" Addison asked.

# 3.

Maybell said, "Mariah, Addison, thanks for inviting me to break-lunch."

Addison was pretty sure that meant she had not eaten yet that day. She leaned forward until her face hovered above her plate. Then, she wrinkled her nose at the smell of the food, sat back, and looked at Hope. Addison saw her eyes soften. He was pretty sure the emancipated woman was going to say something harsh and biting to him, but the child's presence seemed to remove the hard edges of what she was thinking.

Maybell's words weren't soft, however. "So, Addison, you decided not to volunteer for the militia because Mariah is going to have a baby. Then you talked Jibway into staying here because I'm carrying one also?"

Jibway began, "That's not—"

"Hush!" Maybell glanced at the child again. Hope had picked up a green bean and bit off the end. "I want to hear what Addison has to say."

Addison found Mariah staring at him. *Are you enjoying seeing me squirm?*

He'd considered saying to her, "You are carrying our baby." But that bore the implication that Hope was not theirs, rather, she was Mariah's and Orson Seiling's. There was a strong impetus to get his mouth talking, to get himself out of the single hot sunbeam Maybell had focused on him.

"Mariah. You are my wife. You are carrying a brother or sister for our first child. Nothing on earth is more precious to me than the three of you. Protecting you, keeping you safe, those are things God expects me to do for you. For us.

"Maybell. Slavery is an abomination. It is an evil in our land. I do not want that evil to be something Hope and our new little one, our new little ones, have to face. It is my duty to protect my family. It is my duty to protect my blood brother and his family. It is my duty to protect Brotherton. What I see at this moment, while Orson and others are rushing off to the border to join the militia, some of us need to stay here until we see what being at war means for Brotherton."

Maybell said, "Huh." She picked up her fork, scooped up a smidgeon of mashed potatoes, placed it in her mouth, grimaced, and swallowed. For a moment, a question hovered over her. Was the bite going to stay down? It did, and lunch-fast proceeded in a civilized manner.

After they had eaten, Addison offered to change Hope and get her ready for a nap. Mariah said, "Maybell and I will do it."

Addison and Jibway took chairs and cups of coffee to the front porch. They sat and sipped.

"War," Jibway said. "In missionary school, we learned of a promised land that would flow with milk and honey. This land flows with blood and bullets."

Addison frowned. During much of 1859, both Preachers, Larrimer and Cromwell, ended their services with a prayer for peace. God had granted what they prayed for, but now He wanted Brotherton to pay for that year of peace by suffering through a war!

Jibway stared at Addison as if he was reading what his blood brother was thinking. He said, "Blood Brother, you one silver-tongued white man. Maybell accused you of failing to do your duty. You replied with the only words that could get you off the hook. You could talk stripe off skunk. Would be better, though, next time you talk to skunk, talk stink out of him."

Addison hadn't seen it this way before. Not only was a blood brother's life more important than your own, but a blood brother's soul was also more important than one's own. Addison prayed: Thank You Great Spirit, Father, God, Lord of heaven and earth for sending Jibway into my life. And forgive me for questioning your ways. Then he said, "Maybell is a tougher, fiercer warrior than most of the men of Brotherton. It seems strange to watch her around Hope."

"It is as if Maybell is not only carrying an infant, she is also growing inside herself the infant soul of a mother."

"You one silver-tongued Injun, Blood Brother."

The two raised their cups as if both arms were driven by a single mind.

Addison looked down Main Street, toward the center of town. There was no one about. "I wonder if the meeting is still going on."

"Maybe the mayor decided to throw a lunch-fast for everybody."

Addison said, "I'm not sure you should have told the women what Orson said to me. What those two might come up with to get back at him, well, that worries me."

"You may not be sure, but I am. Maybell was going to find out, and when she did, and she knew I was there in the Meeting House and did not tell her, there would have been hell to pay in Jibway Jim's house."

Addison nodded and said, "Yeah," as if the statement needed double affirmation.

Jibway. The most self-sufficient man on earth. Until the people of Brotherton buried the sheriff of Prairietown and freed his slaves, and he married Maybell.

Then it was as if Maybell, once the chains of slavery were cast off, needed the ability to stand on her own two feet, didn't know how, married Jibway, and took his self-reliance. Of course, it hadn't been like that. Jibway did not have his independence taken from him. He gave it up to her. And, on her side, she didn't need Jibway's strength, she leaned on his for a time; then she developed her own. And once she learned to shoot a pistol, as long as she drew breath, no man would ever make a slave of her again.

"What are you smiling about, Addison?"

"Jibway, is it all right with you if I ask Maybell to be my blood sister?"

"Blood Sister?" He shook his head. "Easier to understand a squaw than to understand white man." Jibway rubbed his chin, in a very white man way. "Yes, it is okay with me, but only if it is okay with you If I ask Mariah to be my blood sister."

At the sound of hoofbeats, both looked to the right. Just past the church, a rider had turned his bronc onto Main Street and headed for them.

"Reedley's horse," Addison said.

"Joshua's riding it."

They both turned to their left. Jibway had taught him to: "Always check behind you, especially when something in front of you has latched onto your attention hard."

They saw no threat and turned back. Reedley was halfway to them, horse at a canter.

"Wonder if the meeting's over?" Addison said.

"No. He's come to fetch us."

Reedley reined up. "Need you two to come back to the Meeting House."

"I'll tell Mariah we're leaving."

"She's already there."

"What?"

"Maybell's there, too. Come."

Addison looked at his blood brother. Jibway shrugged, the way white men did sometimes. Then, he untied the reins of his big black, swung up onto the saddle, and headed toward the church at a gallop. Addison followed. Reedley ate their dust.

When the men took their coffees to the front porch, Mariah,

Maybell, and Hope had left the house by the side door and walked down Second Street, taking turns carrying the child. At the Meeting House, they entered through the kitchen. Hope rode on her mother's hip.

There was a fair amount of commotion in the room as women cleared plates from tables. Mariah scanned the room and spotted Orson. He stared at her as she wended her way through the plate gatherers until she faced him. Then, she turned and handed her daughter to Maybell.

Orson was on his feet when she turned around again and slapped him, hard.

He raised a hand to his cheek. Surprise, chagrin, and a few other shame-laced emotions flitted across his face, to be replaced by cunning.

"I was right about him. He's afraid to face me and sends his wife."

Maybell grabbed Mariah's shoulder, pulled her back, and thrust Hope at her with, "Take her."

Wisp of a woman Maybell balled a fist and shot it up at Orson's chin as he flinched. The fist caught his nose. There was a snap, like when you break a deadwood twig.

Addison and Jibway learned all that from Marshal McTavish in the office in a corner of the Meeting House. The mayor, Reedley, Marshal McTavish, and Preacher Larrimer were there as well.

The preacher said, "Addison, after Orson insulted you, the way you handled it showed fortitude, forbearance, faith in the Lord to guide you righteously. Aside from a handful of misguided youth, vaulted into prominence with no idea as to how to handle it, no one in Brotherton doubts your bravery. You handled that situation as well as anyone of us could have hoped."

"Right," the mayor said. "After you left, Ziggy told us he and his wagons had been commandeered by the Union army. We can run our own supply wagons, but what we'll miss is Hostetler's news. Ziggy has promised to put Mr. Reedley here in touch with his informants."

"Hopefully," Marshal McTavish said, "Joshua can get those sources to trust him as well as they trust Ziggy."

"Addison and Jibway," Reedley said, "will you come with me?"

Jibway said, "Yes, Joshua Reedley, we will ride with you."

"Mr. Mayor," Addison said, "have you decided what to do about Sylvan Waverly?"

Gallant Argyl replied. "We have settled on a way to deal with the mature but irresponsible Sylvan Waverly and another to deal with the immature and irresponsible Orson Seiling."

Addison thought about the answer. He nodded. "One more thing, Mr. Mayor. Mariah and Hope will be by themselves there on the east end of town. Can you have someone move them to where they are safe, please?"

The mayor smiled. "That, too, is already taken care of."

Addison listened to the mayor's plan; then he bolted out of his chair. "What? Maybell is moving in with Mariah, and you're putting Sylvan Waverly in the end house on Second Street? And he's to protect them?"

Jibway pulled Addison's arm until he sat back down.

The mayor said, "Mariah and Maybell decided to stay in your house."

"We'll be gone about a week," Reedley said. "Week and a half at the most."

The mayor kept his eyes on Addison as he put his hand on Reedley's arm. "Maybell and Mariah do not want to be treated as if they are helpless and crippled."

Addison wanted to shout: But that's what they are! And Maybell with them, too sick to even eat, made them more vulnerable. While it was true that pro-slaver attacks had come from all directions, east still seemed the most dangerous. Pro-slavers and abolitionist haters lived in that direction. Then having the traitor Waverly there as protection—

"Addison," Marshall McTavish said, "I will ensure the women and your daughter are safe. If you do not trust me with that responsibility, you don't have to accompany Joshua. It is just that you, Jibway, and Reedley work so well together."

Addison's chin dropped onto his chest. He sucked in a big breath and huffed it out, along with a bit of his bellyful of indignation. "Jibway said we'd ride with him."

Reedley stood. "Ziggy's already left. I'm going after him. You two get your gear and catch up."

When Addison stopped by his house to gather his bedroll, Mariah and Hope were there. "Daddy," Hope said, and it struck him like the sword of grief that pierced the mother of Jesus' heart.

Mariah said, "I know you are worried about us, but I, we, worry about you when you are away. We both have our duties. As does Maybell. She will be with us. Together, we will watch out for each other. And Maybell, when we decided she'd move in with us, it cured her nausea. She gobbled down a whole plate of leftovers at the Meeting House before she went to get her things to come here."

Arguing further, he knew, would be pointless. War. The worst thing about it was this war gave him too much time to think. Since the start of the Holy Crusade began, he'd faced … many dangers. With almost every one of them, there had been no time to think, only time for immediate reaction.

He embraced his wife, kissed her, knelt, and kissed her tummy. Then he kissed Hope on the forehead. He rose and headed for the door.

"Bye, bye, Daddy," twisted the sword of grief piercing his heart. He stopped with his hand on the doorknob for a moment. Then he left.

# 4.

Jibway had also left ahead of him. Addison rode past the hidden lookout post without looking in its direction. At the Delaware River ferry crossing, he and Outlaw rafted across. He didn't want his horse expending energy swimming.

On the east bank, Addison mounted and set off down the road to Atchison at a canter. Instantly, he was transported into an 1859 watchfulness. There was no war, or armies with cannons to threaten him, but there was the possibility of pro-slavery ambushers hidden along the two ruts gouged out of the prairie grass by iron-rimmed wagon wheels.

Addison said, "I'm sure my lookout skills have gotten rusty, Outlaw. Have yours?"

The horse kept to his pace and didn't answer.

Maybe ninety minutes earlier, Ziggy had passed this way. He always employed scouts. Reedley and Jibway had ridden this way also. If bushwhackers hid beside the road, odds were good the two of them would have found them. Still, he watched for pro-slavers while Outlaw ate miles.

Addison rode for forty-five minutes, then walked beside his horse for fifteen.

"A reasonable division of labor, eh, Outlaw?"

Outlaw snorted.

They traveled that way for three hours. Addison turned in the saddle to check the sun. It sat as a ball of red-orange fire just above the end of the world. As he turned front again, Outlaw stopped. The horse stared slightly to the right of the wheel ruts. Addison pulled his long gun from the saddle holster. To the right, in the distance, the tall prairie grass was disturbed. His eyes wanted to stay there, focused on that something-is-not-right-there indicator, but he forced them to move to the left of the road.

To the left of the road and twenty-five yards ahead, a man rose out of the thigh-high grass. Addison aimed his rifle without taking the time to raise the butt up against his shoulder and cocked the hammer.

The man had his hands up. He said, "You just might make a decent Injun someday. In the distant future, of course."

"Jibway! I was this close—Addison jerked his finger away from the trigger and raised his thumb and index finger—held about an eighth of an inch apart—to pulling the trigger!"

"If I had my hands up, I was pretty sure you wouldn't shoot me."

Father God, Who art in heaven! I was this close to shooting my blood brother, and he was pretty sure I wouldn't.

Then Addison understood. Jibway was worried his blood brother's mind was so focused on Mariah and the baby, he wouldn't see danger even it was a Conestoga wagon coming right at him right down the middle of the road with the driver whipping the team and hollering to wake the dead and trailing a cloud of dust that looked like a tornado that decided to lay down for a nap.

"Okay to lower my hands?"

Addison shook his head side-to-side, but he meant yes.

Jibway lowered his hands.

Addison returned his rifle to the saddle scabbard. "Thanks."

Jibway nodded his head once. It meant: Think nothing of it.

Both of them also knew Addison would do a lot of thinking about what had just happened.

They caught up to the wagons as the men were dousing their cooking fires. Ziggy liked to stop for a rest and a hot meal before the sun set. At night, a campfire showed a long way over the flat prairie. Unless there was a mighty good reason, Ziggy always stopped at this creek. Hostetler's men called it the Ziggy Ditch.

"We kept some grub fer ya," Ziggy said. "Best get to it. We're fixing to leave shortly."

Two men unsaddled Outlaw and Jibway's big black and led them to water. Addison and Jibway sat on wagon tongues to eat. The mules and horses had been watered, hobbled, and left to graze as the men cooked. Now, as the two late comers ate, the men rounded up the animals, saddled the riding stock, and harnessed teams.

Joshua Reedley and a Hostetler man had departed earlier to scout ahead of the train. Addison and Jibway were to sleep in one of the wagons for four hours. Then they were to take over the lead scout duties.

The blood brothers woke when the wagons stopped. The animals needed to rest a spell, and the sleepers and scouts needed to trade roles.

Jibway rode fifty yards in front of Addison for thirty minutes. Then Addison rode out front for the same period.

The stars in the moonless sky seemed to glory in having the whole place to themselves. The stars had so much happy glow, each of them spilled some on earth. Addison looked behind him. Jibway's silhouette stood out, dark black and sharply defined.

He thought: *I'm a bushwhacker. How would I take Jibway and me out?*

*What I'd do is take my long gun, line up the front and back sights just to the side of Jibway's silhouette, where the starlit backdrop would enable me to see the sights. Then I'd move the barrel ever so slightly to the center of the dark shape and squeeze. I'd try a hundred-yard shot on Jibway. Then I'd shoot me as I tried to ride away. If I were a bushwhacker, I could kill both of us.*

With all the starlight, it was daylight dangerous. Addison gigged Outlaw into a gallop and doubled the distance of his lead. Then, he settled his mount into a walk again. Behind him, Jibway had allowed the space between them to increase. He'd understood. With this spacing, the lead rider was in a bit more danger, but the possibility that they could both be killed was lessened considerably.

Addison took no comfort in having worked out the better spacing. Rather, he chided himself for not realizing it right away. He also appreciated his blood brother anew. Jibway would have seen the necessity for the greater spacing, but he'd wanted Addison to figure it out on his own.

The watch passed uneventfully, and the blood brothers slept in a wagon again. When they were rousted to take their next turn to scout, it would be just before dawn, and they'd be riding into the rising sun.

But Ziggy had a different plan. He delayed stopping until after the sun was above the horizon. Then he halted the train, and his crew watered and set the animals to grazing as others lit cook fires. By the time they set out again, the sun would be high enough it wouldn't be quite as blinding as just after its rise. After they had eaten, and as Addison saddled Outlaw, he watched Ziggy's crew unhobble mules and draft horses and lead them, two by two, to the wagons. Men harnessed teams. Others doused fires and stowed skillets and coffee pots. No one got in anyone else's way. Even the animals cooperated in the orderly breaking of camp.

"Look!" Jibway pointed to the southeast. A column of smoke rose into the blue sky, leaning to the east. "Probably three miles."

Reedley said. "Ziggy, give me two of your men. I'll take Addison and Jibway. We'll ride down the road to Atchison till we're due north of that smoke. Then Jibway. Addison, and I will see what's burning. Your two will scout for you."

On Ziggy's wagon trains, Ziggy was boss. But, in this case, he grunted; then, "Arnold, Jasper, you go with Reedley."

When they departed the wagons, Reedley stayed on the road,

his horse at a walk. Addison and Jibway rode on his flanks. Arnold and Jasper trailed them by a hundred yards.

As Addison rode out on the northern flank, the brim of his hat was useless as a shield from the low-slung and eyeball-frying sun. All of them would be blind looking directly ahead. The way Reedley had spread them out, though, each of them could cover the blind spots of his partners. Somewhat. But, somewhat was better than not at all. And, as usual, the winds were from behind them rendering Outlaw nose-blind as well.

Addison dredged up some of his math lessons. Three miles to the smoke was the long side of a triangle. They'd have to ride down the road a bit more than two, but less than three. As Outlaw clip clopped them along, Addison kept his head turned to his right and his hand raised to shield himself from the vision-denying intensity of the ball of fire.

They came to the point where the smoke column was off Addison's shoulder, and due south. Roughly.

Reedley kept his horse plodding along, however.

Then Addison understood. If anyone were still there at that fire, the sun would be in their eyes—somewhat—as the Reedley crew approached.

When Joshua stopped, Addison figured they'd come at least five miles from Ziggy's camp. Reedley reined his horse around till it was pointed southwest. Then, he hand-signaled Jibway to cross from Reedley's right to his left. Then he signaled Addison to switch sides also. Once his flankers were in their new positions, Reedley gigged his mount into a trot, headed right for the smoke.

They rode for about a mile when Reedley stopped and motioned the other two to come to him.

"Jibway, take your long gun and proceed on foot. I'll follow you by a hundred yards. Addison, you lead Jibway's bronc and trail me."

Once again, Addison chided himself for not thinking of the best way to approach their target on his own. The year of peaceful living had dulled his senses and instincts, and they were coming back to him way too slowly.

*But thank You, God, for Joshua and my blood brother!*

As soon as they set off again, ahead, at least two hundred yards, Addison spotted a figure pop up out of the grass and raise a long gun to his shoulder.

Jibway's rifle boomed, and the figure fell.

Reedley gigged his horse into an all-out run. Close to where the man had fallen, another figure popped up and lit out toward the smoke. Addison let go of the reins to Jibway's black and said, "Outlaw," and his mount charged after Joshua.

Blood Brother's shrill whistle sliced through the sound of hooves and grass swishing past. Addison didn't have to turn and look to know that the black was running toward its rider.

Reedley came up on the runner and kicked him in the back. The man's arms flew up, and he fell on his face. Addison raced by the sprawled unmoving body. Jibway would take care of him.

Now Addison could make out the source of the smoke. The remnants of a barn. A couple of sheds stood beyond the barn. A one-story house was to the right of the ruins. Two men ran out the front door. One had his arms full of blankets. The other jerked a woman, a girl, by the arm alongside him.

Blanket Man shifted his load to one arm, drew a pistol, and fired.

Reedley hauled back on the reins, and his mount squatted and skidded to a stop. Blanket Man fired again. As did the one with the girl. Reedley raised his long gun and fired as Addison and Outlaw raced past.

Blanket Man dropped his armful; then he dropped.

The one with the girl fired at Addison. Addison shot his pistol, aiming high. He didn't want to risk hitting the young girl, but he wanted the bullet to scare her captor. It did. The man released her and tore off around the corner of the house.

As he neared fallen Blanket Man, Addison hauled back on the reins, and Outlaw skidded to a stop. Addison jumped to the ground, ran to the house, shifted his pistol to his left hand, removed his hat, and peered around the corner.

The man had his pistol aimed. Addison jerked back as a bullet tore splinters from where his head had been. He immediately stepped forward with his handgun extended and fired as the man was thumb cocking his. Addison tried not to kill him. The bullet struck its target on the right side, causing him to drop his weapon and spin half around. Addison ran to the man, grabbed the back of his shirt, smashed him face-first into the side of the house, and flung him face-first to the ground. Addison took the man's second belt gun and a knife and tossed them beside his dropped weapon. Then, he pulled off the man's boots and found a derringer in one and a knife in the other.

Addison knelt on the prone, moaning man's back and scanned all around for more threats. Four saddle broncs stood, ground-hitched at the rear of the house. Odds were good that with four men down, the threat had been neutralized. Still, it didn't cost much to check.

*All clear.*

Addison stood and hauled his prisoner to his feet. When he stood, he moaned. "Take it easy. I'm hurt bad."

Three scratch marks lined the bushwhacker's cheek. "I am taking it easy. Like you were taking it easy on the girl."

Addison held a pistol in his right and a handful of the man's shirt in his left, and he shoved his prisoner toward the front corner of the house. The man took a step and stopped.

"I'm hurt bad."

Addison kneed the man's leg, and he went down hard onto his wounded side. He screamed. Addison pulled off one of the screamer's socks.

"Open your mouth!"

The supine wounded glared at his captor with hatred and defiance.

"Open your mouth." Addison tapped the man's nose with the barrel of his pistol. "Or I'm going to bust your nose. Then, I'm going to get this sock into your mouth. And, you know, you might not be able to breath. What with your mouth full of sock and your nose full of blood."

It was as if someone lit a lamp of fear light in each eye. The mouth opened, the sock went in, and Addison jerked his prisoner to his feet and shoved him around the corner of the house.

Reedley held the girl in his arms as she sobbed. Jibway stood behind the man Reedley had kicked to the ground.

Joshua said, "Find out who these bushwhackers are," and he led the girl inside the house.

# 5.

Jibway cocked his head to the side and rubbed his chin. As if
puzzling something beyond his mental reach. "Joshua Reedley
say to find bushwhacker names. Yours have sock in mouth. He tell
name by sign language, maybe?"

Addison shook his head at his blood brother. "The one you shot?"

"Dead." With the barrel of his rifle, Jibway prodded the one
Reedley had kicked next to the one Joshua had shot. "Him dead,
too." Harder this time, he jabbed his prisoner in the back. "Name!"

Addison's prisoner ripped the sock from his mouth. "Don't tell
'em nothing!"

Freeman smashed his fist into the wounded man's ear, and he
went down screaming.

Addison pulled his knife, knelt beside the screamer, and pressed
the tip of the big blade beneath the man's right eye.

Between a tick and a tock, the yowl went from hurt-your-ears to
utter silence. Yowler's body went rigid. Again, fear light shone from
the wide-open eyes.

Addison thought the young man—and, he realized, all four

bushwhackers were probably less than twenty years old—had two personalities: brazen bravado and abject terror.

At the tip of the blade, a tear of blood sprouted. "Name! Or your eye!"

"Able. Able Bloom."

Jibway's prisoner volunteered, "I'm Billy Bob Nelson. The other two's Harlen Peters an' Jack Knight."

Jibway: "Why'd you shoot at us?"

Billy Bob: "That was Jack Knight. He's—was just a stupid kid."

Bloom: "He shoulda' waited. Till you got closer."

Addison: "Shut up, Able Bloom. You're bleeding. Shut up while we talk to Billy Bob. Then I'll bandage you up. If you ain't bled out by then."

Jibway: "Billy Bob, you bushwhackers from Missouri?"

"We ain't bushwhackers. We's Free Staters from North of Atchison. We was on the way south. They's fightin' down there. We was gonna join the Kansas Militia to fight agin the rebels. They's bushwhackers."

Jibway: "Why'd you attack this farm. Didn't see signs these people kept any slaves?"

"Able said he knowed these folks was rebels. They was for the South."

Addison: "So you killed them because you thought they were rebels."

Jibway: "They killed them to rob them, and that's why Jack Knight shot at Reedley. He thought we'd try to stop them."

Addison: "At least they got that right."

Jibway: "The only thing they got right."

Billy Bob, Addison noticed, grimaced and reached a hand up to his side.

Jibway. "Busted rib."

Addison: "Who else did you find here? Where are they?"

Able Bloom: "Don't say nothin'—"

Addison, still on a knee beside Able, pricked the skin beneath the eye, creating another blood tear. Able screamed and reached his good hand up toward the wound, and Addison slashed the palm. "Don't **you** say nothin' unless I ask **you** a question."

Jibway to Billy Bob: "Who else did you find here?"

"A man, a woman, and a boy. Coupla' years older'n the girl."

"What did you do to them?"

Billy Bob looked at Able Bloom. Able was looking at his hand pressed to his chest over a big blood stain. "Able said we should hang the pro-slave man. He had Jack rig a rope to the hay hoist in front of the barn. Then he put the rope around the man's neck and put him up on a horse. The woman ran at Able and scratched his face. He shot her, and the horse bolted. The boy then came at Able. Able shot him, too."

A cloud of silence so heavy Addison thought he could almost see it settled over the four men. Addison had assumed the scratches on Bloom's cheek had come from the girl.  Seconds passed.

Jibway: "Then what?"

Billy Bob: "We cut the man down and piled the three bodies on some straw inside the barn. Able poured coal oil on them and lit them on fire."

The silence again. Billy B. looked stunned. By his confession? Addison wondered, *by realizing in the admission that the sin that had been committed was as much his own as the one who did the shooting.*

Jibway: "What else?"

Billy took in a big breath and huffed it out. "We was gonna stay here and sell what we could from in the house. And there was the cows and horses and pigs and chickens. Able said we'd be fools to pass up this chance to make a stake before we went on to join the militia."

Jibway: "What about the girl?"

The girl and Reedley stepped out of the house and into the yard.

Reedley: "We don't need to talk about that now."

The girl: "They were going to take turns with me."

Addison almost said "Judas Priest," but the silence had returned, and he did not want to be the one to bust it.

That reticence did not forestay Joshua. "This is what we're going to do. By the way, this is Winifred Martin. She says we should call her

Winnie. I'll take her with me, and we'll ride back to the road and hook up with Ziggy. I want to get his thinking on this situation. Jibway, I'd like you to come along with us. You okay with that, Addison?"

Addison nodded.

Winnie reentered the house. Addison and Jibway bandaged Bloom. Besides the blood on his shirt, he'd left a puddle of it on the ground. He was too weak to stand, so they helped him to the front porch and left him in the shade there.

Reedley sent Jibway to fetch the body of the man the Indian had shot.

Addison told Reedley the names of the bushwhackers.

Reedley: "Addison, you and Billy Bob take this Harlen Peters behind the house and to the other side of the garden. Bury Peters and Knight there."

Winifred's statement of the bushwhackers' intentions had set rage to smoldering in Addison's soul. Those sparks had blossomed into a barn-consumed-by-coal-oil-fire inferno. "If they'd shot us, they would have left us for the crows to pick our bones clean."

"We ain't them, and we ain't gonna' become them!"

Addison looked down at the ground. *Judas Priest! One instant I'm too much of a sissy. The next I'm a Godless, savage heathen.*

Reedley took his hat off. "Father God, Lord of heaven and earth. Help us to discern justice and righteousness, and for **those** to be our guiding lights." He put his hat back on. "Now do what I told you."

Addison looked at Billy Bob. He held his left hand over his ribs on the other side. "I'll get … Harlen up on my shoulder. Walk in front of me."

"I'd like to help. Please. I need to help."

Addison nodded. Billy Bob walked to the dead man, bent, and grabbed one of Harlen's wrists. Addison took the other arm, and they started dragging him around the side of the house. Addison did most of the pulling, but Billy Bob gritted his teeth and contributed some effort to the job.

When they cleared the rear corner of the house, Billy B. stopped. Addison did too, but he wasn't going to turn his back on his prisoner.

He dropped the dead man's arm and took two steps farther before turning to see what had captured Billy's attention.

Two rose bushes had been planted to each side of the rear door into the house, and each plant bore different color flowers: red, pink, yellow, and white.

Billy Bob: "I ... I feel like we shot **my** maw."

The rear door of the house opened outward. Winifred stood on the stoop with a hand on the knob, and wearing a ponytail, a-bit-too-big-for-her pants and shirt, and her size work shoes. "You shot **my** maw. And Paw. And brother." Her eyes snapped to Addison. "I want to bury my family there, beyond the garden. Put the murdering trash in the ground behind the sty."

Winifred informed Addison there were shovels in the tool shed beyond the outhouse. He should take one to dig a hole for the murderers. She would dig graves for her family.

Before anyone moved, Reedley rounded the far rear corner of the house. He'd been gathering weapons.

Jibway walked his big black into the back yard. He sat behind the saddle with Jack Knight's body in front of him.

Reedley: "Winnie, do you have your things packed? I'd like to get joined up with that Hostetler wagon train."

Winnifred locked eyes with Joshua. "I'm going to bury my family. Then I'll decide what I'm going to do."

Addison, just a few minutes ago, had seen the girl in Reedley's arms crying like a ... well, like a girl. Now she was talking tougher than Bravado Able Bloom, and her words froze Reedley statue still.

Growing up in the Found Grace Church community, Addison knew Mr. Reedley as the quietest, most reserved person in the congregation. If someone said hello to him, he'd tip his hat, or if indoors, nod. It was easy to forget he was there. Once Preacher Larrimer launched the Holy Crusade, however, and it became obvious their wagon train would be lucky to make Kansas before the turn of the century, Reedley stepped forward and assumed the role of wagon master. He transformed Preacher Larrimer's bleating, milling aimlessly flock into a disciplined crusade, teams hitched and logging miles before the sun came up. Everyone was surprised at the Wagon Master's assertiveness, but they did what he said and didn't waste any time doing it.

Now this snippet of a girl, this Winnie, was telling Joshua Reedley that she was going to decide what she'd do.

Addison watched the Wagon Master think. The original plan had been for Reedley, Jibway, and Addison to accompany Ziggy Hostetler back to Atchison and to meet with Ziggy's source of information.

Reedley: "Here's what we're going to do. I'm going to join up with Ziggy and meet his source of information. Jibway, Addison, you stay with Winifred and help her. If you decide you need to leave, and if she argues with you, tie her up and gag her, and you all head back to Brotherton with her and the two wounded bushwhackers."

Jibway: "One wounded. Able Bloom is dead. I just checked on him."

# 6.

Beyond the remnants of the barn, to the east, Addison and Jibway dug and pitched the dirt to one side. The three bodies, young bodies, lay on their backs on the opposite side of the hole. Winifred and Billy Bob, with considerable frosty distance between them and their backs to the house, stood by and watched the dirt fly. They dug the hole three bodies wide. When they had it knee deep, Addison asked Jibway if he'd fetch the bedrolls from the dead men's horses.

Addison: "And take Billy Bob so I don't have to watch him with one eye and direct my shovel with the other."

Jibway nodded and climbed out of the hole. Billy Bob started walking toward the left corner of the house. Addison went back to spading.

Winnifred: "Teach me how to use a handgun."

Addison looked up. "We're going to bury … them. Then we can work a pistol."

"You shoulda' just drug them away from here and left them to the buzzards!"

Addison took a moment to ensure the words he was formulating were his own, not Joshua Reedley's. He stared back at her. "We are going to bury them. They are human beings. Maybe young and stupid. But human. We're going to bury them. Then we can shoot."

Winifred turned and stomped back to the house.

Addison watched her and recalled the three men—the first three men he killed—back in Thompson Township at the start of the Holy Crusade. He'd needed Joshua Reedley to help him deal with the enormity of taking men's lives. Winifred needed help dealing with the enormity of having the lives of her mother, father, and brother taken away from her. And, of course, there was what the stupid young men were going to do to her. Winifred needed to speak with Maybell and Mariah. After the burying. And the shooting. And the trip back to Brotherton.

Burying the young stupids.

After the hole was dug, and the bodies placed in it shoulder-to-shoulder, Winifred came out of the house, returned to the grave, looked down into it, and scowled at the ground-cloth-covered bodies.

Addison: "What's wrong?"

"You covered them. I want to shovel dirt on their faces. I'm going into the hole and take those tarps off them."

Addison stood a yard and a half away from her. "No. No you're not."

"Try and stop me and I'll scratch your eyes out!"

Jibway: "You go after my blood brother, I shoot you. Then we bury you with them."

Winifred snapped her eyes, brimming with hot hatred, at the Indian. He mirrored her look back at her. Again, she spun and stomped off toward the house. This time, she walked around the right side to the rear.

From behind the blood brothers, Billy Bob sucked in a couple of short, sharp inhales. They turned in time to see a tear leak out of one eye and slither down a cheek. "Jesus. We came to fight against the evil of slavery … . What we did was a worser evil." More inhales. "We taught a beautiful, innocent, young woman how to hate." He looked down into the grave. "I'll see you guys in hell." Then the tears flooded, from his eyes and nose and mouth. His shoulders shook.

It took some moments for the mountain of remorse to shrink to foothill size.

Addison: "Ask the Lord to forgive you."

"I don't deserve His forgiveness."

Jibway: "None of us deserve it, but we are all sinners, and He forgives us anyway."

Surprise shouldered aside the grief stamped on Billy Bob's face.

Addison: "My blood brother attended what he calls a missionary school. The lessons took. At times, it seems he's more a Christian than I am."

Jibway: "Ask him, Billy Bob. Ask Him to forgive you."

Billy Bob walked to the mound of loose dirt, knelt, picked up a handful, and dropped it onto a body. "Jesus, Lord, please forgive Able Bloom." Another handful. "Jesus, Lord, please forgive Jack Knight." Another handful and a plea for Harlen Peters.

Then Billy B. picked up a clod and drew a cross on his forehead— like Preacher Larrimer did on the foreheads of his congregation with ashes at the start of Lent—and he asked for forgiveness for himself. He stayed on his knees as Addison and Jibway filled in the grave. He stood when they began tamping the loose, mounded dirt with the back of their spades.

The sound of riders approaching from the north reached them. Addison and Jibway dropped their shovels. Two riders trotting their mounts.

Jibway: "Ziggy's men." A few moments later. "Harvey Montag and Larry Klein."

Addison watched the riders while Jibway checked behind them.

Hostetler's men reined up and stayed on their saddles.

Montag: "Reedley thought you'd need help getting this business sorted."

Klein hooked a thumb at Billy Bob. "You shoulda' shot him and buried him with the others."

Jibway: "We chose not to."

Montag broke the awkward silence. "We came to help. What can we do?"

Addison: "We got more burying to do." He nodded toward the grave. "Those guys killed the Martins. Man. His wife and son. We'll bury them next."

Jibway: "The daughter survived. She's in back of the house. We need to see what she's doing." He picked up his shovel, handed Addison his, and started toward the side of the dwelling.

Addison prodded Billy Bob to walk in front of him. Before, Addison wanted him in front because he didn't trust him. Now he wanted him in front because he didn't trust Larry Klein.

When they rounded the rear corner of the house, Addison saw Winifred hip deep in a hole. Dirt flew out of it onto the growing mound, propelled as much by anger as by the shovel in her hands.

Addison: "Miss Martin, we'll finish digging the grave."

She had just stomped the spade into the ground, stopped, and turned. "**The** grave? My parents and my brother will each get their own."

Jibway: "Okay. We'll start on the other two."

"I'll dig them myself."

Addison: "We're doing the others. You want them in a row?"

She sighed. "One next to this one. The other a couple of paces farther on."

Jibway: "Farther away from the house?"

She glared at her tormentor for a moment; then she dug more dirt.

Jibway dug the hole farther on.

Addison asked Montag to work the one next to where Winifred worked. Then, "Billy Bob, get a rake from the tool shed and bring it to the barn." And, "Klein, follow me."

Klein followed but mumble-grumbled the whole way while leading his horse around the house and to the ruins of the barn. Wisps of smoke rose from remaining hot pockets under the ashes of what had been a substantial structure.

Addison could see the bodies … . No. They weren't bodies. They were the remains of bodies.

Billy Bob brought the rake. Addison took it and sent him to fetch the bedroll from his horse. He did as bidden. "Klein. Get the roll from Outlaw. Also pick up the pile of blankets laying there on the ground."

A sullen look first. Mumbling second. Then he followed orders.

Addison used the rake and uncovered a few glowing embers and scraped them to the side creating a path to the remains. When his errand runners returned, he told Billy B. to fetch Jibway. "Tell him to **not** let Winnie see this. Do it as quietly as you can, otherwise that woman—."

Billy nodded and left.

Addison: "Klein. There, just beyond the pig pen, a wagon, see? And horses in the corral beyond that. Hitch a team to the wagon and bring it here."

Larry Kline started to mount his steed, but Addison told him to leave it.

"What the hell for?"

"Cause I told you to."

Kline lost the stare down.

Jibway came to Addison, and together they moved the remains onto ground cloths and dragged them clear of the ruins. The third ground cloth came from the roll behind the saddle of Larry Kline's mount. The mother they identified by the remnant of her dress beneath her. The size of the other bodies determined father and son.

The blood brothers covered each of the deceased with a blanket, then wrapped them in the ground cloths, and secured their shrouds around them with rope.

Klein whoa-ed the team and stopped the wagon next to the three ... Martins.

Addison and Jibway loaded the mother. Klein stepped to the ground. The blood brothers loaded the father. Klein walked around the team to his saddle bronc as the son joined his parents.

Klein spun around. "You took my bedroll for these damned pro-slavers!"

Addison: "I needed it now, and I'll replace if before **you** need it."

Jibway: "They **were not** pro-slavers, and they **are not** damned."

Klein started toward Jibway. "No damn Injun—."

Addison grabbed his arm, and Klein swung a roundhouse punch at him, which Addison parried; then he shot a sharp left jab. The fist landed on Klein's mouth. Ziggie's man fell to the ground with an "Ow!" and curses. He raised both hands over his mouth. Blood leaked between his fingers.

"Ow, ow!" More swearing. "Oh, Jesus! I can't … can't close my mouth. Oh, Jesus."

"He calls on Jesus between strings of cuss words. Missionary School Injun no pray that way. White man, however—." Jibway knelt beside the cursing supplicant. "Take your hands away from your mouth." He did not comply.

Addison squatted beside the man, pulled his left wrist away from his face, and pinned it to the ground.

Jibway pinned the other arm. "Hold still!" The tone froze Ziggie's man. "Now, I'm going to look at your teeth. If you bite me, I will cut your nose in half and slice off an ear." Klein eyes got big, and he went still.

Jibway lifted the bloody lip. "One upper front tooth is bent behind the lowers. I'm going to straighten it. It may come out, but maybe it can be saved." He reached a finger toward the bent-back tooth. "Do. Not. Bite. Me."

Jibway stuck his finger in behind the tooth and pulled it straight. Klein went rigid, but he didn't scream. "Be very careful with it, and you might save it. Now, go to the front porch of the house and sit. Don't move from there until we tell you to."

Addison and Jibway climbed aboard the funeral wagon, and Addison drove them to the rear of the house. Billy Bob walked behind the wagon. He stopped at the rear corner of the house.

Ziggie's other man, Harvey Montag, was helping Winnie climb out of her brother's grave.

Addison parked the rig, and he and Jibway unloaded the Martin boy and placed him beside his grave.

Winnifred looked up from brushing her pants legs. "I want to see him."

"No," Addison and Jibway said in unison. "No, you don't."

Winnie's brittle façade shattered. She sobbed. From behind her, Harvey Montag placed his hands on her shoulders, and she spun around and leaned against his chest. Montag's hands didn't seem to know what to do. Finally, though, they rose to the girl's back, and, it seemed to Addison, Harvey's hug began to heal the hurt girl.

Her sobs subsided slowly. Then she pushed back gently. Harvey's hands flew away like startled doves that, somehow, had learned to flee without making a sound. Winnie turned around. "We best get to it."

The blood brothers and Montag worked together. Two of them climbed down into a grave and lifted the ground-cloth caskets from the sides of the graves and placed them, reverently, on the bottom. When the three rested in their final places, the three men and the young woman stood beside the father's grave. Winifred looked at Harvey Montag. A look, almost of horror, ran down from his eyebrows over the rest of his face.

Addison said, "Allow me, Miss Winifred."

She didn't indicate refusal.

Addison bowed his head. "Father, Lord of heaven, Lord of earth. Our Father, receive our brother, Your son, into Your Holy Home in Heaven. You gave him, Lord, tasks to accomplish here: To be a husband; to be a father; to till the soil. He discharged these duties well, Lord. And though we did not know him in life, we know him through his daughter Winifred. Through her, we know him to be a good and God-fearing man."

Winfred's shoulders shook, but her sobs remained silent. The men waited, watched her, wondered if she would regain control.

After a long moment, she sucked in a long breath, held it an instant, and eased it out. She wiped her nose on the sleeve of her … her brother's shirt. Then, she walked around the pit to the mound of dirt, picked up a handful, and dropped it in. She flinched at the sound the dirt made when it hit the ground cloth. Then, she looked at Billy Bob by the corner of the house.

Billy Bob, Addison could see, was crying.

# 7.

Jibway said the words over Mrs. Martin.

Miss Winifred stood beside the pit, dropped a handful of dirt on her mother, and then closed her eyes. Weighty silence fell on the prairie.

A fountain of emotion gushed from the pit of Addison's belly. His eyes saw not the girl Winnie burying her family, rather, he saw his mother. Maw said, "Addison, you're five. You're a big boy now, and big boys don't cry."

Paw had just spanked him, not for the first time that day. And it wasn't the last time he cried after Paw spanked him, but close to the last.

Addison's eyes opened, even though they hadn't been closed. He saw Winnie wobble a bit and took a step to grab her, but Jibway stopped him.

Winifred's eyes did open. She said, "I'll speak for my brother."

After commending her younger brother into the Lord's keeping, she insisted on helping the men fill in the graves. When that was finished, the sun hung low above the horizon. Winifred looked at Addison. "Now teach me how to shoot a handgun."

A T-shaped frame of wood draped with a sun-bleached man's shirt, with a sack of straw for a head festooned with black buttons for eyes, and a floppy black hat stood guard over the garden. Addison uprooted the scarecrow, then replanted it beyond the smokehouse sitting near the corner of the garden.

"We'll fix supper." Jibway started toward the house. Montag followed him.

Addison pulled his sidearm and explained its workings to Winnie. Then, he took careful aim and fired. The left sleeve of the scarecrow twitched.

"You were aiming at the sleeve?"

He nodded and handed her the weapon. "With your finger off the trigger, cock the hammer."

Click.

"One more."

Click.

"Now. Like I explained. Aim. Take a breath. Hold it. Squeeze the trigger. Don't jerk it."

"Able Bloom!"

The pistol fired, and Addison took it from her.

"At least you didn't hit the smokehouse."

By the time the horizon had eaten the bottom half of the ball of fire and daylight, Winifred Martin had learned how to manage herself with a pistol in her hand.

"Tomorrow morning, Miss … Winnie, see if you can make yourself remember half of what you learned here."

"I'll remember all of it."

She handed Addison his pistol; then she turned toward the three mounds.

Harvey Montag dished stew from a cast-iron pot on the stove into bowls. "Klein, I made you some broth. Take it out on the porch. Billy Bob, here's your stew. Porch also."

Winifred marched to the table and assigned seats to Montag, Jibway, and Addison. She took the fourth chair; then she said a before-meal prayer, and another for the souls of her family. After she took a spoonful, the others began to eat. The clink of silverware on dinnerware was their conversation. When their plates were clean, Harvey poured coffee.

Winifred said, "Mr. Montag, how much does this Mister Hostetler pay you?"

Addison cut in. "This is what is going to happen in the morning. Miss Winifred, you, Jibway, and I will depart for Brotherton at sunup. Mr. Montag will stay here with Klein and Billy Bob. They will tend the animals and take care of the place. Once we get to Brotherton, we'll talk with the town council about your situation, and we'll see if we can figure out if there is a way we can help you stay here."

"Safely," Jibway added.

"If Mr. Montag will work for me, we'll be safe."

"No, Ma'am," Harvey said. "We can't even tell our friends from our enemies here. You told us your paw was against slavery, but he was also for States' Rights. For the right of states to determine things like is slavery good or bad."

Jibway: "Winnie, about half our country thinks slavery is evil. The other half thinks it's not. We cannot have a nation where half the population thinks the other half is evil. We've gotten ourselves into a war to try to settle this thing. And on your place here, you'll be smack dab in the middle of it."

Addison repeated what was going to happen in the morning.

Winnie's jaw firmed. "I want a pistol of my own."

"Not tonight," Jibway said. "Tomorrow. If you come with us willingly. No deal if we have to tie you up."

With dawn nudging dim daylight above the Missouri/Kansas border, Jibway and Addison saddled three horses. Then, Jibway rounded up a spare mount for each of them as Addison went inside to fetch Winnie. She was up, wearing pants, and had a flour sack stuffed with things for the journey. He handed her a belt gun and the derringer he'd taken from Able Bloom's boot.

Winnie strapped on the holster, pulled the pistol, made sure five chambers in the cylinder were loaded, and that the hammer rested on an empty chamber. She led Addison outside and across the front porch, and she and her companions mounted and nodded farewells to the three stay behinds. Then, she gigged her heels into her horse's belly.

When she cleared the rear corner of the house, Winnie stopped her mount.

During the night, wooden crosses had been planted over the fresh graves. Names and death dates had been painted onto the crossbeams, which had been lashed to the uprights so hammering wouldn't wake Winifred and spoil the surprise.

The woman hung her head for a moment, then she raised it and looked behind her with what was most likely a smile on her face. Facing west again, she said, "Giddup," and guided her bronc past the outhouse and tool shed and aimed at the endless prairie.

Winnie wasn't leading them directly toward Brotherton, but she was headed west, which the blood brothers figured was good enough for the start of their journey.

They reined up in front of Addison's and Mariah's house a bit before noon. Maybell opened the front door, stepped onto the porch leading Hope by the hand.

Addison's daughter squealed, "Daddy!" and ran to him as he tied Outlaw's reins to the porch post. He scooped up his daughter and hugged her. Then, he felt Winnie's eyes pressing on the back of his neck. He forced joy to drain from his face, and he turned and introduced Maybell and his daughter to Miss Winifred.

Winnie appeared to have been petrified into a stern-faced equestrian statue. Addison figured she'd been prepared to face a new Able Bloom with a new crew of evil-intentioned lackies, and, perhaps, even relished the thought of confronting such riffraff with her pistol and derringer. But, he was sure, she had not been prepared for such a scene of father/daughter affection. Then she muscled up the hint of a smile. "Pleased to meet you, Maybell. And, I'm **very** pleased to meet you, Miss Hope."

Jibway dismounted. "I'll take care of the horses. Maybell, why don't you take Hope? Then, we can feed Winnie some lunch while Addison visits Mariah and the mayor."

Winnie stepped to the ground. "Will you come to me, Miss Hope?"

The little girl hesitated, then she reached out her arms toward her new friend.

Addison walked down Main Street to his mother's house. He knocked on the front door.

"Come in." Mariah's voice. She used her mother-in-law's house for seeing the sick and injured of Brotherton in her capacity as healer.

Maw and Mariah sat at the table together. The person who had been the most important woman for most of his life with the female who had supplanted her. His eyes connected first with New Number One and drank in the love she shined back at him.

His mother. She loved him, too, but, he also saw she understood her place in his heart and that her understanding had not come without pain.

He closed the door behind him, crossed the room to the table, kissed Mariah on the lips, and his mother on the cheek.

Maw: "We just ate, but there's some left for you. Sit."

Mariah rose to fix a plate for him.

When they were all seated again, Addison said a silent prayer, then took a bite, chewed, swallowed, and sipped from his water glass. "We were half a day from Atchison, thereabout, when early in the morning, as we were closing down breakfast, Jibway spotted smoke."

Another forkful, chewing, swallowing, sipping. He told the story a forkful at a time.

When only crumbs of the crust remained of the peach pie, Maw said, "If Jibway hadn't spotted the smoke, if you all had not gone to see what caused it … ."

Mariah: "But thank the good Lord, you did, and you saved that young woman."

Maw: "You said the Young Stupids were anti-slavery just like we are. Why did they shoot at you?"

Addison explained his and Jibway's interpretation of what passed for thinking and conscience on Able Bloom's part.

Mariah: "And this … Winifred, her parents had an isolated farm less than a day's ride from the Missouri border, and she wants to go back to it?"

"According to Winifred," Addison said, "once Kansas joined the Union as a free state, her paw figured it was safe to move from Missouri. And because of all the violence that had rampaged through the area, there was farmland for the taking."

Maw: "But then war broke out."

Mariah: "And after what happened to her family … ."

Maw: "And what almost happened to her … ."

Mariah: "She still wants to go back there?"

Maw: "She'll be lucky to survive two days."

Addison: "I have an idea."

The women in duet: "What is it?"

"I want to talk to the town council. They may not support the idea. I'll tell you about it after I talk to them."

Mariah: "Addison!"

"Later."

The women exchanged a glance laden with exasperation, commiseration, and resignation.

Addison: "I guess a goodbye kiss is not possible?"

Mariah: "Oh, come here." She shook her head. "Young Stupid."

# 8.

Addison left his mother's house and walked down C Street to Sixth, to the marshal's office.

Addison: "I request a meeting, Marshal, with you, the mayor, and the two preachers."

"What for?"

Addison explained.

"Are you crazy?"

"You all may decide I am, but I'm asking for the meeting."

McTavish frowned, rubbed his chin, and shook his head; then he checked his pocket watch. "I can't see the town council approving this … idea of yours, but we, Brotherton, owe you a listening to."

Addison: "I'll notify the preachers."

McTavish frowned again. "So, you want me to notify the mayor. What did Orson Seiling call you? Oh yeah. Fraidy Cat."

The meeting was supposed to convene at two thirty, but everyone was there by five past the hour. So, it started then.

Addison sat on one side of the only occupied table in the big Meeting House. The mayor, the town marshal, and the two preachers faced him from the other.

Mayor Gallant Argyl: "You want us to uproot twenty families from Brotherton and move them to this spot close to the Missouri border?"

Marshal McTavish: "Because this young woman, Winifred, insists on staying on the farm where her parents were killed?"

Mayor: "Bring the woman here. I'll tell her I'm sorry her parents were killed. But we are not moving citizens from the safety of Brotherton that far east."

Marshal: "The closer you are to the border, the more dangerous it is."

Addison: "Our first full year here, distance from Missouri gave us no additional safety whatsoever. What saved us that year was vigilance."

Preacher Cromwell leaned forward and planted his elbows on the table. Preacher Larrimer sat upright, stiff as a board.

Mayor: "Still, because this young woman is stubborn and refuses to leave her parents' farm, it's no reason to uproot our people."

Addison: "I agree, Mr. Mayor. However, one of the factors which contributed to our survival through 1859 was the way Otto Vogelsang laid out our town. The farms are located outside of Brotherton, but all the farmers have houses bunched together here inside town. We'd have been wiped out if we'd all lived on farms with a lot of distance between them. Mr. Vogelsang's plan was good, but there is a size limit to this concept. New families continue to join us, and their farms are a long way from town. One other thing, Mr. Martin located his farm in the middle of a big stretch of excellent land for farming."

Preacher Cromwell sat back. "You want Otto Vogelsang to go with you and lay out a new town for twenty families from here?"

"Yes, sir."

"My wife and I will go with you," Preacher Cromwell said. "And I'm sure I can get a dozen families to come along."

Mayor: "Just hold on here! We are not making that kind of decision now. The whole town council needs to weigh in on this."

Marshal: "And I want to hear what Joshua Reedley thinks about this ... this idea. When's he due back?"

"I don't know, Marshal. He went with Ziggy Hostetler on to Atchison. When we left here, we didn't know how long we'd be gone. Now, when Reedley finds Ziggy's source of news, and heads back, I'd expect him to stop by the Martin farm to check on what's happening there."

Mayor: "So, a couple of days before he's back?"

Addison: "Maybe three."

Mayor: "Well, I want to hear from him before we make a decision. We'll wait for him, but we will have a town council meeting tomorrow. Right after morning church services."

Marshal: "We'll need you there, Addison."

Mayor: "And bring Jibway."

Marshal: "And this Winifred."

Preacher Cromwell: "I'll talk to my parishioners, see if some of them really would be willing to move."

Mayor: "Let's not rush into this thing. Wait till after the meeting tomorrow."

"I'm going to talk to my parishioners, Mr. Mayor. If I'm wrong about them being willing to move, we should know that. Even if Joshua Reedley supports Addison's idea, we are not going to force people to move, are we?"

Preacher Larrimer: "We are not."

Preacher Cromwell: "Addison is right about how far out new farms have to be located."

Gallant Argyl: "Job must have been a mayor, else he would never have been able to establish the biblical benchmark for patience."

That night, Hope slept in her bed. Jibway and Maybell slept in theirs. Winifred slept in the second bedroom in Addison's maw's house.

Mariah and Addison were in their bed, but they weren't asleep. They both lay on their sides. She had her back to him. He held her close and had a hand on her tummy.

Everything, Addison thought, felt right and good and proper. Everything in the entire universe, all the way from God in His heaven to the two of them on His earth, felt all the way to holy. Actually, he reminded himself, it was the four of them. Hope and New Baby were part of it, too.

Mariah rolled onto her other side to face him.

Hope cried, "I poopy."

Addison started to get up. Mariah grabbed his arm. "We're moving to this new town of yours, aren't we?"

The next morning, Mariah left church for Maw's house to tend those who needed her healing services. Addison, Jibway, Maybell, and Winifred joined the parade of town council members headed next door to the Meeting House.

Inside, three rows of chairs for the town council had been lined up in front of the speaker podium. Mayor Argyl occupied the center of the first row. Addison stood behind the podium. Winifred was on a chair beside him.

Most of the Brotherton citizens went to their farms or tended to other business. A few sat in on the proceedings. They dragged chairs to behind the council. Among them, Maybell and Jibway.

Mayor: "Addison, introduce Miss Martin and tell us how you came to meet her."

He started the story with Jibway spotting the smoke and concluded it with the burials of the Young Stupids and of the Martin family.

Mayor: "Miss Martin, it is my understanding you intend staying on … what was your parents' farm. Is that correct?"

She stood. "Yes, Mister Mayor."

"By yourself?"

"No, Sir. I intend to hire some help."

"Men?"

"I'll help her," Maybell cut in.

"Maybell Jim. I've told you numerous times. If you want to speak at these proceedings, request the chairman's permission to do so. Now, do you wish to say anything else?"

"Don't need to say it agin."

It was clear, Addison thought, the mayor had a way in which he wanted the

Winifred Martin story rolled out. Maybell had not derailed his plan. Clearly, though, she had annoyed him. Addison fought the urge to smile.

The mayor moved the story forward. Sixteen-year-old Winifred wanted to stay on the Martin farm. With a couple of hired hands. A single-family farm: an un-survivable entity. The Holy Crusade had that as a guidepost before they began planning the layout of Brotherton. What happened to the Martin family proved the validity of the concept.

"But Addison J. Freeman has an idea. Move families from Brotherton to establish a new town around the Martin farm. Preacher Cromwell says he has more than twelve families willing to relocate to the new town. But, at present, Brotherton is Main through Eighth Streets with a dozen houses on each.

"So, this new town would be no bigger than just one of our streets. This will obviously not be a large enough town to defend itself the way we did, and do, here."

"Mr. Mayor."

"The chair recognizes Marshal McTavish."

"What about Joshua Reedey? Have we heard from him? Do we know when he'll be back?"

The front door of the Meeting House opened, and Joshua Reedley's boots clunked their way to the center of the large room.

Maybell: "Speak of the devil!"

The mayor jumped to his feet and turned to face Maybell.

"Gallant," Reedley said. "I need to talk to you. Now."

Addison's maw, on the end of the second row of chairs, said, "You want us to leave?"

The mayor's mouth hung open.

Joshua Reedley replied, "No, just stay here please. We won't be long. There's a matter I need to tell the mayor and Marshal McTavish." After a moment, "And the preachers. And Addison and Jibway. We'll use the corner office." He tacked on, "We won't be long."

"I'm coming, too!"

"Maybell," Reedley said. "Sit!"

# 9.

Inside the tiny Meeting House corner office, Jibway and Addison crowded in last. Feet shuffled as the older men packed themselves closer together.

Mayor: "You said this wouldn't take long."

"It won't. I have the name of Ziggie's source of information. I am only going to tell that name to those of you in this room. Do not tell it to anyone else. Not anyone! Understand?"

The blood brothers nodded assent. The others mumbled theirs.

Reedley: "Thomas Theismann is Ziggy's source. Now he's ours, too. His information about Bushwhacker intentions comes from a man named Barney Wainscott. This Barney is in with a group of pro-slavery killers located in western Missouri, a ways south of Kansas City. His insider reports, according to Theisman, are worth a saddlebag full of gold. However, we must ensure neither of these names gets out. I need you to promise me you will guard them with your lives. Will you do that?"

Mayor: "We will. Now can we go back to the Town Council meeting?"

"Not yet. Theismann thinks a small town built around the Martin farm would be a good idea. It would expand the Union's control of northeastern Kansas. With Barney's information coming to him regularly, he figures he'd be able to deploy Kansas militia to keep the town safe. And, if Wainscott finds out about a threat to this new town, he could ride directly to it and warn those of us there, without taking the extra time to go through Theismann."

McTavish: "Setting up a new town that close to the Missouri border, that's the craziest thing I ever heard of."

Preacher Cromwell: "Craziest thing I ever heard of was folks uprooting themselves from the east coast and moving all the way to Kansas to vote against the abomination that is slavery."

Joshua Reedley's select group returned to the hall, where he, Reedley, reminded the Council of Addison's idea to move families from Brotherton to establish a new town. He finished with, "If you approve this proposal, I will go with the wagon train."

Preacher Cromwell supported the proposal and announced he now had fifteen families who agreed to move to the new town. Preacher Larrimer sat stiff and straight in his black and white. He nodded his assent. The mayor supported the proposal.

Marshal McTavish: "I am not enthusiastic about moving any of our people east, but I won't vote against."

Maybell: "Vote, then."

Slowly, the mayor rose. Slowly, he turned. "All."

From his position at the side of the speaker podium, Addison could see the mayor was staring at Maybell. She stared right back.

The mayor snarled, "In favor."

A tiny smile appeared on Maybell's face.

The mayor turned away from her. "Say, aye."

"Aye!"

"Opposed?"

Pin drop silence.

"What's next, Joshua?"

"You, Mr. Mayor, I request that you and the marshal get together and draw up a list of concerns you have. Concerns over who's going and what we will take with us. I don't think we will be leaving Brotherton at risk, but I want to be as sure as I can.

"And me, I want to meet with Otto Vogelsang and lay out detailed plans for the materials and people we need to take with us. To figure out how long will it take to get the builders and lumber loaded and ready to move?

"One last thing. I want to take Addison and Jibway with us, but I haven't had a chance to ask them."

"We're going."

Mayor: "Maybell!"

Jibway: "We're going."

Addison's maw fixed supper. Everyone was seated when she placed the stew kettle on the table and took her chair.

Winifred: "Otto thought it will take a week to get things ready to go."

Maw: "Winifred. Prayer first. Then talk and eating."

Winfred blushed, lowered her head, and said the before-meal prayer.

They all Amen-ed. Hope tacked on her tiny echo.

Addison: "Winnie, in all of Illinois, Missouri, and Kansas, nobody knows more about setting up a town than Otto."

Jibway: "It's not just the lumber and other building supplies, it's the men and women who are experts at slapping together a meeting house, a church, and homes. Some of his builders will have to line up help to take care of their farms and families."

Maw held out her hand, and Winnie passed her plate to her. Maw filled the plate, passed it back, and went around the table serving her guests.

Mariah: "Winnie, you got one big thing today. You got the Town Council's approval to build the town of Martinsville."

Maw: "Thank You, God, for that."

Another Amen tail-ended by a tiny echo.

Mariah: "You know, don't you, Winnie, that this is the only way we could go along with you returning to your parents' farm.

Leaving you there with nothing but a couple of hired hands would have been the same as sentencing you to die a horrible death. Just have a little patience."

Maybell: "People what don't need no patience call it a virtue."

Winifred: "Thank you, Mrs. Maybell Jim, for pointing out to me, in your own unique way, that I need to dredge up some of that particular virtue."

Hope: "Amen."

It was as if the little girl's word released a pleasant atmosphere into the room, making them feel happy and blessed to be together.

Jibway looked at his wife. "Out of the mouths of babes."

After they finished eating, the men washed and dried the dishes, and the guests departed. Jibway and Maybell headed down C Street toward their place.

Addison stood beside his mother's house and watched his blood brother and blood sister walk, hand-in-hand. "The most natural looking sight in the whole world. This evening. Here in Brotherton."

Mariah squeezed his arm to her. "Yes, and before we joined the Holy Crusade … ."

Mariah's family joining the Holy Crusade! Such mention always triggered, try as Addison might to suppress it, a full-blown picture forming in his mind, of Orson Seiling with Mariah. He flinched.

"Oh, Addison, I am so sorry. Sometimes my mouth starts talking before I think about what I'm going to say." She huffed out a breath. "I'm just a Young Stupid."

Addison faced her. "You are not any kind of stupid."

He knelt beside their child. "Thank you, God, for … ."

Hope: "Mommy."

Mariah: "And?"

"Daddy."

Addison stood. Hope raised her arms. He picked her up.

Hope: "No! Horsey."

Addison handed his hat to Mariah and hoisted the girl to his shoulders.

"Gid dup."

Due to the hour, Addison whispered his whinny and started walking.

Addison: "You were going to say something about Jibway and Maybell walking together?"

"I was. Before we joined the wagon train, my imagination could never have dreamt up an image of an Indian and a darkie married to each other. Indians were savages roaming the prairie like beasts. And darkies, that was just as polite a name as we could put to a slave. Jibway and Maybell, they have been an inspiration, a revelation. I believed baptism into my church back in Illinois made me a Christian. Actually, it was meeting and knowing Jibway and Maybell that baptized me."

Addison stopped and kissed Mariah.

"Gid dup!"

"Clip, clop, clip, clop."

Mariah: "Winifred was profoundly affected by Maybell and Jibway. She said she finally understood something Jibway told her the morning you all left her farm to come here."

They walked in the dirt street so their heels on the boardwalk wouldn't disturb anyone.

"She said her father expected her brother, when he got a year or two older, to fight for the South, for state's rights. Her father figured no bunch of fancy-pants old fogeys way back east should have the right to decide what's right and wrong for folks hundreds, even a thousand miles away from them. Winifred said she believed her paw until she spent an afternoon with Maybell. It surprised her to discover she was a person. Not a darkie. Not colored. Certainly not a slave.

"Then I told Winnie what that sheriff from Prairietown had done to Maybell."

Mariah's petticoats swished as they walked.

"Cip, cop, Daddy."

"Clip, clop. Clip, clop"

"After I told Winifred, she left the house, walked down Second Street all the way to the Meeting House, and returned. When she got back, tears streamed down her cheeks. She said, 'I've been so upset over what the Young Stupids were going to do to me. Maybell actually endured something much worse. And look at her! She is the strongest woman I ever met.'"

Addison: "Winnie's strong, too. But she's still learning how to use that strength."

Then, they were home.

Addison reached up to set his daughter to the porch.

Hope: "No. Ride horsey."

Mariah: "Hope, Darling, I don't allow horses inside the house."

Hope: "Oh."

The next day, Maurice Reedley informed his father he wanted to go with those moving to set up the new town.

Joshua Reedley: "Eunice is in the family way."

Maurice: "Baby's not expected for another two months. I asked Eunice. She said I can be gone for a week."

Addison: "What if it takes two weeks?"

Maurice: "One week or two. I'll still be back in plenty of time."

"Ask her."

Maurice sighed.

Six days after the Town Council approved the plan to establish Martinsville, Preacher Cromwell conducted the last service in his church on Sixth Street. Many of the furnishings would be moved to Martinsville.

Once the service concluded, the citizens of Brotherton dedicated the rest of the day to moving thirty-two wagons, nineteen for the families moving east and the others for builders and lumber, to the Delaware River ferry to the east of Addison's house. The wagons crossed the river one at a time to join the staging lot Reedley had formed on the other side.

Otto Vogelsang used logs attached to the sides of some wagons to float them across. Otto had used that same scheme during the early part of the Holy Crusade.

Addison was particularly concerned with one wagon. The blood brothers had urged their wives to wait for a later wagon train to travel to the new town. Both refused. Jibway spoke with Otto, and he mounted two hammocks to the bed of a wagon. "Oughta be lot easier on dee wimmen folk dan dat travois rig you talked about."

Addison knew he worried too much about Mariah and her condition. The thing was, she did not worry enough about it.

Into Your hands, Lord.

The next morning, Addison woke Maurice Reedley and Orson Seiling well before Joshua Reedley whanged the horseshoes to rouse the wagon train. Addison was the lead scout for the ride-into-the-sunrise shift. The Wagon Master, Joshua Reedley, considered most of the young men with this new crusade capable of serving as scouts in most conditions, but he considered only Addison and Jibway capable of scouting while riding into an eyeball frying sunrise. And Jibway would be leading Otto Vogelsang to the Martin farm early that morning. Jibway and Otto were up and preparing to leave also. No surprise to find the two of them up early. Addison was surprised, however, to discover Preacher Cromwell up, with a fire going and coffee brewing.

Cromwell: "You scouts, bring your cups. Have some coffee before you go."

Addison: "One cup, and don't dawdle over it." Those words had been aimed at Orson Seiling. They hadn't been needed for Joshua Reedley's son.

Across the staging lot, Addison saw another breakfast fire, and he walked to it. Mariah, Maybell, and Winifred sat eating breakfast from tin plates. Neither he nor Jibway slept with their wives the night before. Both planned to rise early, and both wanted their wives to get as much rest as possible. As usual, Mariah and Maybell had their own ideas about how much rest they needed.

As Addison approached the fire, Mariah looked up at him. He could tell she expected criticism for having gotten up so early. He said, "Just wanted to say good morning and wish you, and your companions a good first day of travel. The second shift scouts take over at 08:30, so I should see you around nine."

He tipped his hat to Maybell and Winnie, and said, "Ladies." Then he bent and kissed Mariah on the forehead, spun about, and started marching back to where Maurice and Orson were drinking Preacher coffee. That's when he realized he hadn't taken a cupful for himself.

*Ratsnot!* he thought, but said, "Let's go."

# 10.

The second shift scouts took over twelve minutes early. Reedley's philosophy about scouts on his wagon trains: "If next shift scouts don't relieve the on-duty scouts fifteen minutes early, the next-shifters are late."

Wally Wilson led the second shift scouts. Addison had scouted with him during the Holy Crusade and trusted him more than enough to spot him three minutes. Plus, Joshua Reedley was with Wilson as the second scout. Other than for the rising-sun shift, two scouts sufficed. The Wagon Master, periodically, rode with his scouts to see if they needed instruction, or advice, or to be replaced.

Now, as Addison rode west to rejoin the train, Orson Seiling was behind him, and Maurice Reedley was behind Orson. With Maurice behind Orson, Addison trusted the arrangement of his fellow scouts.

Riding into a rising sun—or a setting one for that matter—was never comfortable, but he'd found that morning's time on duty as uncomfortable as his very first time scouting for the Holy Crusade. Because this morning, Orson Seiling had been behind him the whole time. Of course, to do his job, Orson had to be behind him.

"Outlaw," Addison said, "I'm going to talk to Joshua Reedley about Orson. I don't trust him and don't want to work with him again. But even more, if I don't trust him, I don't want him assigned to work with someone else even more. I'll talk to the wagon master when we stop at noon to water the animals,"

The horse craned its neck enough to get its eyeball on its rider.

"Yeah, yeah," Addison said. "You'll get a sip of water, too."

Outlaw snorted.

Ahead, Addison saw the line of prairie schooners and Conestogas seeming to stretch all the way back to Brotherton. Hooves and iron-rimmed wheels stirred up a thin haze of distance-dimming dust. He guided Outlaw onto the grass beside the packed dirt road. The horse stopped facing the oncoming wagons. Its tail swished flies.

Addison felt the nine o'clock morning sun on his back ... like warm, soft hands. *Like Mariah's hands.* He allowed himself a moment for tender reflection. A moment.

Maurice and Orson stopped their mounts on the grass beside Addison.

Reedley's wife drove the lead wagon with both sets of wheels on the grass on the north side of the road. There, she stirred up less dust. Addison reined Outlaw around to get out the way. So did Maurice. Orson Seiling stayed put.

Until Maurice wheeled about, grabbed the cheek strap of Orson's mount, and jerked it clear of the oncoming wagons.

As Mrs. Reedley drove past, she frowned at Addison. He was sure she had seen Maurice pull Orson out the way of the wagons.

Addison felt the frown as a slap to his face. He was lead scout. He was in charge of his three-man team. He was responsible for Orson's behavior. But, he had to be careful. There was history between he and Orson. He could not allow hot anger to rush him into action when cold calculation was screaming to be heard.

There was the history with Mariah and Hope, and the hot-blooded passion that subject always evoked, and how hard he had to work to generate cool, logical, and dispassionate thinking. There was how aggravating Orson had been throughout the Holy Crusade and the first year in Brotherton, but then he'd seemed to grow up, mature, become a dependable, **trustworthy** citizen. And as far as Addison knew, Orson had stayed that way until Orson had insulted him when Ziggy announced the start of the war between the States.

Addison had to be sure he was not using any of their history as an excuse to exact revenge.

As calmly and dispassionately as he could, Addison considered the history, the present facts and came to one overarching conclusion: Addison J. Freeman did not trust Orson Seiling.

Then, a moment ago, Orson had sat his horse in the way of Mrs. Reedley's wagon, and he wouldn't have moved out of the way without Maurice forcing him aside. This reassured Addison that he was taking into account more than just his personal feelings about Aggravating Orson.

*Orson Seiling was not trustworthy.* That was clear.

*The members of the wagon train needed to trust each other.* Very clear.

Addison moved Outlaw to beside Orson and shoved him out of the saddle. He fell to the ground and glared up at Addison.

"Why did you do that?" Preacher Cromwell demanded as he stopped his wagon next to Addison.

"Preacher, either keep your wagon moving, or get down and have your wife drive."

"I need to know why you pushed Orson to the ground."

"Maurice," Addison said, "have the wagons go around the preacher. Keep them moving."

"We need to stop here. We need to summon Joshua Reedley. We need to discuss this situation."

"We will stop at noon. That's the plan. And I am not summoning Joshua Reedley."

Maurice had the wagons on the north side of road take to the roadway to pass the Cromwell's stopped schooner. Then Addison asked Maurice to find Lorelei Seiling and to ask her to park her wagon behind the preacher's.

Addison dismounted and took Orson's handgun from his holster. Then he pulled the prone man's boots off and removed a knife from one a small pistol from the other.

Preacher Cromwell was now on the ground beside his wagon. "Addison, what are you going to do with him?"

Addison dropped the boots near their owner, and he turned. "I want to talk to Lorelei Seiling first, Preacher. Then, I'll decide."

"I don't think we ought to be making any big decisions about Orson or anyone without speaking with the Wagon Master first."

"Preacher, thanks for giving me your thoughts on this."

Addison looked up at Mrs. Cromwell in the driver's box. "Ma'am, would you get your wagon moving with the others, please."

It hadn't been intended as a question, and she hadn't taken if for one. She picked up the reins, scooted across the bench, and checked behind her. Then she snapped the reins and said, "Heyup!"

Lorelei Seiling whoa-ed her wagon where the preacher's had been.

Addison: "Lorelei, I am this close to booting Orson off this wagon train, but if you ask me not to, I won't."

Preacher Cromwell looked like he was going to say something but changed his mind.

Lorelei: "Did Mariah tell you what Orson does to me?"

Addison: "No."

"He hits me. I'm scared of him."

Addison waited. Wagons rolled by on both sides of the road. The preacher waited, too.

Lorelei: "Boot him off the wagon train." She snapped the reins and added her own jingle, rumble, and clip clop to the noise of time and miles passing.

Addison: "Orson, pull on your boots and start walking. You no longer belong to this wagon train."

Cromwell: "You aren't giving him his horse?"

Addison: "It's your horse, Preacher."  Then: "Orson, put your boots on and start walking. Now. Or I'll put a rope on you and drag past the last wagon."

Orson lay on the ground glaring.

Addison took the coiled rope tied to his saddle horn and looped it around Orson's ankles.

Orson reached down to pull the rope off himself, when Addison jerked the rope taught, and Orson fell onto his back. Keeping the slack out of the line, Addison mounted and started Outlaw at a canter. There were only a couple of wagons left to pass at the end of the train.

Addison stopped and retrieved his lasso.

Orson lay on the ground staring, glaring. Orson's eyes had shined many things at Addison over the years, but as best he could remember, this was the first time those eyes shined pure hot hate.

Addison kept paper and envelopes in a saddlebag to write to Mariah when he had to be away from her. That morning, he wrote a note to Marshal McTavish telling him about Orson Seiling.

Ansel Fishboch was one of the two men guarding the rear of the train. Addison sent him to deliver the note to the lookouts at the ferry crossing. "Take a spare mount. Deliver the note and get back as fast as two horses can get you here. And Ansel, do not let Orson ride your spare."

At the noon stop, Addison made sure the horses, mules, and other animals were watered in the creek, that cook fires were lit promptly, and that everyone knew he'd holler, "On to Martinsville," at 1:30.

Preacher Cromwell, instead of helping his wife with their team, watched for Joshua Reedley to join the stopped travelers. As soon as he did, the preacher convened a meeting with the wagon master and Addison. He'd unloaded three chairs from his wagon for them to use.

Preacher: "Addison expelled Orson Seiling from the wagon train. I thought we should have waited to talk to you before doing something like that."

Reedley: "Addison?"

"I don't trust him."

Reedley: "Did you talk to Lorelei?"

Addison replied that he had spoken with her, and that he'd given her the opportunity to say, "Don't kick him off the train." She, however, had endorsed the idea of booting her husband from the train.

Reedley: "Anything else you want to say, Preacher Cromwell?"

Cromwell: "It seems that Orson treated Lorelei well until the start of this year. Then he wanted children, but Lorelei was unable to … ."

Addison: "Get pregnant."

Preacher Cromwell blushed but continued: "Orson blamed Lorelei. He began to hit her. Mariah discovered the bruises when she went to the healer about her … problem. Mariah discovered the bruises and reported them to Preacher Larrimer. He invited me to discuss the matter, and we, he and I, and our wives, spoke with the Seiling couple and Mariah and Maybell. The four of us agreed. The Seiling couple needed to separate themselves for a time."

Addison: "After Lorelei met with the preachers, she said she wanted to join those moving to build the new town. Orson said he forbid her to go."

Cromwell: "Preacher Larrimer and I told Orson he longer had the right to forbid her anything. So, he decided to join our wagon train also, but as a single man, not as part of a married couple. I thought with time, and our help, Orson might come around." The preacher sucked in a breath and huffed it out. "How would you have handled this situation, Wagon Master, if we'd given you the chance?"

Reedley: "I'd have spoken to Orson, and if I came to the same conclusion Addison did, that I couldn't trust him, I'd have shot him." The Wagon Master stood. "Addison. Time to whang the horseshoes. And Preacher, you need to reload your chairs."

Cromwell stood. "Addison. You should have let Orson keep his horse."

Addison: "I chose not to." Then he whanged the horseshoes.

Mrs. Cromwell: "Rufus!" Then he started scurrying, too.

# 11.

Addison rose early. He intended to build a fire and make coffee for himself, Maurice, and Ansel Fishboch prior to departing for their sunrise-shift scouting mission. But Wagon Master Reedley already had a fire and coffee ready to serve. He sat on a chair beside his wagon, poured a tin cupful, and handed it to Addison.

"Thanks." The tin cup was hot. He stuck his finger through the loop. "Usually, Mr. Reedley, us scouts are gone before you wake up."

"Actually, young Mr. Freeman," Mrs. Reedley walked around the far side of the wagon, her hands full of reins and harness, "the Wagon Master is always awake before anyone else on the train."

"He just don't crawl outta his bedroll," Maurice Reedley, behind his maw, led a horse, "until the scouts are gone." Then he positioned the draft animal alongside the wagon tongue.

Ansel Fishboch led the other half of the Reedley team. "But it ain't a usual wagon-train morning, is it, Maurice?"

"Nope. This morning, I'm lead scout on the sunrise shift." Maurice grinned. "And Joshua Reedley and Ansel are my assistant scouts."

Addison frowned. *Wait. What does this mean for me?*

"Joshua," Mrs. Reedley said, "Tell Addison what his new job is.

He's worried you're going to boot him off the train like Orson was yesterday."

She was right. Addison J. Freeman felt that very worry, like his belly were a bone and a dog was gnawing at it.

Joshua Reedley didn't tell him. He didn't say anything. Just handed the whanging horseshoes to him.

Maurice: "Scouts. We're headin' out."

The three strode away.

Addison stood and stared at his hands. One held the Wagon Master's whangers. The other that cup of coffee. He drank it down. *Just right. Temperature wise. And taste wise.* He heard a chuckle.

Mrs. Reedley looked at him with a smile on her face.

Addison felt heat blossom in his armpits and on his cheeks. He placed the coffee cup on the chair the Wagon—the former Wagon Master—had used and whanged the iron shoes together. The noise they made seemed loud enough to be heard all the way back to Brotherton. And, for that matter, all the way to the Martin farm. As near as he could figure, they were halfway to their destination.

*A real wagon master would get us there before night swallowed dusk!*

That thought put spurs to the new Wagon Master, and he began to act like the old one. He marched through the wagons, doing way more hollering than walking.

"Get your team harnessed!" "Saddle up." "Light the fire." "Take the young ones to the out-fence."

Otto Vogelsang had erected two three-sided fences around latrine ditches. One for females, the other for males. Otto had said, "On dis prairie, dey is no bushes. Don't have time to build out-houses. So, I build die out-fences."

Addison moved down the south side of the bunched wagons, about to begin his litany again, when he heard, "Get your team harnessed." "Wake up and get moving, or you won't have time to eat." Preacher Cromwell worked the other side of the fleet of anchored prairie schooners.

The Wagon Master figured he'd whang the horseshoes for the morning prayer at five minutes before five o'clock. At quarter till five, however, the wagons were ready to roll. Addison whanged the shoes and hollered, "Morning prayer. Preacher Cromwell, two minutes."

Preacher Larrimer often spoke of how God blessed each man, woman, and child many times each day, but that, "We tend to get so busy we don't see the blessings. We all need to take a moment, several times during our days, to look for those blessings, to find them, and to thank Him."

That morning, his train being ready to roll ten minutes early was most certainly a blessing from God for the brand-new Wagon Master. And giving one of those saved minutes back to Him was Addison's thank You.

Preacher Cromwell used his minutes. The wagon train issued an "Amen," intended to be heard all the way up to heaven.

Wagon Master Addison whanged the shoes once and hollered, "On to Martinsville!"

Mrs. Reedley started her lead wagon team.

Hope sat next to Winifred on the driver's bench of the hammock wagon and said, "Gid dup." Winifred snapped the reins, and the second wagon rolled.

Addison stood next to the road to Atchison and watched and listened to the line of schooners sail past him and Outlaw. Eli Young, his wife Dora next to him on the driver's bench, drove past and tipped his hat to Addison. The Wagon Master frowned back at Eli. A wheel on the Young wagon squeaked.

That squeak snapped Addison back to the start of the Holy Crusade. Then, he had served as a scout for the wagon train but still had everything to learn about how to be one. Reedley had told him, "A wheel needs grease, it'll tell you when. When it tells you, you best tend to it or you will have a busted axel, or maybe it'll catch fire. So, stand beside the road and note any wagons with squeaky wheels. Here's paper and a pencil."

Addison looked behind him, to the south, to the outrider paralleling the road. He pulled a piece of write-to-Mariah paper from his saddlebag along with a pencil. Then he swung up onto Outlaw and rode out onto the grass to give the outrider, who turned out to be the Youngs' son, Billy, a job. "Ride to the front of the train and stop beside the road and write down every wagon needing wheels greased."

"Yes, sir."

"Write your paw's name first."

"Yes, sir."

Billy rode off. Addison watched him. They were the same age. Billy's *yes, sirs,* made him Wagon Master every bit as much as Reedley handing him the whanging irons.

The Wagon Master rode back to the edge of the road and watched the wagons leave the overnight cluster and join one of the two lines forming on the road to Atchison. The last to roll were Otto Vogelsang Conestogas loaded with building supplies. Otto had left his son Hermann in charge. Addison nudged Outlaw into position beside Hermann on the driver's bench. He intended to tell Hermann to have men ready to grease wheels at the nine o'clock rest stop.

"*Vagon* Master, I hear *duh sqveekin'.* I *tink* five vagons be needin' wheels greased. Last five to say dey come wit us, I tink. I have men ready ven ve stop."

Addison tipped his hat, a salute from one seasoned crusader to another, and reined Outlaw to a stop. A wagon master had to think of everything, but once in a while, he got some help with that. Hermann rode ahead. The Wagon Master stayed where he was until he saw his end-of-the train riders were in their proper positions. Then he said, "Outlaw."

When he arrived at the front of the train, he found Maybell in the hammock facing aft. She was knitting! If he'd tried to imagine Maybell Jim fashioning a baby blanket, his mind would not have been able to create such a picture.

Maybell's needles paused, and she looked at Addison. She smiled. His blood sister did not smile often. He thought of her sense of humor as sort of like a winter coat hung in a closet for half the year.

*Addison J. Freeman, Wagon Master.*

*Maybell Jim, Mother.*

He was sure his blood sister had, at those two thoughts, gone to her closet and extracted her sense of humor at mid-season, and smiled.

And it inspired him to think: Mother, and to a lesser extent, Wagon Master, they were two jobs that you had to learn by doing. Watching others, or listening to offered instructions, only did so much for you. The rest you learned by doing. Your doing guided by God-planted instinct.

Maybell took her knitting needles in her left hand. With her right, she lifted the Navy colt from her belly to beside her.

Addison: "*Tisk, tisk.*" Outlaw moved them to the front of the wagon. There, the Wagon Master found Hope sitting on Winifred's lap with her little hands on the reins, too. She glanced at her father briefly, then turned back to the team she was driving.

Behind the driver's bench, Mariah lay on her hammock facing forward. She, too, knitted. She smiled at her husband. Her left eyebrow levitated up while the right remained in place. Addison felt her think: *Look at you, Addison J. Freeman! Wagon Master!*

The Wagon Master felt his duties and his conscience tug him in different directions. His wife was proud of him, and he had to let her know he was proud of her, too. Proud of Mariah the Healer, Mariah the Mother, Mariah the Wife, Mariah the good and Godly person.

Tearing his eyes away from his wife was akin to ripping off a bandage on his arm after the material had congealed with the dried blood and scraped raw meat.

But it was time. High dad-burned time. The sound of thundering hooves came from the east.

A rider rode hard toward the train. Addison galloped ahead to meet him. It was Ansel Fishboch. Joshua Reedley sent—no. Lead scout Maurice Reedley sent Ansel back to report something.

Addison stopped a couple of hundred yards ahead of Mrs. Reedley's wagon. Well away from the road.

Ansel pulled up next to him. His horse lathered and breathing loud. "I'm s'posed to tell you Mud Bottom Creek is dry."

Not a surprise. The creek hadn't held much water when Jibway, Winnifred, and Addison had crossed it on the way to Brotherton.

"Tell Maurice we're stopping there anyway. Got some wheels needing grease."

Ansel reined his mount around.

Addison hollered, "Wait! Get a fresh horse before you ride back. Swap yours for one of those behind Mrs. Reedley's wagon. I don't have to tell you to do the swap without making her stop, do I?"

Ansel said, "No, sir."

# 12.

The Wagon Master had a plan to silence his squeakers.

There was no water in Mud Bottom Creek, but the streambed was axel-deep, suck-your-boots-off sludge that smelled like pond scum. Gravel had been dumped to create a ford, but it was narrow. The train would have to cross single file. As they neared the ford, Addison directed squeaky-wheel wagons onto the grass to both sides of the road.

When the wagons bunched at the ford to form the single file, men handed the reins to their wives, and they climbed down and joined one of the five teams for greasing axels. Hermann Vogelsang had appointed a leader for each.

Addison watched the first squeaker stop short of Mud Bottom Creek. The driver, his wife, and children climbed down, unhitched their team, and led it onto the grass to graze. A six-man grease team swarmed the stopped schooner and removed water barrels and other heavy items from inside. A man with a wrench and hammer loosened the axel nut on a wheel. Three men pulled a thick plank from a Vogelsang lumber Conestoga, placed it to act as lifting lever, and raised the wheel off the ground. Wrench Man removed the axel nut and pulled the wheel off. Another man slathered grease on the axel. The wheel went back. The nut was tightened. The wheel was lowered to the ground. The team moved to the next wheel.

Addison tried to keep the smile off his face, but he couldn't. It was a good plan. Greasing the squeakers this side of the ford was his idea. The rest of the plan, Hermann created.

Addison left Hermann to supervise, and he guided Outlaw between two wagons and crossed the ford.

Mrs. Reedley and Winifred had bunched the schooners into lines of five wagons on the grass to the north and south of the road to Atchison.

"When the train stops, bunch the wagons for protection." A Joshua Reedley dictum, readily adopted by the new Wagon Master.

The sunrise scout team, Maurice Reedley, with his father and Ansel Fishboch, waited in the center of the road for the new Wagon Master. Addison nudged Outlaw to join them.

Maurice: "There's a group of men, about twenty, waiting where you said we'd stop for noon." Actually, Joshua Reedley had said where they'd stop. At the spot where the train would leave the road to Atchison and head directly for the Martin farm. "Saw them through the glass, but we couldn't tell if the men were pro-slavery or anti-slavery."

Addison looked at Joshua Reedley. He stared back.

Addison: "Maurice, you're wagon master till I get back. Take a half hour to water the stock. Then get them moving again. But Hermann Vogelsang is greasing five squeakers on the other side of the ford. If Hermann isn't ready to move yet, wait for him. It's more important to keep everybody together than to save minutes. Uh … to a point."

Maurice: "Right. Keep the train together, but don't take all day to do it."

Addison: "Mr. Reedley, Joshua, ride with me, please. First though, we water these horses and switch saddles to spare mounts. And, Maurice, find me a fishing pole."

Lead scout, Don Carlson, a couple of years older than Addison, stood next to the road peering through the spy glass. He turned as Addison and Joshua approached and reined up next to him.

"One a them's got a glass on us, too." Carlson handed the telescope to Addison.

Addison peered through the glass for several ticks and tocks. Then he handed it to Joshua. "Most likely Missouri bushwhackers. But they could be like those young free state outlaws who killed the Martins."

Joshua looked, adjusted the focus, looked again, and said, "Cannon. Two of them. Probably brought home after the war with Mexico. Twenty men. And, yep. Most likely bushwhackers."

Joshua Reedley handed the glass back to lead scout Carlson.

Addison dismounted, grabbed a long-sleeved long john shirt from a saddlebag, and started tying it to the fishing pole he'd brought.

Joshua: "Tie your white flag to your rifle."

Addison stopped tying, thought a moment, pulled his lever-action repeater from the scabbard, and turned to the lead scout. "Any of you have a single action long gun?"

The Emigrant Aid Society had supplied Brotherton and other Free Staters with repeating rifles. Missouri bushwhackers prized these weapons, and their way to obtain them was to kill Free Staters and take theirs.

Don Carlson answered the new Wagon Master's question. "Yeah. Sylvester Dinwiddie has one."

Joshua: "You should take the repeater."

Wagon Master: "Don't want to risk it falling into their hands."

"Let me go."

"Maybe next time, Mr. Reedley."

Addison gathered the scouts and Joshua. First, he took Dinwiddie's single-shot long gun and told him to ride back to the train. He was to ride hard. When he got there, he should find all the wagons across the ford and moving. If that were not the case, Dinwiddie should tell Maurice Reedley to consider abandoning a wagon or two, and to get the rest across Mud Bottom Creek as quickly as possible.

Addison raised a thumb. Dinwiddie was to tell Maurice to turn the train south out onto the prairie.

When Joshua Reedley served as Wagon Master, and he had a series of instructions to issue, he used fingers to count them off. "Using fingers helps a person remember. And it helps me remember to stop giving jobs to a fellow when I run out of fingers."

Index finger raised. "Maurice should push the teams hard for five hours, then turn the wagons east."

Middle finger rose. "Someone from the scouting party should reach the train before it's time to turn, but if no one shows up, turn and keep rolling."

Finger four elevated. "Maurice should deploy fifteen outriders, all armed with repeating rifles, and positioned to be between the train and the point on the road to Atchison where they had planned to stop for noon. Those outriders should be five hundred yards from the wagons."

Wagon Master: "Sylvester, repeat those instructions back to me."

Dinwiddie raised a thumb. "If the wagons ain't across Mud Bottom Creek, git 'em across. Then head south."

Fingers elevated one at a time to trigger the remaining parts of the Wagon Master's instructions. As Sylvester recited, Addison took a piece of paper and drew the road to Atchison with the bushwhackers' and the ford through Mud Bottom Creek positions X-ed. Martinsville was also drawn onto the crude map.

Addison handed the spyglass and the map to Dinwiddie. "The glass is for the fifteen outriders. Get a new long gun when you get back. Now go. Ride hard."

Sylvester reined his horse around and spurred it into an all-out run.

Addison mumbled, "Should'a told him to not kill his horse getting there."

"I think you should let me go meet the bushwhackers."

"Mr. Reedley, thanks. But I have to do this."

"Tell me how you're going to do it."

If anyone else, even Mariah, had asked him that question, he wouldn't have answered. To Joshua Reedley, he said he was riding a spare horse, and he asked Joshua to look after Outlaw. Then, holding up his single-shot long gun like a white-flag banner, he'd ride toward the bushwhackers. When he got to within a hundred yards of them, he'd stop. If no one came out to see what he wanted, he'd wave his banner in invitation. If still no one came, he'd turn his horse around and hightail it back.

If the bushwhackers did send men—they'd never send just one, or just two—if they sent more than four to palaver, he'd hightail it.

Reedley nodded. "Two things. Tie your white flag to the rifle with string. If you knot the sleeves to the barrel, you won't be able to use the sights. Second, take your repeater."

Neither was a question. Neither was a suggestion.

Neither did the new Wagon Master argue either point with the old one.


A hundred yards short of the bushwhackers—probable bushwhackers, Addison reined up.

And waited.

He felt the forty eyeballs and the two cannon all staring intense malevolence at him.

He held the pole for his white flag aloft with his hand through the cocking lever. The hammer was cocked, his finger next to the trigger guard.

The bushwhackers stood bunched around the cannon. Behind them was a covered wagon and their horses.

Addison waved his white flag back and forth, back and forth. He hollered, "Couple of you come out. We'll parley."

One of the bushwhackers standing next to a cannon turned, and said something Addison could not hear. After a minute, four riders set out toward him, walking their mounts. One of them held a long gun pointed at the sky, except his rifle had no underclothing tied to the barrel.

The four bushwhackers' horses plodded, heads bobbing, toward where Addison waited. He wished he were astride Outlaw, although he hadn't, and didn't want to expose him to the danger of waiting there. In the middle of the road. Exposed. He felt like he was a target on a shooting range.

Still, talking to Outlaw would have helped just then. And talking to the spare horse he rode, well, it would have been easier speaking with a woman he didn't know and to whom he hadn't been introduced. But speaking soft and slow would calm the animal. So, he whispered softly and slowly, "Can't believe those yahoos are riding bunched together."

The four rode abreast, and close enough so all four horses fit on the road. As soon as he got the words out, the yahoos separated putting a distance between them of about the width of the scoured of grass roadbed.

When they were about forty yards from him, Addison's mount grew nervous, did a little dance, and shifted weight from one front leg to the other. "Guess I shoulda' kept my mouth shut," he whispered. "Those dumb Missourah boys woulda' never thought of putting distance between them on their own."

As they neared, Addison grew nervous. He felt like he needed a set of eyeballs for each of them.

At about fifteen yards from him, Addison said, "Stop!"

The rider on the edge of the roadbed to his left raised a hand, and they reined up.

Raised Hand lowered it. He was maybe twenty. Or fifty. Scruffy beard. Greasy-looking, stringy hair hung to the shoulders of his dirty shirt. "Whaddaya want?"

Addison: "What do **you** want? Alla' you bunched up beside the road. With cannon. What do **you** want?"

Greasy Hair: "What I want is for every stinkin' one a you murderin' abolitionists to be swept from the face of the earth! I bet you're the ones killed the Martin family so's you could take their land and build you nuther stinkin' abolitionist town. That ain't gonna happen. So, y'all got a choice. Turn around and go back where you come from. You got wimmen 'n kids. We'd rather not kill them like you murdered the Martin wimmen."

The bushwhacker glared pure hot hate.

Addison worried. They might have already killed Jibway and Otto Vogelsang. And Winifred's two men.

"In case you're wonderin'," the outlaw said, "those men at the Martin farm, we ain't killed them. Yet. Figger to hang 'em after we git done with y'all." He pointed a finger at Addison. "Now. You do what I tole yah. Go back where yuh come from!"

Greasy Hair turned to his companion with the long gun. "Watch the bastard. Don't let him shoot me in the back." He reined his horse around and galloped it back toward his gang.

The one with the long gun started lowering the weapon to aim it at Addison.

Quick as a flash, Addison dropped his rifle into position and fired.

Long Gun Bushwhacker tumbled backward out of the saddle. His mount bolted, heading north.

To Addison's right, one of men's horses reared, dumped its rider, and ran off heading south. Still Mounted Man drew a pistol.

Addison ducked, rolled out of his saddle, landed on his knees, and levered a round into the chamber. A pistol popped. Addison's horse collapsed onto the ground. Without raising the butt to his shoulder, he fired. Pistol Shooter flew off his saddle.

The three downed bushwhackers lay still. Addison tore the undershirt from his rifle, raised it, aimed at Greasy Hair hustling back to rejoin his gang, and squeezed the trigger. Greasy Hair slumped, then tumbled to the ground.

Addison stood in the road, the smell of gun smoke and horse sweat … and his own filling his nose. There was ringing in his ears. Then gunfire drowned that out.

The bushwhackers fired at him.

Addison ran onto the grass, to the one who'd carried a long gun. He lay with his eyes open and staring. At nothing. A dark blotch over his heart stained his tan shirt.

Addison grabbed the single-shot long gun, and with a rifle in each hand, ran to the pistol shooter's mount. Which waited. Ground hitched.

He took the barrels of both rifles in one hand, grabbed the saddle horn with the other, and swung up onto the saddle. The bushwhackers still blazed away; their pistols ineffective at that distance. But with all those bullets flying, one of them might be a piece of lucky lead.

Addison reined his mount around and dug his heels in the animal's belly. It launched into an all-out run away from the shooting.

# 13.

Joshua, with Outlaw on a rope, and scout Don Carlson, leading a spare horse, galloped toward the wagon train. Addison gigged his—the bushwhacker's mount with his heels. He thought the animal was running full out and spurred it so it wouldn't slow down. It didn't slow. It sped up another notch.

*A fine piece of—.* Addison stomped on the thought, thinking he was being disloyal to Outlaw.

When he came abreast of Joshua Reedley, Addison slowed. He expected Joshua to tell him what to do. *Oh! I'm the Wagon Master.*

Wagon Master Addison moved back next to Outlaw, slid his repeating rifle into the scabbard, and, while hanging onto the single-shot long gun, switched onto **his** horse. Then he hollered to the scout, "Don. Give Joshua your repeater. Take this single shot and the spare horses and rejoin the train. Tell them what happened. Tell them to expect a passel of angry bushwhackers."

Addison checked behind them. No pursuit. Yet!

He came up alongside Joshua again. "I think those bushwhackers are mad as all get out. I think they'll come after us with everybody they got left. What do you think?"

"Yeah," Joshua said. They'll come after us. Probly four will stay with the wagon and cannons."

"So, a dozen. They'll ride hard. They'll think we're running away from them. Grass here is knee high. Enough, I think, for an ambush."

Joshua said, "You want the extra repeater rifle?"

"You keep it. You're a better shot. Slightly better."

They reined up, walked their horses into the grass to either side of the road, and pulled their mounts down onto their knees, then rolled them onto their sides. Both riders lay across the shoulders of their horses and waited, rifles in hand, for their pistolero enemy.

They didn't have to wait long. Vibration in the ground and the thunder of hooves reached them. Joshua spoke soft, reassuring words to his horse. Addison purred comfort to Outlaw. The gaggle of riders raced down the middle of road, all packed tightly together, all coming hell bent for leather.

Joshua looked at Addison. Addison nodded. Reedley would fire first.

Joshua rose onto a knee, aimed, and fired. A rider in the middle of the pack fell, and the pack split apart and moved onto the grass. Reedley's next shot unhorsed the right-most bushwhacker.

Addison hoped the pro-slavers would think they had a single shooter against them and keep coming. They kept coming. Reedley fired again as Addison triggered his first round. Then, it was fire, lever, aim, fire. Lever, aim, fire.

Pandemonium arrested the bushwhacker's charge. Horses reared. Riderless horses ran in all directions save at Addison. One pro-slaver helped an unhorsed one up behind him and headed east.

Addison focused on the bushwhackers headed north. He worried those might try to flank him and Joshua from that side. He aimed and fired at the farthest out onto the grass and dropped him. Then his rifle was empty. Joshua was firing his second repeater. Addison loaded two rounds and dropped a third to the ground when Reedley hollered, "Time to go!"

Addison said, "Outlaw!" and he got his hooves under him. Addison checked on the bushwhackers. Five horses raced east.

Reedley mounted and said, "Now what?"

"The bushwhackers won't quit. They'll figure our wagon train will be close. Once they find it, they'll stop and cut loose with the cannon and blow up everyone and everything."

Joshua spurred his horse into a run down the middle of the road.

Huh! Addison would have ridden south heading for where he figured the wagon train would be. But Reedley, he was sure, thought there might be a wounded bushwhacker who would see them head out onto the prairie. That could be enough to make the pro-slavers stop and think. Then they'd be harder to ambush.

*Johua Reedley. A pretty smart hombre.*

Addison and Joshua reined up about a mile and a half east of the ford across Mud Bottom Creek. There, the wagon train had turned onto the prairie and cut a blatant sign of their passage.

Addison: "You think Maurice has headed the train east by now?"

"If not, close to it."

Reedley spurred his mount down the middle of the path of beaten-down prairie grass. Outlaw tore after him.

They ran their horses for a time. Addison hadn't thought to count the minutes. Then, Joshua pulled up. Addison stopped Outlaw and saw it. Directly ahead, the canvas covers of the prairie schooners, distance and haze dimmed, but visible above the wake of flattened grass.

Addison wondered if Maurice halted the train for lunch. By the sun, it was two p.m.

Reedley: "They're watering the horses."

Addison: "We've got to get them moving. And in a line, not bunched up like I said earlier. Not with the bushwhackers and their cannons after us."

Joshua looked at the new Wagon Master. Expectantly.

Addison: "We'll go slow from here. Maurice will have lookouts posted." He shook his head. "Wish I hadn't thrown my long john top away."

"You still got the bottoms."

Addison's face grew warm, but he pulled the new white flag

material from a saddlebag and tied the legs of the garment to the barrel of his repeater. He wasn't worried about obscuring the sights.

The new Wagon Master led the way with his new white banner raised, Outlaw at a walk. As they closed the distance, Addison could see the wagons had been bunched in five rows. *Just like I said.*

At about two hundred yards short of the train, a voice hollered, "Stop! Don't reach for no gun!"

Maurice Reedley rose from the grass holding a repeater rifle. "Addison J. Freeman. You wet your pants and are using your long gun like a clothesline to dry your longies?"

To Addison's right, Ansel Fishbock stood up. "Pee Pants Freeman! Heck of a name for a wagon master!"

"Shut up, Fishboch!" Addison barked as he untied the legs of his white flag. "This wagon train ain't big enough to hold two wiseacres." To Maurice: "Do you have the map I drew?"

Maurice pulled the paper from a shirt pocket. Addison dismounted, dropped the reins, hustled to take his drawing, motioned the others to gather round, and unfolded the map. He had Ansel turn around and used his back as a desk to draw in where he and Joshua had staged their ambush, and where Maurice had turned the train off the road to Atchison. Then he showed the map to the others.

"The bushwhackers," Addison said, "are driven by how much they hate us, and not much else. They will come down the road fast as they can drag their cannon. They won't know we've left the road until they see the trail through the grass."

Maurice: "So, they think they're going to meet us on the road to Atchison and attack us from our front, but they'll actually be chasing us from behind."

Addison: "Mr. Reedley, you know anything about cannon?"

Joshua: "The cannon will slow them down some. But, depending on the kind of carriage under the big guns, they could still come at a good clip."

Ansel Fishboch: "How far can those cannon shoot, Mr. Reedley?"

Joshua: "Don't know for sure. I expect they'd be pretty accurate at five hundred yards. Specially shootin' at a wagon. And if they can fire exploding balls, they could hurt us bad from maybe even a half mile."

Addison pointed behind him. "When you all turned south, you flattened the grass and made an arrow pointed at where we are right now. The bushwhackers will follow that arrow."

Maurice: "Instead of meeting us head-on, they'll be chasing us from behind. Is that good or bad?"

Addison: "Good. Mostly. It helps us figure out where to place our riflemen. Did you pick fifteen men with repeaters?"

Maurice nodded.

Ansel: "You said you ambushed them along the road to Atchison. Think they'll let themselves ride into another?"

Addison: "I think they want to kill us all so bad, they ain't doing much thinking."

On his map, Addison traced the train's southbound route with his finger. "At some point, the bushwhackers will be able to see the wagons. Then, they'll turn toward us and whip their teams to bring their big guns in range.

"Maurice. Get the train moving. Fast. Push the animals hard. Put them single file."

The stand-in wagon master hurried off.

"Mr. Reedley. Gather the riflemen. Give each of them two repeaters. Have them afoot and wait where the train is stopped now. And bring me the spyglass."

Joshua hurried off.

Addison studied his map. He tried to imagine bushwhacker speed and how that meant miles and minutes. He placed his finger on the spot where Joshua had spotted the covers on the wagons. However, the bushwhackers had a spy glass. He moved his finger back toward the road to Atchison. The finger stopped. *About right.*

He knew how he'd string out his riflemen in a line. He'd place Joshua Reedley at the right end. Addison would anchor the line on the left. Addison and Reedley would have horses. Both of them could hide their mounts in the grass.

The plan was set.

*Please, God, be with us. I'd rather have You with us than any plan.*

# 14.

Addison dropped to a knee and stared through the spyglass until it felt like the glass was trying to suck his eyeball out. He lowered it and rubbed his eye. Then he turned to his right. No head showed above the prairie grass.

The riflemen had placed themselves fifty yards apart.

Addison said—loud enough to carry fifty yards, but not much farther: "Clear." The echo, "Clear" came back to him as a whisper. It would take a minute for the message to be relayed to Joshua at the other end of the line.

He faced forward and brought the telescope up to his left eye, but he couldn't blink his eyes independently like Mariah could, and it was frustrating trying to focus, so he placed the glass to his overworked right. And saw the canvas cover of the bushwhacker wagon. Then he spotted the darker shapes of scouts in front of the wagon.

Addison lowered the glass, turned to his right, told himself to control the volume of his voice, to limit his messages to a handful of fingers, and said, "Four scouts. Two near, two far. Odd near. Even far."

Each of his riflemen had been assigned a number. The one next to Addison was number one. Number fifteen was next to Joshua. His odd-numbered riflemen would aim for the near scouts. The evens would shoot for the far.

A five-finger message would take a minute to travel through his shooters.

Addison checked through the spyglass. The bushwhacker near-scout to his right had stopped his mount and was peering through a telescope. Addison worried the man might have seen him kneeling. But the scout closed the telescope, stuck it in a bag slung from his saddle horn, turned, and spurred his mount into a gallop back toward the bushwhackers' cannons. Addison was sure, pretty sure, that meant the bushwhacker had seen only Hermann Vogelsang's rearmost wagon.

Addison waited for the nearest bushwhacker scouts to arrive within one hundred yards. He fought his inclination to aim at the scout with the spy glass, the leader, he thought, and instead, concentrated on the near scout to his left.

*There! A hundred yards!*

"Fire!" Addison hollered. The word packed a fair amount of its own unrestrainable urgency. Still, he managed to count to fifteen, before he raised his rifle, aimed, and fired. Leftmost near-scout tumbled backward out of his saddle.

Rifles banged. Bushwhacker scouts near and far fell. Their horses ran toward Mud Bottom Creek. Addison checked through the glass.

The teams towing the cannon had swung around and stopped. Bushwhackers were busy rolling cannon off their carriages and pointing them at the rear of the wagon train.

The bushwhacker wagon stopped between the two cannons.

Addison got Outlaw up, mounted, and rode toward the cannon. He glanced to his right. His riflemen were running forward, as well. After twenty yards, the Odds would stop, aim, fire, and run again. Then the Evens repeated the drill

Addison could see four bushwhackers around each cannon, working to load and aim them. He hauled back on the reins. Outlaw squatted and skidded to a stop. The driver of the bushwhacker wagon raised a rifle and fired at Addison. And missed. The driver reloaded and was raising his long gun when Addison aimed and fired at him. The driver dropped his weapon and collapsed onto the bench.

Addison's riflemen fired a volley, and men around the cannon fell. Addison fired at the cannoneers. The riflemen fired another volley.

Three cannoneers remained standing. They all raised their hands.

Three mounted bushwhackers raced away from behind the wagon, heading for the road. Addison pointed Outlaw to run after them. *Please, God. Don't let my own riflemen shoot me.*

They didn't.

Joshua was also chasing the fleeing bushwhackers. And he was closer. He reined up, aimed, and fired. A bushwhacker tumbled to the ground. The horse kept running.

Addison raced on. He was gaining on his enemy, but he judged Outlaw was tiring. He reined up, aimed, and fired. A second bushwhacker fell. Addison levered a new round and fired and missed. Levered, aimed, fired, and missed again. From behind him, Joshua Reedley fired. The last of them fell from the saddle.

Joshua rode up beside Addison.

Addison: "Joshua … uh. Mr. Reedley. Ride back to the train. Have Maurice stop and gaggle up the wagons like we usually do. Then bring horses back for our riflemen. I'll check the last three of the bushwhackers. To see if any of them are still alive."

Joshua, Mr. Reedley swung his horse around and followed orders.

*****

All the bushwhackers Addison and Joshua had chased were dead. As soon as he found the last one, he rode to where the wagons were bunched and looked for Mariah. She should be fine, but he had to set eyes on her. And Maybell. He found his wife and Winifred around a fire, working on supper. Hope sat on Maybell's lap. He'd been in battle, and the bullets no longer ripped through the air, but he hadn't felt safe until he laid eyes on his wife and daughter.

Addison and Mariah came together and held each other fiercely.

Hope hopped to the ground and ran to her parents and hugged her Daddy's leg.

"Addison," Maurice Reedley said. "One of our riflemen was wounded. Can Mariah take a look at him?"

The Healer stepped back and said, "I'll get my bag."

Addison picked up Hope and went to the wagon, where he retrieved the medical bag for his wife. Then, Mariah followed Maurice. To do her duty. Addison handed Hope back to Maybell, and he went to do his duty as Wagon Master.

He gathered a team of men and boys to bury the dead bushwhackers. Preacher Cromwell went with them.

He sent men to load the bushwhacker cannons on their carriages again.

Then, the Wagon Master picked four good cowboys to round up any bushwhackers' horses they could find. Missouri outlaws were known to have good riding stock.

"Mr. Reedley," Addison said. 'let's get a cup of coffee and talk about what happened."

Winifred had coffee ready. They each filled a cup and sat on chairs. Around them, the camp bustled with women cooking and tending to children.

Addison sipped and said, "If the bushwhackers had all been armed with long guns, we'd have had a very bad day."

Joshua: "Yes, but their main tactic is to wait for their enemy in ambush. When their target is spitting distance close, they charge out of the woods firing pistols and howling like crazy. Probably scare as many to death as they kill with bullets."

Addison: "When they decided to make a daylight raid into Kansas, I wonder if they thought the cannon would carry the day for them?"

Reedley: "We need to question the three survivors. But before we do that, what are we going to do with them in the end? Parole them? Kill them?"

"We'll question them and then decide what to do with them."

The three live bushwhackers were bound with hands behind

them and propped against wagon wheels. The O'Riley brothers and their hound guarded them.

Two of the prisoners leaned against the front wheel. One was clean-shaven and appeared to be a couple of years younger than Addison. The man next to him was older, maybe mid-thirties. A frown wrinkled the man's brow. Above his bushy black beard, his dark eyes blazed with a hungry ferocity and scanned left and right, and left again. As if he were a predator with a dozen prey before him and he was trying to decide which one to eat first.

Addison walked up to Clean Shaven and tapped the sole of his boot with the toe of his own. "What's your name?"

Hungry Eyes snapped. "Keep your mouth shut. Don't tell these sumbitching abolitionists nothin'."

Joshua Reedley strode to Hungry Eyes and smacked him on the jaw with the butt of his rifle. The bushwhacker fell onto his side, moaned once, coughed, and spat out a mouthful of blood.

Joshua said, "One of you O'Reillys, come help me."

One of them did. Reedley rolled Hungry Eyes onto his back: then Joshua picked up a leg of the moaning man and indicated that his O'Reilly helper should take the other leg. Together, the two of them dragged the bushwhacker past the rear of the wagon.

Clean Shaven had watched what had happened to his compatriot with his mouth hanging open.

Addison toed the man's boot again. "What's your name?"

Clean Shaven's eyes opened wider. His mouth clamped shut only to open again. "Ruben. Ruben Fleming."

Addison glanced at the man tied up and leaning on the rear wheel. He'd been staring at Addison, but he looked away. The man was also young, also afraid.

"Ruben, how did you know we had a wagon train heading for the Martin farm?"

"Oscar, the one they drug off, had been with our troop awhile, but he said we weren't killing enough Yankee soldiers, so he was quitting the war and moving out west. He joined a wagon train, and it stopped at Dobb's trading post. He heard what you all was doing in Brotherton, an he quit that train and hightailed it back to us. We'd just come by two cannon, and Jubal, he was our leader, figured we'd blow your wagon train all to hell, an then we'd do the same to Brotherton."

As Ruben spoke, it was as if his words, infused as they were with bravado, elevated the speaker's spirits, rather than the speaker injecting those emotions into his words. Then he had nothing more to say, and nothing to hold fear at bay.

"Where'd they take Oscar? What're they going to do to him?"

Addison didn't answer.

"What are you going to do to me?"

Addison didn't answer. He moved to stand opposite the bushwhacker propped against the rear wheel, and stared down at him. "How old are you?"

"What're you gonna do to me?"

"That depends on you. Answer the question."

"Fifteen."

"Name?"

"Wally. Wally Winkelpleck."

A picture popped into Addison's head. Zeke, Adam, and Matt. Third-grade bullies who'd welcomed him, the deacon's brat, to first grade by stealing his lunch. He wondered what they'd have done to a Wally Winklepleck. Zeke and his cohorts were good at hiding their misdeeds through watchfulness for the teacher and threats to their schoolmates, but they were eventually spotted. Preacher Larrimer then came to school to administer spankings and assign the boys clean-the-school-after-class duties for the rest of the year. Plus, Larrimer's sermon the next Sunday was on "Loving your neighbor as you love yourself." Starting immediately after that sermon and during lunch in the hall next to the church, the entire congregation took up the task of civilizing what Maurice Reedley, the Wiseacre, called The Unholy Trinity. The next school year, Zeke, Adam, and Matt were model citizens.

Addison said, "Wally, why were you riding with the bushwhackers?"

It was as if a bucketful of fiery hot anger was dumped over his head, washing away the fear on his face.

"Blue Bellies! I was out rounding up the cows for evening milking when Blue Belly soldiers come and shot my paw and my brother. And they took Maw and my sister away with them. Probably shot them, too, after—." Wally looked away. His breath rasped in and out, as if he'd been running till he couldn't anymore. Then he turned back and glared at Addison. "Blue Bellies, Abolitionists, John Brown Jayhawkers! You're all alike. Y'all need to be shot and burned. Sure wouldn't feed you to the hogs. You'd ruin the taste of their bacon."

Joshua Reedley stepped around the rear of the wagon. "Wally, why did you stop fighting and raise your hands?"

Wally was fair-complexioned. "I—I—" His blush set fire to his cheeks.

# 15.

Wagon Master Addison Freeman assigned Ruben Fleming to ride in the O'Reilly brothers' wagon. Wally Winklepleck rode in what the young men in the train called the Wimmen Wagon. His hands and feet were tied, and he sat in a rear corner propped against the tailgate. He glared up at his guard, recumbent in her hammock. Maybell stared right back.

Winifred said, "Hey up," snapped the reins, and the wagon lurched into motion.

Maybell said, "Mistuh Winklepleck, sure hope I don't have to shoot you. If'n I do, we'll have to write on your grave marker: 'Wally Winklepleck, a white man shot dead by a pregnant colored woman married to an Ojibway Indian.' Why, that'd take three boards to hold alla that. You reckon you be worth three boards, Mr. Winklepleck?"

Wally's mouth dropped open, like he'd just heard his grade schoolteacher tell the class that the world was round, and Wally wasn't buying it, not even a little bit. But then he frowned, and his eyes blazed with dark fury. He jerked and strained at the rope binding his hands.

Maybell raised the Navy Colt and cocked the hammer.

Wally looked up. His eyes grew big and full of so much fear that the fear pushed the hate out. For a moment. Then the hate took over again, and he resumed struggling with his bindings.

Maybell fired the pistol.

"Oh, ow!" Wally cussed and raised his bound hands to his left ear. When he lowered them again, they were covered with blood. He cussed some more.

Addison guided Outlaw to where he could peer into the rear of the wagon. Mariah stood, holding onto the frame of her hammock to steady herself against jiggles, jerks, and jostles as their wagon wheels rolled over the uneven terrain. She handed the wounded man a white cloth to hold over his bleeding ear.

An impulse to say thanks, Addison was sure, washed over Wally's face, but then he clamped his lips together and pressed the cloth to his wound.

Mariah: "Wally, you think you have reason to hate us, but we have reason to hate you, too. You believe it is right and proper for you to own slaves. We believe slavery is an abomination against the laws of God and of man. That's what we believe as strongly as you believe there is nothing wrong with owning other humans as long as their skin color condemns them to inferiority to your almighty whiteness."

The wagon lurched, and Mariah staggered, but remained upright.

Addison: "Mariah, you should get back in the hammock."

She nodded to her husband. "One more thing, Wally. Do you know what you are right now?" A pause. "You're Maybell's slave."

Wally recoiled as if he'd been slapped; then he frowned; then hate again burned hot in his eyes. "******* can't own whites!"

Maybell cocked the pistol.

Wally raised his hands to cover his good ear.

Maybell: "Best lower your hands or you'll lose fingers as well as the other ear."

Wally lowered his hands; then he turned his head to the side.

Maybell: "Good. Rather shoot a nose off than nuther ear."

Wally raised his hands in front of his face. "No! Please?"

Mariah: "Maybell knows full well what pro-slavery white men do to colored women. Do you think it helped her to beg them to let her be?"

"Please! Please don't shoot me again!"

Maybell: "Shut up! Sit there. Real still like."

She lowered the hammer on her Colt.

Mariah: "Hold that cloth over your ear. When we stop, I'll bandage it."

Then she laid back onto her hammock.

Addison reined Outlaw away from the rear of the wagon and to the side, where he watched the schooners and Conestogas trundle and rumble past. He thanked God for Mariah and Maybell. They just may have done the only thing that could reach Wally Winkelpleck. *Please, God, help Wally see the evil infesting slavery. So I don't have to kill him. Or Ruben.* As wagon master, he needed to see some possibility the young pro-slavers could begin to understand the error, the sin resident in slavery. Otherwise, he'd have to kill one, or maybe, both of them. As Wagon Master, it was his responsibility. He could not direct another to execute one, or both, if they refused to bend. Nor could he let Joshua take those additional deaths onto his soul, as he had already taken the responsibility for Oscar.

At the midmorning stop, Addison sent Hermann Vogelsang and Winifred, along with a party of men and women, on saddle horses ahead to the Martin farm. There, they'd prepare the evening meal for the wagon train.

Also, during the stop, Preacher Cromwell took Wally Winkelpleck aside and spoke with him for thirty minutes; then the wagon master hollered, "On to Martinsville!"

When they resumed the journey, Wally Winkelpleck rode with the O'Reillys, and Ruben Fleming rode in the hammock wagon, situated as Wally had been. All the way to Winifred's farm, Addison expected to hear a pistol shot, signaling the creation of a notch in Ruben's ear. But the train neared their destination at midafternoon with no shot having been fired.

Hermann Vogelsang's plan laid out the streets of Martinsville to the north of the Martin farm. So, the Wagon Master planned to line up the wagons near the southside of Winifred's home.

Martinsville was laid out similar to Brotherton. Except Main and the numbered streets ran north/south vice east/west. The Meeting House was sited in the center of Main and would be built sturdy enough to serve as a fort. The church would be built behind the Meeting House on Second Street. The communal barn sat on Fifth Street.

Where the barn would be, Jibway and his two companions built a large corral to hold the horses and cows accompanying the wagon train. His two companions were Billy Bob Nelson and Harvey Montag. Billy Bob had been with the gang of young men who had killed Winifred's family, but had been horrified to discover he'd joined a band of outlaws instead of the Kansas Militia. Harvey Montag, a Ziggy Hostetler waggoneer, had also remained with Jibway at the Martin farm after Winifred traveled to Brotherton with Addison and Joshua Reedley.

At the Martin farm, the Wagon Master ordered Maurice Reedley to line the wagons up. He had to figure out what to do with Winkelpleck and Ruben Fleming.

As soon as Preacher Cromwell stopped his wagon, Addison asked him to accompany him to the rear of the Martin farmhouse. There the two sat on the steps to the rear door.

Addison: "Preacher, since you spoke with the Winkelpleck kid, what do you think of him? Is he a died-in-the-wool Abolitionist hater? Or might he change his thinking about us?"

Cromwell rubbed a hand over his long, lean, clean-shaven face. "Your question makes me feel like I'm in the Roman Coliseum. Down on the floor of the arena, a gladiator has lost his sword, and he's kneeling in front of one with a sword. The one with the weapon is looking at me, and he's expecting me to signal thumb up, or thumb down. And if I don't give him a signal, he'll cut my head off."

The Preacher had stopped talking, but Addison was sure he was still working on his answer.

Cromwell had changed from when Addison first met him as the

spiritual leader of a wagon train of Emigrant Aid Society pilgrims traveling to Kansas for the same purpose Preacher Larrimer's congregation uprooted itself. Practically violent in his defense of his non-violent philosophy. Now, after being part of Brotherton, after engaging in some of its battles for self-preservation, he'd changed. Become practically human even. Addison could not imagine himself asking such a question of Preacher Larrimer.

Cromwell: "Wally Winkelpleck, in one sense, is just like I was when I came to Kansas. Everything I believed in back east, the foundational pillars supporting my mind and my soul, were kicked out from under me. The hate, the violence, the pro-slavery kill lust aimed at us. These were thoughts my brain just could not accept.

"Now consider young Wally. He finds himself held captive by an armed, colored woman, who is with child. And all the rest of us see nothing wrong with the situation. We know what Maybell is capable of. But to Mr. Winkelpleck, a colored woman married to an Indian, and all of us treat them like they are just as white as he is. It's just inconceivable. And she is armed, and he is her prisoner. Inconceivable. She shoots a piece of his ear off, and we do nothing about it. Inconceivable."

Preacher Cromwell stood and stretched and craned his neck one way, then the other. The bones popped and snapped. Then he knelt on the step he'd sat on and removed his black, flat-brimmed hat. "Father, God, Lord of heaven, Lord of earth, help young Wally see, as You helped me see, that the way I grew up was wrong. I looked at the people around me and considered the way they behaved to be right and good and proper, and anyone who behaved differently was dead wrong. Young Wally needs help, as I did, to learn that lesson. Help him see that Maybell is a person, not like he is, but a better person than he is."

Addison: "Amen."

Both men donned their hats and rose.

Addison sighed.

Preacher: "You still have to decide about the other one, Ruben?"

Addison nodded.

Preacher: "After supper."

# 16.

The men, women, and children of the wagon train from Brotherton settled into circles of camaraderie, feasting, and thanksgiving for a safe arrival at their destination, with only one of their number wounded, instead of what could have happened if the bushwhackers had been able to cut loose with their cannons.

Hermann Vogelsang was staking out the houses along Main Street. Addison invited him to join them for dinner.

Hermann: "Tomorrow. First light. Ve begin building Meeting House. Ven dat done, I eat."

Addison: "Stubborn German. I'm going to eat now. When I'm finished, I'm bringing you a plate, and I'm bringing Maybell with me. If you don't eat then, she'll shoot your ear off."

Hermann hammered another stake into the ground.

Addison shook his head and rejoined the circle in front of the hammock wagon.

Preacher Cromwell had waited for the wagon master to join them. Then he began the before-meal prayer. The prayer took a while. Cromwell paused for breath, and Hope's "I hungwy" carried through the evening prairie silence, at the time when the day birds and bugs had stopped their songs, but the nighttime ones hadn't yet begun theirs.

The Preacher cleared his throat and said, "Amen." Echoed lustily and enthusiastically by the travelers. The amen echo died out, and in the pause of a tick and a tock, the sound of a mallet striking wood came from the other side of Winifred's house.

Addison muscled aside his annoyance at Hermann and thanked God for him instead.

Addison and Hope sat on the tongue of the hammock wagon, and Jibway, Maybell, Joshua Reedley, Harvey Montag, Billy Bob Nelson, and Winifred completed their circle. They all walked to the food tables in front of Winifred's house, filled their plates—Addison carried Hope's—and returned to their seats.

There, Wagon Master Daddy tied a made-from-a-flour-sack dishtowel around Hope's neck as she stuck a cheek-bulging spoonful of stew into her mouth. The rest of the circle was almost as hungry as she was. There was no talking, just the clinks and scrapes of spoons and forks on tin plates. Billy Bob finished his plateful first and rose to fetch a second. Addison motioned Winifred to come and sit by Hope, and he hurried after B Bob, as Hope called him.

Earlier, Addison had spoken with Jibway about Billy Bob. His blood brother had only good things to say about the young man. "He works hard. Sees a thing that needs doing and does it without having to be told. And he is happy we saved him from becoming a murdering outlaw instead of a soldier."

Addison caught up to Billy. "You've seen our two prisoners?"

Billy Bob nodded.

Addison: "You have any thoughts about what we ought to do with them?"

B Bob shook his head. "I haven't spoken with them. Jibway did."

Addison: "Jibway told me he asked the two of them their names. Wally replied: 'I ain't sayin' nothin' to no red-skinned—' Wally used a word I won't use. Jibway responded, 'Union soldiers killed your paw, and you want to get even by blowing up women and children with your cannons! You know what that makes you? You are worse than a white—that word again!"

Billy Bob kept walking toward the serving tables.

Addison: "Will you talk to them and let me know what you think?"

B. Bob: "Y'all saved me from becoming a murdering outlaw. I don't want to have anything to do with killing those men."

Addison: "I can't let them go. If I do, they'll be back with other bushwhackers. But I also do not want to have to kill them. I am looking for help to figure out a way so I won't have to shoot them. You haven't met Preacher Cromwell yet. I'll introduce you to him. Talk to him. Then decide if you can help me with my problem."

The next morning, the crusaders from Brotherton were roused from sleep by the whanging of horseshoes. It was still pitch dark out, but the smell of side meat frying seemed to be a better motivator to get people moving than dawn's early light would have been.

The night before, the crusaders had pronounced themselves citizens of Martinsville, that Winifred Martin was their mayor, and Addison Freeman was the town marshal.

The mayor: "Preacher Cromwell, the morning prayer, please. Then, we'll take thirty minutes to eat. After that, we have a burying to do. Once that's done, we have a town to build."

The preacher appended an "amen, to his prayer, and the citizens scurried to fetch plates. Again, there wasn't much talking.

Hope ate. Mariah took a bite. Addison sat there with a knife and fork in his hands but didn't use them. He stared toward the east, where there was an announcement that, that day, the sun would indeed rise once more.

Mariah laid her silverware on her plate and placed a hand on her husband's arm. She looked into his eyes.

In her eyes, he saw concern, caring, a willingness to share his burden. The last thing he wanted was to offload some of what weighed him down onto her. But something like that just happened. His heavy heart felt a bit lighter.

She said, "Addison." Just that. Just his name, but he knew she was reminding him of two years ago, when a sense of duty compelled her to join those fighting another bushwhacker raid, rather than "allowing others to do my fighting for me." She had fought. She had killed, and he had helped her carry the burden of another's death on her healer soul.

Hope: "I still hungwy."

Despite the weights pulling down the corners of his lips, Addison smiled and scraped some of his food onto her plate.

Just before the first edge of the sun peeked over the horizon, Winifred said, "On to the burying."

Addison had dug the grave just beyond where the Martins' barn had stood. He'd wrapped and placed the body in the hole.

Preacher Cromwell stood at the foot of the grave holding the Good Book. The citizens assembled behind him. He waited. The murmuring and shuffling noises died out; then he read a passage from scripture and closed the book. "Father God. Lord of Heaven. Lord of earth. We ask You to receive our brother Wally into your tender mercy. There was the making of a good man in his soul, but that good man was buried under an evil, an abominable morality. A morality infused by the devil into the minds and hearts of Wally, his family, his neighbors, in the whole part of our country that has now gone to war with us. Wally began absorbing this manmade, Satan inspired morality with his mother's milk. As he grew up, he never saw or heard the faintest whisper of Your morality, Lord. One of our members even cut a notch in his ear as a reminder that he should listen to those of us who do adhere to Your morality, Your guide for determining right and wrong. I tried to convince him, Lord, of the evil in some of his beliefs, but he would not listen. He remained firmly committed to the notion that everyone of us abolitionists, every man, woman, and child among us should die, and that our nation's motto, In God We Trust, should be changed to, In The South We Trust."

Preacher Cromwell paused. Addison had his eyes cast down, staring into the hole where wrapped Wally lay. A breeze swept across the grassland whispering of the prairie's expanse, hinting at the vastness of His universe.

The Preacher sucked in a deep breath and let it out. "So, Lord, we ask you, again, to accept the good Wally. And also, we ask You to guard the hearts and souls of all us who must fight and kill to preserve our nation Under God. Help us to find the way between Thou Shalt Not Kill, and There is a time for every purpose under heaven. Help us be ever mindful, that every life we take, is a life that is precious to You. Never let the killing we must do harden our hearts, Lord.

"Amen."

The citizens of Martinsville whispered, "Amen."

Preacher Cromwell turned and walked away. One by one, couple by couple, family by family, the funeral party followed him back to the wagons arranged in rows and columns like soldiers in formation. Silently, they returned to the wagons.

They all returned except for Mariah and Hope. And Jibway and Maybell. And Joshua Reedley and his wife and son.

Hope pulled her hand free from her mother and ran to her father. "Up."

Addison picked her up, and she hugged him tightly around the neck. Mariah moved to his other side, and he put his arm around her. *Love in my arms and death at my feet. Please, Lord, help me handle both.*

"I'll close the grave," Maurice said.

"I'll help," Jibway said.

"I need to do it," Addison said.

"We have a town to build," Joshua Reedley said.

The sound of a stake being whacked into the ground reached the gravesite.

# 17.

That night, Harvey Montag and Billy Bob slept in the hammock wagon. Mayor Winifred invited the two women expecting to deliver in two months, along with their husbands and daughter, to occupy bedrooms in her house.

Addison ensured his family was settled for the night; then he left to confer with Maurice

Reedley about sentry positions and plans to relieve those on watch. Maurice explained the plan he'd developed for rotating the watches; Addison nodded; then the two of them rode to check on all four lookout positions. They also checked on the young man guarding Ruben Fleming.

Addison considered it to be possible that Ruben would see the wrong in his opinion about slavery, to see the wrong in his uncompromising hatred of abolitionists, to see the wrong in waging war on women and children. It was also possible, however, that Ruben faked signs of questioning his former ways to save himself from execution. So, Ruben would remain under guard.

By the time the town marshal climbed into bed, everyone in the house was sound asleep. When he got out of bed in the morning,

Mariah and Hope were still sleeping. He found Jibway and Winifred in the kitchen. The smell of coffee greeted Addison before they did.

Addison tipped the hat he wasn't wearing. "Mayor."

Winifred stopped the coffee cup halfway up to her mouth. "Should we, I, bang the horseshoes?"

"No need," the marshal said. "When Hermann's Poppa built Brotherton, everyone on our wagon train learned to get up at first light, and to be ready to commence the day's work at sunup. On the trail, horseshoes whanging means, 'Get up and get ready to move on!' In Brotherton, and here, too, I suggest, bells and horseshoes means, 'Get up and grab your guns.'"

Winifred: "So we all rise early, eat, and assemble at sunrise so Hermann can tell us what to do?"

Jibway shook his head. "Hermann gave assignments to all the experienced men and women last night. At sunup, he expects to hear hammers driving nails or saws cutting boards."

Winifred: "He didn't give me a job."

Addison: "He figures he's not your boss. You're his."

Jibway: "Hermann will have a *Schule fur zimmerhandarbeit,* he calls it. Grade school for carpenters. It will be set up near the Meeting House. I'm going. Maybe you'd like to come also, unless you already know how to hammer and saw."

"Carpenter School," Winifred said, "I'd like to attend. I should drive some of the nails that build the town named after Paw and Maw."

Winifred reminded Addison of Maybell. The spirits of both young women were formed around a pillar of strength. And, when it was called for, Winifred was strong enough to be humble. The blood brothers exchanged a glance. Jibway admired the mayor, too.

The blood brothers sipped their coffees.

Jibway also admired the black liquid in his cup. "Ah, coffee. White man bring one good thing to Injuns."

Tap, tap, tap sounded from the front door. Winifred opened it to find twelve-year-old Maisie Dom on her porch. Maisie's maw was Laura, a midwife.

"Maw said I should come and stay with Mrs. Freeman and Mrs. Jim. She said if either of the ladies needs help, to fetch her quick. Maw said, even though the ladies were in hammocks, our journey must have been hard on them."

Winifred invited the girl inside and to a seat at the table. "Coffee?"

"Yessum, Maw says I be old enough now."

Addison fetched a cup and poured coffee for the young lady. She spooned in sugar. He went to a bedroom door and peeked inside; then he closed it again. "Still asleep."

The midwife's daughter: "Maw said it be good if'n the two wimmen sleep till high noon."

Addison: "Mayor, if it's all right with you, I'm going to check on the O'Reilly brothers and Ruben Fleming."

Mayor: "Go. Maisie will take care of things here."

The marshal left by the front door and walked to the food serving area in front of the wagons. There, he made a bacon sandwich for himself; then he walked through the wagons to the O'Reillys. Sean, Timothy, and their prisoner/guest, Ruben Fleming, sat on chairs in front of the prairie schooner. All three enthusiastically shoveled in breakfast. Hound, the O'Reilly's dog had its eyes on Ruben, like he might be breakfast.

Sean stood. "Gosh and begorrah! It's Marshal Addison J. Freeman! Take my chair."

Sometimes Sean seemed to want to be known as more of a wiseacre than Maurice. In this case, Addison could understand, a bit, how they looked at him. The brothers had been in their early twenties when he was born.

Ruben also rose. "Take my chair, Marshal. I'll sit on the wagon tongue."

Addison held up his hand. "Stay. Finish eating; then we're going on a little ride."

Timothy O'Reilly scooped up the last forkful and placed his empty plate on his chair. He beckoned for Addison to follow him. Timothy chewed until they reached the rope corral where the riding stock was hobbled and grazing. He swallowed. "Ne'er mind me brother. He still sees you as wearing nappies."

"Sean's not the only one who sees me that way." Addison arranged the saddle blanket on Outlaw. "How'd Ruben behave last night? Not being tied up, I mean?"

Timothy chuckled. "He asked us tie him up and to take our dog away. Said he could'na sleep with Hound's eyes on him and growling at him ever time he twitched."

"Do you have any thoughts about him, about whether we'll be able to trust him?"

Timothy hefted the saddle onto Ruben's horse. "Ruben's kinda like me brother. Sean still sees you in nappies. Ruben has grown up thinking we were the greatest evil on God's green earth. We killed his two companions but not him. He does na' know what to make of us. And you haven't made your mind up about him. But, you must see something in him that gives you hope he will come round."

The O'Reillys didn't say much, but when they did speak, it was generally a good idea to listen to what they said. Except, of course, when Timothy was being a wiseacre.

Sean and Ruben, with Hound between them, cleared the wagons and walked to Addison.

Addison mounted. "Let's go, Ruben. Getting light in the east. We're going in that direction first, and I don't want the sun blinding us. And, Hound, thanks for watching over Ruben last night. Oh, and Sean and Timothy, thanks to you as well."

Outlaw set out at a walk. Ruben rode alongside.

The east lookout station was in a solitary copse of trees about a mile from the Martin farmhouse. Addison wanted to arrive there before the sun peeked above Missouri. *There's time. Just.*

After a minute, Ruben said, "Why'd you kill Oscar and Wally?"

"Because they hated us and were never going to change their mind about us. We couldn't guard them night and day until the war ends. Whenever that might be. We couldn't let them go because they'd have gathered more of you pro-slavers—"

"We didn't own no slaves. We's fightin' for states' rights."

"Fighting for the right of states to decide if it is right or wrong to own slaves. Slavery is wrong. It's against God's laws—"

"People owned slaves in the Bible."

"Two thousand years ago, people did own slaves. But, that's one of the reasons Jesus came to earth. Slavery is one of the sins He died for."

"Them's just words of abolitionist preachers!"

Addison allowed a few seconds of silence. "What did you think of riding in the wagon with Maybell Jim?"

Ruben looked away. Addison was sure he was blushing. "And her husband, Jibway Jim. What do you think of him?"

Ruben faced the dawn and shook his head. There was plenty of light to see that.

"That Maybell, with a pistol, scariest thing I ever seen. A colored woman with a pistol and me all tied up. And her Injun husband, y'all treat them like they's people."

"Because that's what they are."

They were close to the bunch of scrubby trees. Addison hollered his name.

"Come on in, Marshal," the scrubby trees answered in a female voice.

Ophelia. Ophelia and Abner manned this post.

Out of the corner of his eye, Addison saw Ruben shake his head. "We traveled to here in 1858. So we could vote for Kansas to enter the Union as a free state. We had to fight our way here, and then we had to fight to hang on. Through all the fighting, women fought right alongside the men. We'd not have won out without them doing half the shooting."

They rode in silence for the time it took to inhale and exhale twice.

Addison: "You still think blowing up women and kids with your cannons doesn't sound bad?"

Ruben didn't answer.

At the edge of the trees, Addison dismounted and scanned the horizon from north all the way around to south. Then a sliver of fire peeked above the end of the earth.

Addison turned to Ruben and asked him the question: "Turn around. See the Martin farmhouse. Can your cannon fire a ball this far?"

# 18.

It showed on his face. Ruben Fleming was thinking his answer to **the** question would determine whether he lived or died. Addison gave his prisoner time to consider things.

They walked their mounts side-by-side toward the northern lookout post.

For a moment, Captor Freeman put himself in Captive Fleming's position and pondered the choices the man had as to how to answer that question:

*-I could refuse to answer. That would get me killed.*
*-I could lie. That would get me killed, but later. Killed later is better than killed now.*
*-If I answer, and tell the truth, that'd betray my—*

Addison's imagination could not come up with a name for those he'd betray. *Were they friends? He wouldn't call them fellow bushwhackers. Would he think he was betraying fellow soldiers? Or countrymen?*

Off Ruben's shoulder, the sun had climbed above the horizon. And the neighboring state. Which was supposedly Union, but most of the people seemed to be for the South. And Kansans had voted to enter the Union as a free state, but still a goodly number of its citizens remained anti-abolitionist. *At least now, most of the fighting between Missouri pro-slavers and Kansas free-staters is taking place in the south, near the Indian Territory.*

Addison: "I need an answer to my question."

"I won't answer it. That would be betraying my fellow states' rights soldiers."

Addison sucked in a big breath and let it out.

"You gonna' shoot me now?"

"Are you any kind of carpenter?"

"I kin drive a nail."

"Will you help us build Martinsville? Or will that be a betrayal?"

The horses' tails shooed flies.

"I need an answer to my question."

"If I don't help you build your abolitionist town, you'll shoot me?"

"I will, but I see you as a man of moral principles, Ruben. It's just that you believe whites are superior to Negroes and Indians. I think, with time, you'll come to see they are people just like us. If you knew Jibway Jim, you'd see he's smarter than you and me put together. And you've seen Maybell. She's as tough as any white man, with or without a pistol in her hand. My problem is I don't want to divert any builders to put together a jail. We need to get our Meeting House and homes set up quick as we can.

"Will you help us build our town?"

Ruben nodded. "I will."

"I need one more thing." *Addison J. Freeman, are you fooling yourself to think you can trust the word of bushwhacker? I don't think so. Not with* **this** *bushwhacker.* "I need your word that you won't harm any of our people. Will you give me your word?"

"What if I have to defend myself?"

"If you have to defend yourself, we will not consider that to be breaking your promise. The mayor and I will be your judges. So, aside from defending yourself, will you give me your word?"

"I promise I won't hurt any of your people, unless I have to defend myself."

Addison held out his hand. Ruben shook it.

Outlaw bobbed his head up and down.

A smile tried like heck to climb onto Addison's face, but he mind-muscled it into submission. He was relieved he did not have to shoot Ruben, but more importantly, he was pleased to have the possibility to change Ruben's mind about skin color.

He hoped there was a way to win the war without having to kill all the Southerners.


After Addison and Ruben visited the compass point lookout posts, they returned to Martinsville. There, they joined those building the Meeting House. The frames for the sides and front of the structure had been completed and secured in place.

Addison and Ruben joined those assembling the rear wall. Once that was finished, it was raised and secured into place, completing the roofless skeleton of the building.

As soon as the hammer banging ceased, Hermann hollered: "Eat now. But don't vaste daylight. Daylight is for *verking*! One plateful only!"

After gobbling down their food, Ruben belched.

Addison said, "We'll check on the lookout posts again."

They saddled and mounted, and Addison headed them east; then he belched.

Outlaw whickered. Ruben smirked.

Addison turned his face away so Ruben wouldn't see him smile.

Two women manned … occupied the eastern lookout post in the saplings. They had the spyglass confiscated after the fight with the bushwhackers. Addison had the other one, and once they arrived, he used it, while still mounted, to scan the eastern horizon from north to south. Then, Marshal Addison Freeman tipped his hat to the lookouts, and he and Ruben headed for the southern lookout post.

As they rode away, he thought about women **manning** a lookout post. He was surprised to realize the citizens of Brotherton and

Martinsville had their own prejudices built right into their language. There were phrases like: *Takes a man to do that job!* But the Holy Crusade would never have reached Kansas and built Brotherton without every man, woman, and even some children fighting, defending, and building. The same thing was already playing out in Martinsville.

*It would be well, Addison J. Freeman, to remember that inbred condemnation of females to a lesser status than obviously superior males when we are looking at southerners and condemning them for their outrageous prejudice.*

*It would also be well, Addison J. Freeman, to remember that the South declared war on us northerners.* It sounded like Jibway voicing that last thought. Outlaw bobbed his head.

Joshua Reedley had also departed Martinsville at first light. He headed for Atchison. He sought intelligence, more spyglasses or binoculars, lumber, and provisions. He was expected back the next day. Hopefully with spyglasses enough to equip each lookout post.

Otto Vogelsang had returned to Brotherton to lead a second train of wagons loaded with building supplies. That evening, at supper time, the schooners arrived loaded with lumber. Otto Vogelsang drove one of them. Hermann was visibly upset. **He** wanted to build Martinsville, but now with his poppa there, Poppa would be in charge.

*"Ach, Meiner Sohn, du hast kein* reason to be in *eine* tizzy! *Du bist der* boss. *Ich bin deiner verker."*

Hermann humphed and stomped away.

Otto called Abraham Webster, a Colored man from Brotherton, to climb down from his wagon and to say hello to Addison.

Otto: "Abraham *vant* to join your new Brotherton."

Addison: "We'll have to ask Mayor Winifred Martin."

Winifred: "I'm right here. Is Hagar with you?"

"Yessum."

"Welcome, Abraham.

"Addison, tell Hermann to add one more house to the plan."

The wagon Abraham drove did not contain building supplies. It held all the couple's worldly possessions.

Otto also had news for Maurice Reedley. Eunice had had her baby. Very early. The tiny boy did not survive.

Maurice wanted to return to Brotherton immediately.

Joshua Reedley: "Son, wait till morning. I mean it. If I half to tie you up, I will."

Addison: "I'll ask Harvey Montag to ride with him."

The next night, the mayor invited Joshua Reedley to supper. After they ate, he could report on his trip to Atchison. Also at table were Mrs. Reedley, Marshal Freeman and Mariah and Hope, Jibway and Maybell, and Preacher Cromwell and his wife.

After everyone had finished supper, Addison and Jibway cleared the dirty dishes. Winifred carried a cake to the table and returned to her chair. She asked Mrs. Cromwell to slice and plate portions of the dessert. Mariah and Maybell brought cups and saucers. Mrs. Reedley poured coffee.

Winifred forked off a morsel of devil's food with white icing and pronounced it, "Very good." Then she thanked Maybell and Mariah for preparing it.

Hope said, "Berry good," through a mouthful.

Mariah: "You don't speak with food in your mouth, Young Lady."

After that, no one spoke until the dessert plates were empty. Then Mariah took Hope to their bedroom and settled her atop Addison's bedroll on the floor.

Winifred: "You Brotherton people are sure serious about eating."

Preacher Cromwell: "Yes. I, too, noticed that straight away. It seemed they were always moving or fighting. When they had a chance to eat, they set to it."

Addison: "There are times when talking is more important than eating."

Winifred: "So what you're really saying, Marshal Freeman, is now that our eating is finished, we should be talking about important things." She looked at Joshua. "Mr. Reedley?"

Joshua sipped from his cup and returned it to the saucer. He looked at the mayor. "Some bad news, I'm afraid. In the past, our contact in Atchison received intelligence regarding pro-slavery intentions from a couple of men who owned farms just east of the Kansas border. The Union army considered the people who had farms in a wide band of territory stretching eastward from the Kansas border to be pro-slavery. So, the army has driven those farmers off their land. In removing those Southerners, the army also removed our source of information."

Addison: "There were a couple of times when the survival of Brotherton depended on that intelligence."

And no one had to say that Martinsville was so much closer to the Missouri border and danger than Brotherton had been.

# 19.

Joshua Reedley rose from the table, fetched coffee from the stove, poured refills, placed the empty pot on the counter next to the well pump, and returned to his chair. "Since our source of information about bushwhacker intentions dried up, we need to rely on ourselves. I wonder if our builders can make the bell tower on the Meeting House taller, five feet taller?"

Preacher Cromwell: "It's fortunate Otto Vogelsang arrived. We can ask him in the morning."

Addison: "We'll ask Hermann."

Winifred: "But Hermann is young, almost as young as … ." The mayor blushed.

Preacher Cromwell: "Mayor Winifred is right. Otto is obviously the more experienced builder. We should ask him."

Joshua Reedley: "Addison is right, Preacher. In planning Martinsville, Hermann copied the plans his father developed for Brotherton, but Hermann is our builder. We need to show him we have confidence in his ability."

Addison: "He, hopefully, will have enough sense to consult with his father. Will his father's design support the weight of a taller tower?

If Hermann is too proud to ask his poppa, the mayor and I will have to convince him to do that."

Winfred: "Preacher Cromwell, would you lead our after-meal prayer, please?"

The preacher said the prayer. Everyone replied, "Amen."

Then Cromwell said, "Joshua, Addison. After thinking about it, I see you are right about asking Hermann."

When the front door closed on the Cromwells, Joshua said, "Don Carlson is at Fort Scott learning how to care for and shoot a cannon. He could be gone a week."

Under the table, Mariah squeezed Addison's hand.

Later, as the Freemans lay beside each other in bed with their daughter asleep on Addison's bedroll on the floor, Mariah whispered, "Ruben refused to help us learn how to handle the cannons. Since Joshua sent Don to learn how to work them, you're going to shoot Ruben, aren't you?"

"Actually, if he had agreed to teach us how to use them, I'd have shot him. If he had agreed, he'd have done so only to save his life. But he wouldn't help us. I see in that a sense of right and wrong I trust. He doesn't believe he and his fellow soldiers for states' rights are wrong, but, after a bit more time, I think he will see it."

Silence, heavier than the quilt under which they lay, settled on them and remained for several long seconds.

Mariah whispered, "Why is it so important to change Ruben's mind?"

He explained what he'd been thinking about the war with the South. To win the war, would the North have to kill all Southerners? Or could they change their adversaries' minds?

Stillness returned. For a moment.

Mariah whispered, "Father God, Lord of heaven and earth, thank You for bringing this good man and me together. He married me when I was pregnant with another man's child. He loves Hope and me as his own."

She rolled onto her side.

He rolled onto his and kissed her.

Their child kicked his/her father in the belly.

Mariah giggled.

He shushed her and went back to kissing her.

The next morning, Addison went with Hermann to ask his poppa about adding more height to the bell tower.

Otto: "Current design *vill* support *duh veiht, duh* weight, but in storm, we get the high *vinds.* We … you should add more support— He pointed to places on the Meeting House plan where additional timbers should be placed—here, here, and here."

Two days later, Hermann and his builders completed work on the Martinsville Meeting House, except for one task. In addition to the extra-tall bell tower, Hermann and his father developed an improvement over the design of the Brotherton Meeting House. In the former, lookouts had to climb an outside ladder to the roof of the structure, then another ladder leaning against the outside of the tower to get to their post. The Vogelsang's new design included a winding staircase from the vestibule of the building up to the apex of the roof, where a ladder was fixed to the inside of the tower extending to the top. The winding staircase was not yet completed, and Hermann had a crew of six continue that work.

Meanwhile, lookouts used the belltower and accessed it via external ladders. Addison assigned two persons to each shift. Both were equipped with spyglasses.

Marshal Freeman had developed an aversion to use of the term "manned" and decreed lookouts would be stationed in the belltower around the clock. The outside-of-town lookout posts would not be occupied during daylight and good weather, and good weather would be defined by the Town Marshal or his deputy, Jibway Jim.

While Hermann completed the Meeting House, his poppa and a crew planned to raise the communal barn where Fifth Street would be. Currently, though, only three streets of houses were needed. Preacher Cromwell argued, "The church should go up next."

"We use Meeting House for church. We build barn. It go up *qvick.* And *ve* take care of *duh* animals. *Den, ve* build your church."

"Our church," Preacher insisted.

"Our church," the builder said, as if he conceded victory in the argument.

Observing them, Addison was sure, pretty sure, Preacher Cromwell had orchestrated the exchange to help Hermann feel like he was now accepted as the Martinsville builder.

*Larrimer had been the best man as preacher during the Holy Crusade and the building up of Brotherton. Cromwell was the best man for the job of raising Martinsville from the prairie grass. Thank You, Lord.*

Addison assigned Ruben Fleming to work as part of one of Otto's teams, which included Abraham and Hagar Webster. And Abraham was team leader. When informed of his assignment, Ruben cursed.

Abraham said, "My wife ain't offended by your cussin', but I am. Don't do that no more."

Addison noted Ruben eyeing the pistols on the Colored couple's hips. "Ruben, I expect you to get as much work done as Hagar does. At supper, Abraham will tell me how you did."

Ruben's cheeks blazed red as a sunset. His jaw clenched. Addison was pretty sure the words "Just shoot me!" had formed in Ruben's mind, and those words were trying to decide whether they should be spoken or not.

The words weren't said.

At day's end, after Ruben had been returned to the O'Reilly's Hound for the night, Abraham reported to Addison. "That Mistah Ruben, I knowed he was bound and determined to not let Hagar git more work done than him, an' he starts hammering nails and bending most of 'em. I told him, 'Hagar don't be bending her nails.'" Abraham grinned. "He never bent nuther nail all day, and, by suppertime, he got as much work done as Hagar and me together."

Hermann set to work on the foundation of the church, fronted, just as it was in Brotherton, on Second Street and behind the Meeting House. When the barn was finished, he put his poppa and a crew to building homes on Main Street. This crew was to build structures with outside walls and a roof. They would spend no time on inside "finishing work." That would be done by occupants of the home when they had time for such niceties.

By the time Maurice returned, the Meeting House and barn had been completed, as well as three of the six dwellings planned for Main Street. One of the houses next to the Meeting House looked like all the others going up, but it was intended for cannon occupants. They were already in residence.

The marshal and mayor met with Joshua and Don Carlson across a table in the Meeting House.

Addison: "Don, how many men does the Army assign to man each big gun?"

"One man can load, aim, and fire it. If need be. But, best to assign a crew of five to each."

Winifred: "Shouldn't we all learn to shoot the things?"

Addison: "Later, Madam Mayor. Right now, our priorities should be to get the building completed. But you are right. We need to be prepared to use those big guns, so, we'll pick ten of us to learn how fire them. Soon, we'll have to get the winter wheat crops planted. Once the planting's done, Don can finish training the rest of us on how to handle the cannon. Comment, Mr. Reedley?"

Joshua shook his head.

Addison: "Don, get with Jibway and pick out two crews. You can do the basic training in the Cannon House. Then, when they are ready, take one of the weapons to the south of town and practice firing it. Anything else, Madam Mayor?"

"One thing, Don. You and Jibway select the crews. When you begin training them, I'm going to attend your cannon shooting school, too."

# 20.

Hermann's builders completed houses for all of Martinsville's citizens except for Lorelei Seiling. Lorelei stayed with Mayor Winifred Martin. After the sides and roof of the church had been completed, building activity ceased, and planting winter wheat and oats occupied the people.

Addison and Jibway lived in the houses on Main Street north of Cannon House.

Mariah estimated her baby would be born near the end of October. And so would Maybell's.

At the end of September, Mrs. Freeman, Addison's mother, along with Maurice and Eunice, moved to Martinsville. By the time they arrived, Martinsville, was an established and functioning town with the Meeting House on Main Street, the Church of All the Saints on Second, and the General Store on Third. In addition, every family had a home of their own, plus Hermann Vogelsang had built four extra homes expecting additional families to join them. Mrs. Freeman was given the home next to the Meeting House on Main. On the layout of the town, it was the same house she'd occupied in Brotherton.

Mrs. Freeman was joyed—she never used the term overjoyed

because that level of joy was reserved for those in heaven and seeing the face of Jesus—to become a citizen of Martinsville. She was joyed to be with her son and his family. She was joyed to be there in time to help both Mariah and Maybell in the last weeks before the births of their babies, one of them, of course, being a new grandchild. And the wooden signs at the ends of the new town had no bullet holes in them, as did the ones identifying Brotherton.

The townspeople became, not all the way to joyed, but pleased with their newest neighbor. Her first day in town, Mrs. Freeman, with plenty of help, got her furniture and belongings placed in her new house. On her second day, she joined the crew of women and young men who cleaned the church and Meeting House. By quitting time, she was the boss of the *Cleanuppers.* And, on her first Sunday, she also took over supervision of the crew preparing the communal meal following services.

The second last week in October, Mariah delivered. She and Addison named their son Jonathon Ruben. Mrs. Freeman, Addison's mother, began calling her grandson JR, and soon, that became his common name.

Maybell gave birth to her daughter, Glory, a week later.

On the first Sunday in December, Preacher Cromwell conducted services in his new church. After the extra-long service of celebration and consecration of the Lord's new house, the mayor stood next to the marshal and the rest of the town council, greeting the people filing into the Meeting House after church. When Last Worshiper, soon to be Last Diner, passed through the greeters, Winifred said, "Addison, I saw how your mother was engaged in the running of Brotherton, but I never appreciated how people just naturally defer to her. It's like they watch her for a few minutes and then think: 'This woman is smart. If I follow her, I will learn important things.'"

"Maw was like that back in Found Grace Church, too. Of course, Paw was Preacher Larrimer's head deacon. I always thought she did what she did because it was expected of her as Head Deacon's wife."

Addison mimicked tipping the hat he wasn't wearing. "Funny, isn't it, Madam Mayor? Sometimes you need the eyes of others to help you see what was right in front of your own eyeballs for twenty years."

The hint of a smile landed on the mayor's face like a butterfly landing on a flower. Then it flew off again, and she said, "Preacher Cromwell."

The preacher said grace from the rear of the hall. At "Amen!" he sat at one of the tables near the rear wall.

Then Mrs. Freeman's crew of young men and women began carrying plates to tables, starting at the front of the room. Some of her meal servers were also boot cleaners. They, of course, washed their hands first thing upon entering the Meeting House after services.

Addison's Mother had established a crew of young men to clean the boots and shoes of people entering the Meeting House for dinner one rainy, muddy Sunday when Hermann Vogelsang became distraught at how much mud had been tracked into his brand-new Meeting House.

At another of the rearmost tables, Hope occupied a highchair next to where her parents sat across from Jibway and Maybell. The mayor held their daughter, Glory, as she walked around the room, alternating greeting those eating with cooing at the infant. JR slept soundly in a crib in the corner opposite The Ruben Fleming Room.

The design of the Brotherton Meeting House included an office in the left rear corner of the structure, and Hermann built one in the corner of his design as well. The corner office served as an overnight accommodation, not really a cell, for Ruben Fleming. The door was locked, though, when Ruben was in it for the night. One thing was kind of funny. When they started boarding Ruben in the corner office, the O'Reilly's Hound slept on the ground next to the front door of the Meeting House.

Wiseacre Maurice Reedley said of Hound, "You have to be careful around him. His face wears the same look when he's thinking 'I'm going to eat you for breakfast' as when he's thinking 'You know, I really like you.'"

Ruben Fleming also sat at the Freemans' table next to Hope, with places saved for the mayor and Addison's mother.

Addison looked down the table, and Ruben's eyes met his. He almost trusted Ruben. The man was almost his friend.

Hope said, "Mista' Ruben, will you ask Miss Winnie can we sit at a front table next week? My daddy won't ask her." She glanced at her father, then back again to Ruben and appended, "Pease?"

"Sorry, Miss Hope. But your daddy is marshal, and he says we have to let the town people eat first." Then he leaned over and whispered, in a voice everyone at the table, and the one next to them, heard, "But, I'll ask **her** when **he** isn't looking."

Hope replied, "Shhhh!"

Addison thought about how he thought about Ruben. He was not only almost a friend, but almost a good friend. And there was still that *almost trust him*. Joshua and Jibway both reminded him regularly, almost often, that they would not be able to trust Ruben until the bushwhackers attacked Martinsville and they could see how he reacted.

"And," Joshua had said, "they will come. Don't need no *maybe* caboosed onto that thought."

Jibway: "Tomorrow, maybe, or next week, maybe. Next month. Next year."

Joshua: "They will come; then we'll see whether we can trust Mr. Ruben Fleming."

Addison and Mariah had spoken about him also. In a whisper because JR slept in his cradle at the foot of their bed. Mariah said softly, "Hope loves him like an uncle. And he's the only uncle she has. 'Faith, Hope, and Love, and the greatest of these is Love.' Sometimes, it seems to me, Hope—the virtue our daughter is named for—is the greatest."

Then, six-week-old JR yowled.

"Right on time." No need to whisper anymore. "I do **hope** my son, one day soon, will permit the townspeople of Martinsville to sleep when they want to."

1862

# 21.

Every family in Martinsville owned tillable acres. The plowing, planting, and harvesting, though, were not single-family endeavors. Rather, those were community tasks, as they were in Brotherton, and one of the mayor's responsibilities was to organize the fertilizing, plowing, and planting as soon as the weather permitted.

On the first Sunday in March, Preacher Cromwell prayed for an early spring and plenty of rain—but not too much rain.

During the week, however, the talk around town was about bushwhackers and the very good possibility of a retaliation raid for having killed twenty of them—nineteen, actually, since Ruben Fleming had survived. And last year, twenty bushwhackers came with two cannons! What would they bring this year?

Over the week, the talk agitated Ruben more each day. Addison asked him about it.

Ruben sucked in a breath and huffed it out. "I … I don't understand it. The other people are worried about a bushwhacker raid, and they stop talking if I get near them. A part of me thinks: *Hey! I'm one of you. I'm worried, too.* But then I realize I am not one of you. I'm not sure I know what I am anymore."

Addison: "Ruben. I know you are a God-fearing man. He tells us: *Ask and ye shall receive.* Ask Him."

Another deep breath. Another exhale. "I have asked. He hasn't answered yet."

"He will."

A tiny nod from Ruben. "This much I do know. When they, the States-righters, come, I will not lift a finger against them. Even though they will think I am a traitor and want to kill me as well."

"You also promised you would not raise a finger against us, except to defend yourself."

A tiny nod from Ruben.


The second Sunday in March, Preacher prayed for snow. His prayer wasn't answered until the following Saturday. The Ides of March. The prayer was answered with the biggest snowfall of the winter, sixteen inches. As long as there was snow on the ground, the risk of bushwhackers raiding Martinsville was low. Not non-existent. Low. But something for which to be very grateful.

Throughout the day and night of the fifteenth, the town marshal kept all the compass-point lookout-stations occupied. The lookouts were not grateful. "The risk of a bushwhacker raid," Addison had reminded them, "is low, but it is not zero."

Addison reduced the time on station for his sentries from four hours to two, and he and Outlaw rode around to each lookout post at the midpoint of each shift.

Snow stopped falling at four a.m., but the temperature continued to drop, and the sky was clear. Visibility was excellent, so Addison brought the sentries in to man the post in the Meeting House bell tower.

After he brought the sentries in, Addison slept on the floor of the Meeting House next to the corner office.

Sunday morning broke clear with the sky the blue of Preacher Cromwell's eyes. The sun reflected off the white earth blanket with a frozen eye-ball frying fire.

That morning, the sixteenth, Hermann Vogelsang hammered

boards together to make a snow scraper. Then put teams of draft horses and mules pulling his contrivance to clear the streets. His scrapers were the size of a front door for a house. Hermann angled his contraption so as the animals towed them, the snow was plowed to the side and piled into yards of houses lining the streets. Then, the residents had to shovel a path to the street.

Addison walked down plowed Main Street to find Jibway Jim and Maurice Reedley working together to clear a path from his front door to Main Street. Even though he'd been up most of the night, it felt funny, not right to have others do his work for him.

Maurice waved off Addison's thanks and proclaimed, "Thank You, Lord, for this snow. Because of it, early Sunday services moved from the crack of dawn to the crack of noon. Course, it woulda' been nicer if this slave drivin' Injun woulda' let me sleep till the crack of noon."

Jibway hmphed a cloud of white breath, led the way to his and Maybell's house next door, and their shovels went to work again.

Addison opened the door to his house, and the smell of side meat frying greeted him, as did Hope from her highchair, with "Daddy!" His mother shushed her granddaughter, then she smiled at her son.

Hope put a finger to her lips and whispered, "Shhh. Momma an' JR sleeping."

Addison raised a finger to his lips to show his daughter that he had received her order to be quiet and fully intended to obey. Then he hung his belt gun on a peg fixed to the wall and shucked off his heavy coat. Gloves dangled from the sleeves. A cord had been fixed to the gloves in case he had to pull them off to handle a gun. He placed his boots on a rag-rug his mother had given Mariah for the purpose of accommodating wet, muddy, or snowy boots. He smiled, remembering one of Maw's gospels: "Stinky boots stay outside, Mister!" She'd said that to Paw, too.

Maw: "What are you smirking about?"

He told her.

Hope: "Stinky boots! Eeuu!" She wrinkled her adorable little nose.

Addison's heart brimmed over with warmth, with gratitude for the blessing of his house and the pure, unadulterated love bulging its walls. For an instant, bushwhackers and the war and their enemies and the everlasting vigilance watching, waiting, guarding against them remained outside.

He said, "No stinky boots, only snowy."

A mask of smugness slipped over Hope's angel face, as if she were thinking: About time you got enough sense to listen to me, Daddy!

Addison stocking-footed it to his daughter and kissed her on the forehead.

"Cold! Gamma, Daddy need coffee."

Addison stood up and frowned down at his daughter.

"Pease!"

He walked to the bedroom door and opened it quietly. Mariah sat on the side of bed, slipping her feet into slippers, and her smile warmed him. If he'd been a snowman, he'd have melted into a puddle where he stood.

Then, they all ate breakfast together. Except John Ruben. He slept during the day and was awake all night.

"One day, soon, and please, God, very soon," Addison said, "JR will eat breakfast with us, too." He was thinking of his son sitting on the table in the infant seat Hope had occupied for so many meals the family had shared.

After breakfast, Addison put on his non-stinky boots and sidearm—he wore it always except in his house and in church—and coat and hat, and went to his mother's house to scoop a path through the snow to her front door.

By the time he had the path cleared, Maw arrived with Hope.

Hope said, "We paint Gamma's house."

Maw smiled. "Just the living room walls. Until the church bells call us to services."

Back at his house, Addison crawled into the bed in their third bedroom. Hermann had designed all the houses in Martinsville with three bedrooms. His father had done the same in Brotherton.

Mariah slipped under the covers beside him.

"I'm cold," he warned.

"I figured that out for myself."

Then it was quiet for a time, and he felt his heart grow bigger. It had to grow bigger to hold all the new love he felt for this Woman, his Wife, the Mother of their children.

And he wasn't cold anymore when he felt her drift into sleep. Then arms of soft darkness embraced him and pulled him gently out of the world and into a place where only blessed peace abided. He floated there. Until it was time for noon church services.

As the Freemans stepped out of their house and onto the front porch, the church bell clanged, announcing services would begin in thirty minutes. Addison shut the front door and bent to pick up his daughter.

Hope shook her head. "I walk." The path to the street was narrow, and Hope led the way. Her father stepped off the porch and looked to his right, and up at the bell tower to ensure sentries were on station. They were. He walked to the street.

Mariah folded a corner of blanket over the baby's face and followed.

The street was still covered with an inch or so of snow. They proceeded to the Meeting House carefully, taking Hope-sized strides, with Addison holding his daughter's little gloved hand in his big one. His other hand was on his wife's elbow.

A large, yellow-tinged red sun hung above them. Addison imagined it feeling ashamed because of its inability to raise the temperature much above zero degrees, but he was much more concerned with the footing. He did not want Hope to fall, and especially not Mariah with JR in her arms.

Inside the vestibule of the Meeting House, a dozen young boys waited with rags to wipe off boots and shoes. Then they walked to the rear of the building, where Hope happily joined other children her age. JR, asleep and oblivious, raised no objection to being handed over to one of the young women.

*Funny,* Addison thought, *I didn't want women **manning** our lookout posts, but I'm sure glad we aren't leaving Hope and JR with men womanning during-church-services childcare.*

*Maybe Preacher Cromwell can help me figure this out.*

Inside the church, the Freemans, mother, son, and daughter-in-law, along with Jibway and Maybell, occupied the center pew on the left side of the center aisle.

Before Preacher Cromwell opened the service, Addison reflected on Brotherton, the town, the people, and the church there, and thought about how similar Martinsville was to it. And how different.

One difference resided with Deacon Mordecai Goshen. His name when he'd escaped from his master in Georgia, had been Hiram Musterman. After making his way north, a group of emigrants moving from the east coast to Kansas, took him with them with forged identity papers. After they arrived in Brotherton, the emigrants wanted Hiram enrolled as a citizen under his new name. Preacher Larrimer refused to allow a lie to be sanctioned in New Found Grace Church. Two years prior, Larrimer had sanctioned a lie in order to prevent a bigger sin from being committed. He no longer felt that way. "Every time you convince yourself that a little sin is better than a big one, it gets easier and easier to commit the little sin. Soon, you don't even need a big sin nearby as justification. And before you know it, committing big sins comes just as easy as the little ones."

When Otto Vogelsang had traveled to Martinsville to help with building the town, Hiram came with him. In Martinsville, when church services were still held in the Meeting House, Preacher Cromwell had baptized Hiram with the name Mordecai Goshen.

At the baptism, Preacher Cromwell proclaimed: "God has endowed us, his creatures here on earth, with the power to discern good from evil, and as best I am able to use this gift from the Holy Spirit, this is the good and proper thing to do." He poured water, said the words, and Hiram was reborn with a new name.

And in December of last year, the preacher had ordained Mordecai as a deacon in the Church of All the Saints.

Another difference between the two towns, and the two churches, sat in the pew ahead of Addison's. Ruben Fleming sat there with Abraham and Hagar Webster. Brotherton had no citizens who were bushwhackers in the process of reformation. He recalled the caution laid on him by both Joshua Reedley and Jibway: Don't trust Ruben until after the bushwhackers attack Martinsville, and all three of them were sure the bushwhackers would come after them again. Maybe this spring. Or summer. Or fall. Or next year. But they would come. Then would be the test for Ruben, and hopefully, and finally, trusting him.

# 22.

Joshua Reedley, his wife, Abigail, Maurice, and Eunice spent two weeks in Brotherton. Joshua, Abigail, and Eunice returned to Martinsville on May 1. Addison and Jibway met with them in the Marshal's office on Third Street. They sat at a table with the coffee pot.

"First thing," Joshua said. "No one's seen or heard of Orson Seiling since you kicked him off the wagon train."

"Second, the eight young men Orson talked into joining the militia—of course, Orson didn't go with them—returned in late fall, but they are set to sign up again with a unit working near the Indian Territory. Maurice is going, too. He also intends to ask some of his friends from here to come along.

"Third, four of the colored men in Brotherton are planning to join a colored regiment in the Kansas militia. They plan to swing through here and invite Abraham and Mordecai to go with them."

Reedley took a sip from his cup and replaced it on the saucer.

Addison: "Is that all of the good news you got for us?"

Reedley looked at Addison. He interpreted the look to mean: *For now.*

Jibway: "Sentries and fighters. Both towns are going to be short."

Reedley: "You've got a couple of all-women sentry teams. They've worked out."

Addison: "Besides Maybell and Mariah, two other of our women have little ones to care for. And, Eunice came back with you, but she just lost her baby."

Joshua Reedley: "Eunice will be okay. She wanted to jump right into things after we got here, but Abbie and I persuaded her to take a couple more days."

Mrs. Reedley: "So far, women my age have not been assigned to sentry duty. Mainly because there were enough young people to do the job. And the older men are busy keeping up the farms. I'll talk to the women. We can do more."

Joahua: "One more thing. Ruben Fleming did tell us the men who attacked us last year came north out of Arkansas and into southeast Missouri. Then they angled across the state to south of Kansas City, and on to where they set up on the road to Atchison to stop us. I'd like to ride the route they followed and see what I can learn. I'd like Jibway to go with me."

Addison felt like Joshua had snuck up behind him and kicked his feet out from under him, and he had landed hard on the seat of his pants, and now, he looked at Joshua with his mouth hanging open.

Jibway reached a hand across the table and placed it on his blood brother's forearm. "You're the marshal."

"Yeah, but—"

Jibway's smirk stopped Addison's rejoinder at the preamble.

His blood brother always tore into "Yeah But-ers." And not always jokingly.

*Reedley's right. So is Jibway. But I'm not going to admit it till after supper.*

Addison: "When're you leaving?"

Reedley looked at Jibway. "Half an hour?"

Jibway pulled out his pocket watch and checked it. "Thirty-two minutes." He jumped to his feet, stowed the watch, placed his chair against the table, and tore out the door. A moment later, his big black's hooves thundered toward Main Street.

Abigail: "Joshua."

"Yes, Dear," and they left too.

When the door closed on the marshal in his office, he sat at his table for a moment. Then he threw his coffee cup at the cast-iron stove. Joshua and Jibway were going on the exact kind of job Addison had been doing since the Holy Crusade started. Four years ago! But now, Marshall Addison J. Freeman was unable to go. His chest felt empty, as if a bear had ripped him open and eaten his heart.

*Appoint Ruben Fleming Marshal of Martinsville and go with them.*

That thought, so much worse than a "Yeah but," stopped his mental and childish meanderings. Leave a man he didn't **fully** trust to protect Mariah, Hope, JR, his mother, and the people of Martinsville? Even the thought of doing such a thing was the worst sin he'd committed in his whole life.

*Father God, Lord of Heaven and Earth, forgive me. Thy will be done.*

The marshal rose from the table, took the broom and dustpan from the coat closet, and swept up the busted bits of coffee cup. It wasn't right to leave the job for the young woman who cleaned the office every other day.

Ma had given him six cups and saucers for the office. He'd use the tin cup he kept in his saddlebag on the sixth saucer as a reminder that he should just do the job the good Lord put in front of him and not be such a "Yeah-But-er."

The next day, just in time for supper, Maurice Reedley arrived. With him were eight other young men from Brotherton—three other young whites. Also in the company were five Coloreds. The leader of the latter bunch was Ezra Only.

Ezra had been one of the Prairietown Sheriff's slaves, as had Maybell. After the sheriff had been killed and his slaves liberated, someone from the Brotherton war party asked him his name.

"I's Ezra."

"What's your last name?"

"I's Ezra only." He'd meant to convey, "I ain't got no last name." However, his documentation proclaimed him to be Ezra Only.

Normally, there were supper leftovers. That night there were none. If the nighttime sentries wanted something to eat, they'd have to provide for themselves.

At first light the next morning, Maurice Reedley set off with the eight men he'd led from Brotherton, along with eight more from Martinsville. Maurice and his crew headed southeast toward the Indian Territory.

Ezra Only, along with the Brotherton four, and Abraham Webster and Mordecai Goshen from Martinsville, headed northeast for Fort Scott. There, they would join the Kansas Militia Colored Regiment.

The morning was unsettling for Addison. He was used to being a leave-er, not one being left. Since he'd been wagon master during the fight with the bushwhackers, he'd gotten used to telling people what to do, not having to obey orders received from others. Especially not when the others were women.

Mrs. Freeman and Abigail Reedley had organized a women's breakfast gathering in the Meeting House to discuss the situation with lookouts and invited Addison to attend. She had made up a list of the women, young and mature, who handled guns and horses well. "Handle guns and horses as good as a man," was how she put it.

Abigail told Addison, "You feel like you need to jump in and say something, jump in."

He stood in the corner of the room while all the women sat at tables, eating breakfast and listening to Mrs. Freeman. At "good as a man," he shifted his weight from one leg to the other. *Outrageous notion.* That was his first thought. Second thought was: *Some women handle guns better than some men.* In Addison's opinion, Jibway was the best man with a gun he'd ever known. And Maybell, he'd taught her to be as good as him. Third thought: *Keep your mouth shut, Addison J. Freeman!*

Addison had spoken with Preacher Cromwell about his problem of seeing men and women as equal. In his mind, he had no trouble accepting the notion that men and women were equal, but when that notion was sprung on him, his automatic and immediate response was "What a preposterous idea."

Preacher Cromell said, "Think of the Jewish people. They'd waited for a Messiah for a thousand years. Then he shows up, and a lot of people expected a Messiah King. Royalty. They did not expect a carpenter's son, and they crucified their long-awaited Messiah.

"We all grow up with notions like that implanted in our heads. But God created us with the power of discerning right from wrong. Discernment, however, requires time for it to function effectively. Think, then seek the answer, and ye shall find it."

Addison had spoken with Jibway about the preacher's thoughts on discernment. Jibway agreed. But he had a **yeah, but**. "Yeah, but if it's time to draw a pistol, don't think. Draw it."

Mrs. Freeman had just said mothers with infants should be exempted from lookout duties, when Maybell piped up, "You ain't zemptin' me, Mrs. Freeman. I be standing lookout."

"I'm a lookout!" Eunice Reedley, Maurice's wife, to that point, had sat quietly at a table and hadn't said a word.

Eunice had spoken three words out loud, but she'd also said 'I'm not a mother with an infant,' not out loud.

A quiet pause ensued for a moment that grew long.

Then, one of the other women with an infant said she did **not** want to be exempted from lookout duties, and neither did any of the others in her condition, including Mariah. Mrs. Freeman agreed that Mariah could stand lookout watches in the Meeting House bell tower, but not out on the compass point stations when visibility was poor. She was the Martinsville healer, and she needed to be available in town for that purpose.

Then another discussion ensued. If a woman with-an-infant lookout was injured or killed, the other mothers in Martinsville would care for that mother's child.

Addison thought hi8s ma and Mrs. Reedley had organized the lookouts better than he could have. He also thought that, sometimes, women were tougher than men.

The next three nights, Addison and Mrs. Reedley imitated the

Freeman's baby boy. They were awake all night. One of them in the Meeting House with the lookouts in the tower, the other riding around to the compass point lookout posts. Even though the visibility was excellent, Addison felt better if he took a spyglass out to the bad weather posts and checked. Just to be sure.

The next day, Mrs. Reedley convinced Addison that his nighttime excursions were not necessary. Addison agreed, and he took turns with Mariah, sleeping in their bed while the other took care of wide-awake JR.

At two thirty a.m., the Meeting House bell clanging jolted Addison upright in bed. The clanging stopped. Then one clang. A second. And a third. And a fourth.

North, east, south … West. He bolted out of bed and pulled on his pants.

# 23.

Addison jerked open the bedroom door. He expected to find Mariah in the living room holding their night owl son. She held Hope instead. Hope clung to her mother. The warning bell in the middle of the night always frightened their daughter. JR was in his baby basket on the table. He gurgled and cooed as he played with his hands. From the extra bedroom, Maybell's and Jibway's daughter wailed. Maybell would be getting dressed.

"Go," Mariah said, and it was as if he woke up all over again.

He rushed across the living room, headed for his guns hanging on the wall pegs next to the front door. She entered the bedroom with their daughter.

He strapped on his belt gun, slung on the shoulder holster, and put his hat on. Then he grabbed the rifle scabbard, took his hat off again, and slung that strap over his shoulder. Paw appeared in his head and said, "Boy, when you're in a hurry to get something done, the quickest way to get it done is to do it right the first time." Addison shook his head, put his hat back on, and tore out the side door.

Behind the house, Outlaw waited in the pen beside the stable. Addison didn't bother with a saddle or bridle. He opened the gate, hustled to the horse, grabbed a handful of mane, and swung up onto the horse's back. He guided Outlaw with his knees onto Second Street, past the Cannon House, and down the side of the Meeting House. There he stopped and looked up at the bell tower. No moon, but stars aplenty.

"Eunice, what do you see?"

"Four men on foot by the barn."

"The gunshots?"

"The men from Third Street cut loose on them. I think they were going to steal horses."

"What do you see now?"

"Bunch of our folks gathered at the far-right corner of the barn. They just lit a lantern."

"Eunice, check the other directions."

"I did just before you rode up. Marvalee is checking now." A pause. "Clear all around."

Addison thanked Eunice, turned Outlaw, and pointed him toward the barn and the dim light of a single lantern. Then he set Outlaw off at a canter. He did not want to come tearing up to the folks at the barn all hell bent for leather. That would be a good way to get himself—and Outlaw—shot.

Just beyond the barn, he whoa-ed Outlaw near a dozen people who'd formed a circle with the lantern in the middle of them. They were in all manner of dress. A man in long johns with a gun belt around his waist. Night shirts tucked into trousers. Women, too, wore nightgowns stuffed into pants or Eunice skirts.

All of them were armed.

When Addison rode up, those closest to Addison moved aside so he could see the horse thief lying on the ground on his back. "He dead?"

A woman knelt beside the man and placed a hand over his bloody shirt. "Don't think his heart is beating."

Then, the thief's eyes opened.

Addison jumped down and knelt beside him. "Who are you, and what were you doing here?"

"Red." It took an effort to speak the syllable. Addison glanced at the man's hair. Red all right. "Steal horses." He took a breath. "Didn't see." Another breath. "No sentries." Then he exhaled and didn't take air back in.

Outlaw whinnied. Addison turned. His horse stared due west. A couple of whinny answers came out of the dark.

A man said, "Coupla' our riders rode after the hoss thieves. Probly them."

Addison: "Douse the lantern."

"But—"

"Douse the lantern!"

From the darkness, "Hey. It's Arnie Wilson."

"And Ollie Eckle."

"Kin I light the lantern again?"

"I'll tell you when."

Addison noticed how dark it was to the west. Storm clouds building. Probably why Eunice didn't see the horse thieves sooner.

Addison posted Arnie Wilson and Matilda Dinwiddie in the hayloft of the barn as sentries in the west lookout post. He ordered Ollie Eckle, "Ride to the Meeting House and ring the bell to summon everyone. Then relieve Eunice in the bell tower and tell her to wait for me in the vestibule."

When he arrived at the Meeting House, Addison hopped to the ground and told Outlaw, "Home." The horse bobbed its head and cantered that way. Then he joined the lines crowding inside.

Eunice waited beside the steps leading to the bell tower. "Marshal, I am so sorry. I should have noticed it getting dark to the west and warned you so you could post sentries at the lookout post."

"You both were awake and alert and using the spyglasses, right?"

"Well … yes."

"Then you have nothing to be sorry for. At first light, I'm going to see if I can pick up their trail. I'd like you to come along. Unless you're too tired after the midnight lookout job."

"I'm tired but not too tired."

"I hope we get to look around a bit before it rains. Feels like rain's coming."

"Rain?" She smirked. 'I'm feeling plumb tuckered."

It was time to get inside.

In the hall, Addison's maw had things organized. She'd assembled youngsters less than twelve years old in the north end of the building. Most of them were asleep on bedrolls on the floor. Infants were in cradles. Some slept. Some fussed. JR looked around, fascinated with all the people awake, just like he was.

Addison pulled the floor-to-ceiling curtain closed, separating the space into *big people* and *little people* rooms.

Across from him, Winifred stood next to the door into the vestibule, where a couple hurried in. The man said, "Mayor, Ma'am, I think we're the last."

While The Last were on their way to spots at a table next to where Addison stood, the mayor said, "Marshal, what happened this morning?"

He explained about the would-be horse thieves and the approaching storm darkening the sky, so the sentries didn't see them until they were almost to the barn. "Jibway and Joshua are good at telling when storms are coming, but they're both gone."

Behind Addison, a loud banging startled him. He parted the curtains. The noise came from the corner office. *Ruben. Forgot about him.* He strode to Ruben's sleeping room and unlocked the door.

Ruben: "What's going on?"

As they walked back toward the curtain, Addison told Ruben about the horse thieves and approaching bad weather, and how it kept the sentries in the bell tower from spotting them until the last minute.

Ruben: "You didn't know we'd be having storms before sunup?"

Addison shook his head and led Ruben through the curtain. Then he addressed the crowd.

"Madam Mayor, people of Martinsville, I thought we had a good lookout plan, but I did not know bad weather was on the way. If I had known or even suspected, I would have posted sentries out on the compass-point-lookout posts. Ruben just told me he knew rain would hit us before sunrise."

A grumble of thunder drew almost everyone's eyes toward the west.

"Told you," Ruben smirked.

In the middle of the room, Thad Tamber stood. "The wife's good at telling bad weather's coming." He sat back down and popped right back up again. "Number of times I spent all day scything hay and planned to let it dry in the field till the next day, only at supper she says, 'Gonna rain tomorrow.' So I take a lantern and fork up the hay and get the wagon in the barn just before the rain cuts loose."

Marcella Tamber didn't stand up. She said, "I was wrong once. Thad worked all night after I told him it would rain, and it didn't rain even one drop." She paused. "I thought I knew all his cuss words, but I heard some new ones the next morning over breakfast."

A few in the crowd snickered. Preacher Cromwell smiled.

Winifred clapped her hands to shush them. "Anybody else able to predict rain? Reliably?"

Two other husbands offered up their wives' names.

Addison: "This is what I propose. We will place a jar on a table in the vestibule of the Meeting House. If any of you women, and you, Ruben, think bad weather is coming, write on a slip of paper 'bad weather' and put your name and time on the slip and drop it in the jar. I'll check the jar regularly, and before I go to bed. It'll help us keep from putting too much burden on our people who stand lookout. But it will help us stay better prepared to deal poor visibility."

Silas Munson piped up from a table close to Winifred. "We shouldn'ta let so many of our young men join the militia."

Winifred: 'I think we need to support our state. If Kansas fights the pro-slavers where they live, they won't be able to send so many fighters against us. And this morning, we had four horse thieves to contend with. Not twenty anti-abolitionists with cannons."

Everyone in the room faced Silas and Winifred. When the mayor stopped speaking, Addison expected a number of people to turn and look at Ruben. But no one did.

# 24.

Eunice: "'World had nothing to wear this morning but gray.' Paw said that on mornings like this. Ma was grumpy 'til she had breakfast and coffee, and she'd been listening to him say the same thing every rainy morning all thirty-five years they'd been married. She came back with: 'Why can't you just say it's raining?'"

Addison and Eunice stood between their horses, staring out the open west-facing door of the barn. When he'd looked in the direction of the rising sun, Addison had seen the same thing he saw now. Gray. Gray light, and only enough of it to see … not very far in front of them. But with every minute, the sun would rise higher, and visibility would improve.

*Time to get moving.*

"Eunice, why can't you just say it's raining?"

Outlaw snorted. And so did Eunice.

Addison mounted and gigged Outlaw into a walk, into the rain, into the sound of incessant drops pelt the crown and brim of his hat. He could see, he figured, about a hundred feet. He hoped the signs of the horse thieves' passage would still be visible as trodden-down prairie grass.

*There.*

A number of horses had disturbed the grass. Four thieves had headed toward Martinsville. Three ran away. Then Arnie Wilson and Ollie Eckle rode after them and returned.

Addison said, "Outlaw," and the horse set off at a canter. He didn't look back to see if Eunice stayed with him. He couldn't hear anything but the pattering. Eunice'd be where he'd told her to be. He concentrated on the signs, looking for something other than the trampled grass.

Addison figured they'd been riding for a half hour when the pattern in the disturbed grass changed. He reined up. The wide path had necked down to a narrow one.

The gray had brightened some. Rain still fell. Mist and fog limited visibility to about five hundred yards. This was where Arnie and Ollie had turned around. Addison was sure. The narrow trail of beaten-down grass? Probably the horse thieves single filing away. Was it the path they took toward Martinsville as well?

"One of them knew the lay of the land," Addison mumbled. "The others just followed him."

When they'd left the barn, the wind blew gently from the south. Now it came from directly in front of them and drove the rain into his face. He tilted his head down.

And thought: *Ambush!*

Addison turned and rode hard back to Eunice. "I'm thinking there's an ambush not too far in front of us. They could have figured we wouldn't send a big posse after them in these conditions and after this much time. They'd figure we'd do just what we're doing. See if we can figure out where they're going, where they came from."

He dismounted. "Wait here for thirty minutes, then come follow me down that trail they left. I'll be waiting for you, and I'll holler 'It's Tom' when you get close enough to hear me."

"Tom?"

He pulled his long gun from the scabbard and handed her the reins. "Tom."

Addison walked hunched over next to the beaten path. The

visibility, better. Hard to estimate how far he could see. He'd be a hard target for a handgun. Easy for a rifle, though. The rain had let up some. To the west, even though it was past eight a.m., a big half-circle of what looked like predawn glow sat on the horizon. Behind him, where the sun should be making itself known, the sky was still dark.

He kept moving. His eyes did, too. Scanning both sides of the trail. Then look right in front of him and move down the trail, and all the while, scanning the sides.

Addison stopped and knelt on a knee. *Someone's out there. Not far. Shoulda brought the spyglass.*

He rose, hunched over, and started forward again, eyeballing the trail. *There.* Something lay on the trail, but he couldn't make it out.

Addison carried his rifle in his left hand. He'd kept his right under the slicker and in his armpit to keep it warm, so it wouldn't stiffen. Now he grabbed the long gun in his right, cocked a round into the chamber, and started forward again. He saw a flash. A bullet *thwipped* past his ear. Raising the butt to his shoulder, he aimed and fired, levered in a new round, fired, levered and fired. The dark shape of a man rose from the grass and ran down the trail. Addison fired, and missed, and fired, and missed again, and fired again. The man fell facedown onto the muddy trail.

After reloading his rifle, Addison hunched over again and ran down the trail until he came to what he had seen. A boot. On the foot of a man lying beside the trail. A patch of blood stained the back of the horse thief's shirt. Addison rolled him over. Another bullet hole marked the middle of his forehead.

*What the heck?*

Then he knew. The man had been wounded and couldn't go on. If they left him alive, we might have gotten information from him. So, they shot him. And used him as bait for their ambush. Ambush Bait was less than twenty years old. The one shot back at the barn, he was probably early twenties. *Kids. Like the bunch that killed Winifred's family.*

Three of the original pack of four were down. One still out there.

*Eunice.* Even though he told her, "You hear shooting, you ride back to Martinsville," she'd be riding hard toward him.

Addison took off running west down the trail. After he counted to ten, he zigged left into the grass. After another ten, he zigged farther left, then cut right and crossed the trail and came to where the thief he had shot lay face down.

Addison raised his rifle, aimed at a spot in the grass to the right of the trail a good long rifle shot away, and fired. He levered and fired, aiming to the left of the trail this time. Back and forth across the trail he fired rounds until the last one spooked the remaining horse thief to stand, pull his horse, and another to their feet. He swung up onto the saddle and hightailed it, leading the spare horse, and heading south.

Addison loaded one shell, aimed and fired, and missed. Then he checked all around, scanning a full circle, as he reloaded his rifle.

*Eunice!* Looking east, she was riding hard down the trail with Outlaw right behind her. She reined up, her mount skidding on its haunches.

Addison laid his rifle on the grass, faced her, raised his hands, and hollered, "It's Ad—It's Tom! It's Tom! It's Tom."

She hollered, "I believed you the first Tom!"

*Joking? At a time like this?*

Addison picked up his rifle. The odds that another horse thief was out there hiding in the grass were low. Not zero. Low. He checked a full circle around where he stood. Then he stared at the spot where the one he'd shot lay. *Father God, Lord of heaven and earth, I killed another man. Forgive me.*

He tasted vinegar in the saliva coating his tongue, and he remembered what Joshua had told him four years ago, after he'd killed a man for the first time—men, three of them, actually. "If you ever have to kill a man again, and you do not get that ugly taste in your mouth, throw your gun away."

Eunice, holding a rifle in one hand and the reins in the other, walked up to him. Outlaw trailed her horse. "That Tom business, you figured these horse thieves had an ambush set for us, and they might have seen the setup we were using. Then, they could have heard you say your name and let you pass. When I approached, they could have used the name to draw me in closer and shot us. That what you figured?"

"Yes, except after I used Tom once, I would have whispered for you to use the name 'Dick' the second."

"And Harry the third time?"

"No. Third time I'd have used Hezekiah."

Eunice shook her head. "I know you for a good man, Addison. How'd you get so **good** at thinking like a bad one so's you kin fool them?"

"I learned a lot from Joshua Reedley. And Jibway. And we've been fighting them for four years. They've tried sneaking up on us in all manner of ways. But one thing they have all had in common is that they hate us. 'Don't hate your enemies.' Jibway told me that, and, 'Hate blinds you to some of what you could see without hate narrowing your vision.'"

Addison's eyes swept around them again.

It had stopped raining.

Eunice: "These horse thieves. You think they were pro-slavers?"

"Don't rightly know. Chances are they were just—Addison looked at his horse—bandits, criminals, just interested in stealing from us."

"What do we do now? We going after the one what got away?"

"Nope. He had a spare horse. Probably never catch him. Besides, it's time we got back to Martinsville."

Each of them draped a body across their saddle. Eunice insisted on hoisting her own passenger. They mounted and sat behind the saddle and started back toward Martinsville. Eunice guided her mount alongside Addison and Outlaw.

"Addison. You may not know how to smell rain, but you sure are good at smelling bushwhackers."

Addison didn't say anything. The only sound was an occasional *splurp* of a hoof unsticking from mud into which it had sunk.

"When we git back," she said, "I ain't doing another solitary thing till I've eaten breakfast, lunch, and supper all at one sitting."

"First thing when we get back, we tend to the horses. Now, you ride ahead. I'll trail you by a bit. And keep your eyes open and your head on a swivel."

"You think there's more bushwhackers between us and town?"

"Possibility's low, but not zero. Now, you go on. I'll tail you. Keep your eyes—"

"I know! I know! Eyes open. Head on a swivel."

She started her horse forward at a walk.

"Rats," Addison mumbled. "Should'a told her the wind is behind us now. So, her horse won't smell a bushwhacker hiding in the grass. I'll talk to her when we get back."

Outlaw started following Eunice, just the right amount of distance behind.

"You hungry, too?"

Outlaw bobbed his head.

Addison humphed and scanned all around, including behind.

# 25.

Mariah and Maybell served lunch to Addison and Eunice. Then, the marshal and Eunice walked down Main Street to the mayor's house. She invited them in and offered them coffee.

"Madam Mayor, I ask for a town council meeting at 4 p.m. Three things I want to put to them. Approval of Eunice as deputy town marshal." He paused to give the mayor time to comment, but she didn't. "I think we should bury our three horse thieves next to those murderers who killed your family—if you have no objection?"

"No objection."

"Third thing is our lookout plan. We've used two lookouts in the bell tower and freed up six others to work the farms, compared to how it is when we have people assigned to the compass point lookout posts, but, just like with the storm limiting visibility from the bell tower this morning, sunrise and sunset make it hard to see in those directions. Eunice suggested we post lookouts at the appropriate lookout posts at those two times."

Mayor: "The bell tower remains manned—"

Addison grimaced.

"Marshal Freeman. We are at war. War is not a normal state for men and women to be in. Normal is being at peace. Mostly. Our language was developed to serve us during that normal, peaceful state. We do not have time to build a whole new language to serve just the situation we are in now. War says we don't have time for that. War says women can **man** a lookout post."

Eunice: "Right Win … Madam Mayor. Our war says men and women are equal. Course even war can't say men can have babies."

Addison rubbed his stomach. Both women laughed. The marshal blushed.


Two days later, Ziggy Hostetler arrived with a single wagon and four outriders. The wagon was loaded with gunpowder and cartridges for repeating rifles. He wanted to speak with the town council.

In the Meeting House, Ziggy stood behind the podium positioned along a side wall. The Council members sat on chairs facing him. He said, "First thing is I got three letters here from Josh and Jib."

Joshua Reedley and Jibway Jim. Lately, Ziggy—Zig—had begun to reduce acquaintances' names to a single syllable. He believed there were situations where you only had time to say one syllable to give warning.

Addison rose from his chair next to the mayor and took the letters. They were addressed to Mrs. Reedley, Maybell Jim, and himself. He sat back down, intending to distribute the envelopes after Ziggy was done speaking.

Zig went on. "Want all of you to know. Gunpowder and cartridges gonna' be scarce from now on. The army puts claim to most of it. Even so, I'll git you all here in Martinsville a wagon load ever' now and then. What I'd like you to do is share what you git with Brotherton."

Mayor Winifred: "First of all, Mr. Hostet—"

"Call me Zig."

The mayor stared at her visitor for a moment. "First of all, Mister Hostetler—"

By the look on his face, Ad was sure Zig had swallowed a lump of chaw. He kept a chunk between his cheek and gums most of his awake hours. Except when he was eating, of course.

"Thank you for bringing these supplies to us. We will get half of it to Brotherton. Now then, anything else to say?"

Zig swallowed, grimaced, and said, "Ad, how about you read the letter?"

Addison ripped open the envelope, removed a single page, stood, and faced the council.

"Jibway wrote this."

Greetings, Blood Brother,

When we left Martinsville, we headed for Atchison. Joshua wanted to see if the man we used to get us word about bushwhacker intentions was still there. He was and was glad to accompany us. I'll call him Information Man. He wanted to see if his friend, the one he got information from, was still alive. I'll call him Still Alive?.

From Atchison, we headed south till we cleared Kansas City by a half-day's ride. Then we headed east. Information Man was anxious to check on Still Alive?'s farm, which was not far into Missouri.

We came across a farm where the house and barn had been burned, and another place, which had not been burned. Someone had come in and tore the house and barn apart for the lumber. One of the burned ones belonged to Still Alive?. I lost count of how many burned and pillaged farms we passed. Joshua said we came thirty-five miles into Missouri before we came to an inhabited, still functioning farm.

Those first farms we came to, the people were armed, and they did not want to talk to us. They did not even let us water our horses.

We eventually came to a place where the people let Information Man tell them he was for states' rights, and that he'd had a friend, Still Alive? who'd had a farm close to the Kansas border, and he wondered if these farm-people had heard of what had happened to him.

No one at that farm had heard of his friend, but the oldest man did allow us to water our horses, and he even told his wife to fix us something to eat. During the meal, the farmer told us the "Blue Bellies" patrolled that stretch of land back to the Kansas border, and if they encountered anyone, a male was asked to profess adherence to the Union. If he refused, he was shot and buried in an unmarked grave. And women and girls accompanying a man who refused to swear allegiance to the Union were taken to Kansas City and placed in a home for widows of states' rights advocates.

According to Information Man, most of the people we will encounter as we proceed will be for states' rights. If there are any pro-Union folks along our way, they won't admit it.

Joshua and I will proceed on our journey. Information Man is returning to Atchison, and he will get our letters back to you through Ziggy.

Addison folded up the letter. "Anything else, Zig?"
"Two things. One, I'd like to trade my wagon for one of yours with a fresh team."
Eunice: "I'll see to it." She got up and hustled out.
"Second thing. We may get some information as to bushwhacker intentions again. It won't be as good as before, but it'll be a lot better than no information at all. And that's all I'll say about that."

Ziggy tipped his hat and started to walk toward the front door. Addison also left and stood by him on the boardwalk.

Ziggy looked around and whispered, "The man Jib called Information Man is on his way back to the area where he found that hospitable farmer. He's going to try to hunker down there and see if he can worm his way in with the local bushwhackers and get word back to us if he finds out anything that might threaten us. Information Man will write a weekly letter to Z. Hostettler. He'll tell folks he's writing to his wife, Zoe, an' that she had to change her last name, 'cause she lives amongst a buncha' free staters."

At the rumble of a wagon coming down C Street, Ad tipped his hat to Zig and walked back into the Meeting House and to the seat he'd vacated. "Madam Mayor, council members, I think we can start practice firing our weapons again tomorrow. But we should make it a policy that if we get down to only enough powder for fifty rounds from the cannons, we stop practicing with them. Handguns and rifles, everyone should have at least ten spare rounds for each of their firearms."

Mayor Winifred: "Anyone object to the marshal's proposal regarding the minimum amount of spare ammo we always have on hand?"

No one objected.

Mayor: "Good. We still have some daylight left. I'm going to fire a cannon. Now."

The first Wednesday of the month, usually at supper time, two supply wagons arrived from Atchison, each with a driver and rifleman, and four outriders.

As usual, Addison waited for them on the boardwalk in front of the Meeting House, but this Wednesday, eight outriders accompanied the Conestoga. David Isaacson drove the lead wagon. His family had been part of the Holy Crusade. David reined up his team and greeted the marshal.

"The extra riders," Addison said. "Were you expecting trouble?"

"No, no. Those four fellas back there"—he hooked a thumb over his shoulder—"caught up to us a couple miles back. Said they're on the way to join the Kansas Militia down by the Indian Territory. They wanted to know if we were going far. They thought it would be safer if we traveled together. Told them we were only coming here."

Four in-a-line horsemen pulled up on the far side of the wagon. The first tipped his hat. "I'm Matt. You the marshal here? David says the town marshal always meets the wagons."

Matt was clean shaven. His clothes looked too neat and clean for being on the trail. The other three sported scraggly beards, and long stringy hair hung from under floppy, sweat-stained hats. Their shirts and pants were overdue for stuffing into the rag bag. Addison guessed their ages at between eighteen and twenty-five.

"I'm Marshal Freeman."

"Was wondering, Marshal," Matt said, "Would you all be willing to feed us and give us a place to bed down tonight? We'd pay you for your trouble."

Addison's eyes passed over Matt and the others. Matt looked back at him, smiling, confident, one good man speaking to another. The others, though, when Addison looked at them, they looked away.

Eunice walked out of the Meeting House and stood on the step above the boardwalk. She cradled a rifle in her forearm.

Addison: "Matt, we'll feed you and put you up for the night, but only if you give up your guns right now. You'll get them back in the morning. When you leave."

Matt: "These wagon men have to give up their guns, too?"

Addison: "I've known Dave Isaacson all my life. And the men with him, I've known them long enough. You all, not near long enough. So, hand over your guns or ride on."

Matt: "All right, Marshal. We'll—"

A Floppy Hat said, "I ain't!" and he started pulling his pistol.

"Stop!" Addison hollered and drew both pistols.

Floppy Hat paused with his pistol half cleared of the holster. Then he jerked the weapon free. Addison shot him off his saddle.

Eunice's rifle barked, and Matt tumbled backward. He held a pistol in his hand.

The other two floppy hats gigged their mounts into all-out runs heading east. Eunice levered a round into the chamber, aimed, fired. Another Floppy Hat fell. The last of them began jerking his reins left, then right, then left again. Eunice fired three more times, but the last Floppy Hat Bushwhacker got away.

Addison: "Eunice, get some help and gather up the bodies."

# 26.

Marshal Freeman told David Isaacson to let his men unload the supplies they'd brought and take care of their horses and mules and invited him to come to his office.

After walking there, Addison prepared a pot of coffee. "What else do you know about those men who latched onto you?"

"The only one I talked to was Matt. The others kept their mouths shut and looked like guard dogs itching to be free of the leash so they could eat your heart. Matt did say they came from up around St. Joseph. Matt's paw runs a hotel there. He said the others were from farms around town."

"Did you trust them?"

"No. That Matt was way too slick, and his sidekicks were way too not slick enough. I put two of my outriders behind them." David shook his head. "I'm sorry for leading them right into the middle of town."

"Nothing to be sorry for. I bet Matt knew enough about us to know we would have seen him coming and met him outside of town. I sure would not have let them spend the night. They reminded me too much of the gang that killed Winifred's family, except there was one decent man among that bunch."

"But, when I brought them to you, you said they could stay. Why?"

"They could stay **if** they gave up their guns. Then I planned to separate the four of them and to question the three shabby-looking men one-by-one."

The door to the sheriff's office opened. Addison turned.

Eunice stood in the doorway but did not enter. "Preacher Cromwell will hold a burial service for our two bushwhackers in fifteen minutes. I brought horses for you."

Preacher Cromwell's graveside service lasted less than fifteen minutes. An hour later, a communal supper was served in the Meeting House.

Mayor Winifred spoke to the guests before the preacher gave the blessing. "Mr. Isaacson, welcome to you and your men. We consider the things you bring us on Wednesdays **in** your wagons as blessings. Today, what you brought **behind** your wagons, we do not think of as blessings. Until Marshal Freeman gave us his slant on things and said I should thank you.

"He said, 'Those bushwhackers would have tried to find some way to sneak up on us, in the dark, in bad weather. As it happened, though, we got to deal with them in broad daylight and face-to-face.'

"So, thank you, Mr. Isaacson." Mayor Winifred turned to the table next to hers. "Preacher Cromwell, if you please."

The next morning, David Isaacson promised Addison he'd never again allow a passel of men to join his two-wagon train prior to entering Martinsville. Then, he and his men departed for Atchison.

It was haying time, and everyone pitched in with the scything, raking, and hoisting it into the loft of the communal barn. Even Preacher Cromwell joined the effort. He'd just learned how to handle a pitchfork. Mayor Winifred already knew how to handle one, and she helped build a haystack. A few of the older men grumbled about "all the young men being gone to play soldier boy." Forty-seven-year-old Albert Fishbock invited Addison and Eunice to do something useful. "Climb down off your horses and grab pitchforks."

The mayor chimed in. "Mr. Fishbock, twice now in a very short time, men have tried to rob us or do us harm. If one were to sneak close and shoot you, we'd have to stop work in the hayfields to hold your funeral. Just think of all the working-in-the-field time we'd lose if that were to happen." The mayor turned to Addison. "What did you want to say to us, Marshal Freeman?"

"It's important we get the hay in. That's why I haven't called for our compass point lookout posts to be manned, but it's even more important that all of us stay alive."

All the hay workers wore gun belts around their waists or across their shoulders. Except Albert Fishbock.

"Mr. Fishbock, do you have a gun with you?"

"Rifle's in the wagon. On the driver's bench."

"We've told everybody to have both a rifle nearby and a pistol to hand when working on the farms."

"I am not good with a pistol."

"Eunice, teach Mr. Fishbock how to fire a pistol."

"Mr. Fishbock," Mayor Winifred said. "It's your fault we are wasting haying time, not the marshal's."

Addison reached behind him and pulled out a long john top and a pistol from a saddlebag and handed them to Eunice. "Take a couple of pitchforks and rig up a scarecrow target. Use all the rounds except leave him with a loaded pistol at the end."

Addison called Ansel Fishbock, Albert's son, to come over to him.

Ansel jabbed his pitchfork into the ground and did as bidden. Addison handed him a spyglass. "Every fifteen minutes, pause in your haying work and scan the horizon with this. At the end of the day, put the glass on the table in my office."

A pistol popped behind him. Addison gigged Outlaw into a canter and headed south. He passed men and women loading more wagons and building more haystacks. Some of the women wore dresses and bonnets. Some wore pants and hats. Some of the women's hands, he figured, would be wearing blisters the next day.

Leaving the hay workers behind, he rode on beyond the south lookout post. The sky was clear and blue. A pleasant breeze wafted from the west.

Outlaw stopped abruptly. Cold-footed bugs crawled up the nape of Addison's neck. He reached into his saddle bag to pull out his spyglass, but it went dark. Not the world. Inside his head. And then he had the sensation that he was falling.

And then the darkness snuffed out, too.

# 27.

Addison's head hurt something fierce. He opened his eyes. Light stabbed hot pokers all the way into his brain. The lids slammed shut. He heard himself moan.

"Marshal Freeman!"

A female voice.

He turned his head in the speaker's direction, and a new pain sliced into his brain behind his forehead. The pain subsided, and he peeked to see who was with him, but the light hurt too bad.

"Too bright!" he heard himself say.

"Oh! I'll close the curtains."

*Who's this woman? Where am I? What happened?*

The glow hovering just on the other side of his closed, tight eyelids dimmed. He risked another peek. The woman was a girl. Maybe twelve. Lucy. From one of the families in Preacher Cromwell's party. He could not dredge up her last name.

"Jasper!" Lucy hollered, and her loud voice hurt his head as much as the bright light had. "Run to Mrs. Freeman's house. Mariah will be there. Tell her, the marshal is awake."

Little boots clumped across the floor. A door slammed. Addison grimaced.

"Sorry, Marshal. I should have told Jasper to not slam the door. That's the only way my brother knows how to close one."

*Lucy. Jasper.*

Then he knew. "Lucy Abramson."

The girl smiled. "Do you want anything? Water, maybe?"

"Water."

The girl walked out of the bedroom door.

He noticed the clock on the wall. *My bedroom?*

He intended to prop himself on his elbows and look around, to see for sure where he was, but a flash of new pain shot through his right shoulder, with his eyes pressed tightly closed, he saw falling stars.

"What in thunderation happened to me?"

"You got shot," the Lucy girl said.

*Shot?*

Then he remembered haying time. He and Outlaw checked on the farmers gathering hay, then rode on to the southern lookout post. He remembered blue sky, a pleasant breeze, and Outlaw carrying him along at an easy trot. Suddenly, Outlaw stopped.

He remembered the sensation of bugs on the nape of his neck. Then darkness. Not outside. Darkness inside him. He remembered falling, as if he'd stepped off the end of the earth.

"How'd I get here?"

"Marshal. You have to lie still, or you'll hurt yourself even worse. Please. Lie still."

"Outlaw! Was Outlaw shot, too?"

"Your horse is safe. Please lie still. Mariah said your shoulder is broken, and if you move even a little bit, the shoulder won't mend right." She held up the water glass in one hand and raised her other one. "Now, just stay still. Let me hold this for you."

There was only a little water, and he had a big thirst. She leaned over and held the glass to his lips and allowed him a sip. But it was the best-tasting sip of water he'd had in his whole life.

"More, please."

The glass returned to his lips, and he raised his left hand and emptied it.

The front door opened and banged against the wall.

"Daddy!"

Addison choked on the gulp of water and started coughing—it was as if he'd set his head and shoulder on fire. Pain, like he'd never felt before, in his head, his neck, the whole right side of his body from his waist to Adam's apple. It was as if his left side and legs were no longer a part of his body.

"Addison."

He cleared his throat. "Mariah."

She stood in the doorway holding Hope's hand. His daughter wanted to come to him. "No, Dear. Daddy's hurt. We have to be very careful."

Mariah entered the room, walked to his side, restraining Hope, and leaned over him, studying him. Concern and worry masked her beautiful face. He raised his left hand and caressed her cheek. He sucked in a breath of comfort and exhaled his cares and concerns. That didn't hurt at all. Mariah was there. And Hope. *JR? Oh yeah. It's daytime. He's asleep.* Daytime sleeping seemed like a good idea.

Addison woke. The wall clock read seven past three. Mariah sat on a chair next to the bed, absorbed in a book. He turned his head slightly. It didn't hurt his neck too bad. Afternoon sunlight haloed the bedroom curtains.

So, it was afternoon, but he had no idea how long he'd been out. Minutes? Hours? Days? Weeks?

But that didn't really matter. What did matter was looking at his wife read her book. He drank her in.

Then her eyes rose and met his. A look of concern flashed over her countenance.

He said, "I. Want. A. Dink. A. Waddi!"

Mariah rose. Her book dropped to the floor. Tears flooded down her cheeks.

"I'm so sorry, Mariah. I was trying to make a joke."

"A joke! Oh, Addison, it was the most wonderful joke I've ever heard."

A month or so before JR was born, Hope had awakened them with the "Dink a waddi" line at three in the morning. Addison recalled the incident and made a joke of it. Those two factors, Mariah said, alleviated **some** of her concern for him.

She fetched him a glass of water and helped him drink it.

Then she told him what had happened. A bullet from a buffalo gun had creased Addison's forehead and knocked him out. He'd evidently fallen like a sack of potatoes and landed on his shoulder and smacked the ground with his head. He'd been unconscious for two days. Mariah had worried he might have suffered brain damage.

She shook her head. "I guess you think since Maurice Reedley is gone, you have to be his deputy wiseacre." Then, "The mayor and Eunice want to speak with you. I sent Lucy Abramson to tell them you're awake."

Before they arrived, Mariah moved a kitchen chair into the bedroom. Then she started moving the corner chair next to the first one.

Addison said, "That's your chair. Bring another from the kitchen, please."

When they arrived, the mayor sat, but Eunice stood behind her chair. Both seemed only capable of solicitude.

Addison: "I got shot in the head. Fell off Outlaw. Busted my shoulder and banged my head. What else do you know about what happened?"

The mayor nodded to Eunice.

"I was showing Albert Fishbock how to shoot a pistol, when his boy, Ansel, came running up to us. He'd heard a large caliber rifle fire. From the south. So, Ansel and I rode out there. We saw Outlaw and found you on the ground near him. You were on your back. Unconscious. You had a head wound. Your left eye was a puddle of blood. You were breathing. I tried shaking your right arm, and it moved real funny. Something was busted bad. Your arm or shoulder, I wasn't sure."

Eunice's story wasn't short. She'd sent Ansel to find Mariah and tell her what happened. Eunice stayed with Addison. For a few minutes. Then she decided she couldn't really do anything for him, and walked around where Outlaw stood, looking for sign. About twenty yards away, she found a circle of flattened grass with a man, Orson Seiling, on his back. A buffalo gun lay beside him.

His eyes were open, but they weren't seeing anything. A bloody imprint of a horseshoe scarred his forehead. In one hand, the dead man had a leather strap. A piece of a rein.

What in tarnation had happened? Had Orson shot the marshal? Seemed likely. Eunice noticed a trail leading due south from the circle of beaten grass. A faint trail. Made by one man. Orson. But it was time to get back to Addison.

He was still breathing, just as she'd left him. She checked Outlaw and found the left rein missing.

Eunice said, "I turned and saw a wagon coming from Martinsville, heading right at us.

"Your wife, your maw, and Mrs. Reedley were in the wagon. Ansel Fishbock rode alongside. It took all of us to get you into that wagon without hurting you too much more."

Mariah: "Back at the house, I got two more women to help move you into the bed here."

Eunice: "Ansel and I followed that trail through the grass. About a hundred yards from where you lay, we found the spot where the shooter fired. Then, more than a mile farther, we found a small cluster of saplings and a horse tied to one of the trees. So, I figure the horse belonged to Orson. He tied his animal there and crept to within a hundred yards of where he shot you. After he shot you, since his mount was a mile behind him, he thought he could ride Outlaw to make his getaway. Outlaw did not agree with that plan.

"Orson must have grabbed your horse's reins. Outlaw reared, and one rein snapped off. I found it in Orson's hand. Then Outlaw kicked him in the head and killed him."

After a pause, Mayor Winifred said, "Marshal, I saw on the trip here from Brotherton that there was some … antagonism between you and Orson. What was that about?"

Addison looked at Mariah.

She answered the question. "Mayor Winifred, a little about Orson. He had this devil-may-care attitude about him. Some people were attracted to him. I know I was when I first met him. Then I found out his attitude came from not caring about anyone but himself.

"Life forces most of us to grow up at some point. Whether we want to or not. Orson refused to grow up. At the start of the Holy Crusade, his mother asked Joshua Reedley to take her son and help him do that. Grow up. Mature. Be responsible. Joshua gave the job to Addison.

"But that isn't what you asked about."

Mariah nodded to her husband.

He picked up the story. "I tried reasoning with Orson, I tried threatening him, I tried hitting him. He didn't seem to care that I hit him. He wouldn't fight back, and I was ready to give him back to Joshua, but then the sheriff of Prairietown sent a bunch of killers after us in Brotherton. We stopped them, and then we went to confront the sheriff. There was fighting, and Orson behaved … well. And I thought he'd finally done it. Grown up. He even married Lorelei. Then, last year, he started behaving like his old self again."

Mayor Winifred said, "I spoke with Lorelei."

# 28.

"Eunice, close the door, please." The mayor's voice was soft, but at the same time, hard with authority.

Eunice eased the door shut.

"Mariah," Winifred said, in a voice scraped clean of emotion, "I thought you should hear this, too.

"I went to see Lorelei, to notify her that Orson had been killed. I was … nervous. I'd never had to do that sort of thing before. And the circumstances—

"I knocked on her door. She ushered me to the table and served coffee. Then she sat and said, 'This is about Orson, isn't it? What's he done?'

"I told her the story, what he'd done to you, Marshal, and how he'd been killed. She said, 'Please, God. Don't let Addison die.'

"We talked for quite a while. Lorelei told me everything from when Orson courted her, through their first happy months together. Then, when Lorelei could not get in the family way, he changed. He grew bitter and claimed it was Addison's fault. He had ruined his first marriage to Lizbeth. Then he stole his second girlfriend,

168

Mariah, and Mariah could bear children. And Orson wound up with a barren woman."

Addison tried to come up with something to say, but everything he imagined, well, it wouldn't be right.

"That," Mariah said. Outrage gilded her voice. "Is not—"

The mayor held up her hand. "Lorelei also said," her voice, again, reined in, "whenever something happened, Orson always blamed someone else."

Eunice said, "Before our Holy Crusade, shoot, the whole time we were growing up together, Orson was always off by himself. When we played games, he never joined in."

"Then," Addison cut in, "he turned fourteen and figured out girls and boys are different. The way Maurice the Wiseacre put it, 'Orson figured he oughta git hisself onea them there girl things. Sort of like 'Raymond got a puppy. I want one too!'"

Addison paused. "I just thought of something. Those four horse thieves. I wonder if Orson was the one who got away. And the four who caboosed themselves onto David Isaacson's wagon train, I wonder if he sicced them on us, too."

"The way I see it," Eunice said. "I think it's likely Orson was with the horse thieves. The other four, remember Jibway's letter, and him mentioning how many young men run wild and loose in that swath of Missouri just east of the border? Nothing for them to do but be outlaws.

"Back to Orson and the horse thieves. I can see him figuring he couldn't sneak up on us in a gang of four, so he'd try it by himself."

Addison: "Eunice, how'd you get so good at figuring out how bad people think?"

"I had … have a good teacher."

"In view of what's happened, any ideas about sprucing up our lookout plan?"

"I have, Marshal. I was going to suggest you talk to the O'Reilly brothers and see if they'd visit all the lookout posts with their hound— when we don't have them manned—at midnight thirty."

Addison frowned. "Midnight thirty?"

"Yes. I couldn't decide if midnight or one o'clock was better."

"Solomon couldn't have come up with a better solution. And, Eunice, you talk to the O'Reilly brothers."

Then Eunice frowned.

"Now would be a good time."

Eunice walked out.

Addison wished Joshua and Jibway were with them, but for the first time since he was properly awake, he did not think *I SURE wish Joshua and Jibway were back.*

Mariah confined Addison to bed for ten days; then she allowed him to rise, if he allowed her to help him dress, if he promised to be very careful and not disturb the bindings around his shoulder, and to keep his right arm in the sling. He promised and was on the boardwalk with Mayor Winifred in front of the Meeting House when the supply wagons arrived.

Isaacson reined up next to the two of them and tipped his hat to the mayor. "Got a couple of letters for yuh, Ma'am ... uh, for your people, Ma'am." He pulled two envelopes from a sack behind the driver's bench and handed them to the mayor. One large, the other small. "What happened is Zig made a supply run down to the militia near the Indian Territory. He brought that letter back, along with some others.

"I started supplying Union Army units working near Independence. The smaller envelope is from there."

Looking over the mayor's shoulder, Addison saw that the larger had been addressed to Eunice Reedley. From her husband, Maurice.

The mayor slipped the small envelope on top. It was addressed to Hagar Webster.

Addison: "Hagar doesn't read ... not well, yet. Maybe Maybell should read it to her."

Mayor: "I'll ask Maybell to go with me, and I'll read it to her."

Addison: "I can take the other to Eunice. She's in the sheriff's office."

Mayor: "I can have someone else take it to her."

"I can do it. Mariah doesn't want me on a horse, but walking is good for me, she said. Long as I'm careful. I'll be careful. Otherwise, she'll strap me back in bed again."

That evening, the communal dinner began as it always did, with a Preacher Cromwell blessing.

After the "Amen," the mayor rose, and said, "Eunice and Hagar received letters from their husbands today. They've agreed to share … well, parts of their letters. What would you rather do first? Eat or hear the news?"

"News" drowned out "Eat" by a fair margin.

Mayor: "News it is."

Just above the buzz of voices in the hall, Addison heard, "That was wimmen and kids voting. Wimmen and kids ain't got the right to vote."

Winifred heard it, too. She gripped the sides of the podium. "They do have the right to vote, because I gave it to them. To make sure, we'll vote again. News, or eat?"

If there was a single "Eat' in the roar, Addison didn't hear it.

Mayor Winifred invited Hagar to go first.

Hagar rose and walked, arm-in-arm with Maybell, to the speaker podium. Maybell stepped behind her.

Hagar cleared her throat and looked back at Maybell, who nodded encouragement.

"Abram wrote him'n Mordecai Goshen be fine. An so's all the men from Brotherton."

Once she got past the first couple of sentences, the story flowed out smoothly. Most of what the Colored Regiment did was to ride patrols around Independence. It was a rare patrol when they did not encounter a band of secessionists or just plain outlaws, looking to rob and plunder. The gangs they'd encountered ranged in size from two to fifteen.

"Abram finished his letter saying he hoped the bushwhackers would keep their attention on Independence, and maybe you all back in Martinsville won't be bothered."

Hagar turned away from the podium and stepped toward the door out into the vestibule. Maybell stopped her. "We's stayin'."

Behind Hagar, the mayor started clapping, and the crowd joined in until the applause was every bit as vigorous as that second vote had been. Maybell placed her arm around Hagar and guided her back to their table. When they took their seats, the mayor raised her hand, the clapping died out. She gestured for Eunice to come forward.

Eunice walked behind the podium and laid some papers on it. Then, she scanned the crowd and said, "I know those of you who voted to eat must be getting powerful hungry, so this won't take more than an hour and ten minutes."

Someone hollered, "Can we vote one more time, Mayor?"

Eunice looked pleased at the reaction. Then she spoke for only ten of the seventy minutes she had promised.

In his letter, Maurice said none of the men he was with were writing letters, because until Ziggy showed up, there was no way to get the letters back to Martinsville or Brotherton. But he had gotten into the habit of writing a page to Eunice every Sunday evening. Except for one. The secesh had figured out that the Kansas men had church services at nine on Sunday mornings, and the rebs attacked the militia camp at nine thirty. So, Maurice had been unable to write that day as it was taken up with fighting off the biggest rebel raid they'd experienced. It took most of the day, and the militia lost some men and had some wounded, but in the end, they'd driven them away.

Scattered through Maurice's jottings was news of the other militiamen from Martinsville. All of them were well, although, one man had been wounded in the leg and had to work for the cooks for three weeks while he mended.

We have to fight off a rebel attack every six or eight weeks or so, he'd written. Mostly they come up out of Arkansas and try to sneak up on us. So far, it hasn't worked for them. But they keep trying. And please, God, they keep failing.

Oh, you can tell the others that their men are writing letters now, and the next time Ziggy comes, he'll have a passel of mail to cart back to Martinsville.

There was one part of her letter Eunice did not share. Orson showed up at the Kansas Militia camp and sold the quartermaster four horses. Eunice figured that it was three days after the failed attempt to steal horses from Martinsville. Addison advised her to not share that bit of news. Lorilei would be in the crowd. Or hear of it.

When she'd showed Addison that part of the letter, he said, "I wonder if he used the money he got from selling the horses to buy that buffalo gun?"

# 29.

In the sheriff's office, Eunice offered to fetch coffee for the two of them, but Addison insisted on doing the fetching.

"Helps me feel a little less crippled."

"Mariah would like it better if you felt a little **more** crippled."

He imagined Zig telling him: *Shut up and pour, Ad.*

He poured, sat, sipped, and set the cup on the saucer. "The midnight-thirty ride with the O'Reilly's hound?"

"Sean and Timothy, and Hound, all knew what to do. I wanted to be with them the first time, though. The dog growled near the west lookout post. Sean O'Reilly said it was a fox fixing to raid a hen house. That's the only thing that happened."

Addison sipped. "The buffalo gun. How many rounds do we have?"

"Nine."

"Pick four who are good with a rifle and have them each fire one round with the buffalo gun. Albert Fishbock's good with a long gun."

"The mayor appointed him Farm Manager."

"Right," Addison said. "And he thinks that's all he should be doing. How many jobs you figure you're holding down, Eunice?"

"A hundred."

"Right. Albert can handle two."

That afternoon, Eunice took her four potential sharp shooters to the south lookout post, placed a target where Orsen had fired at Addison, and had each of them fire one round from where she'd found Outlaw.

At the same time, Addison walked across Main Street and out onto the prairie about a hundred yards, jammed a pitchfork into the ground, and thumbtacked a piece of cardboard, the size of a man's head, onto the top of the handle. Doing everything with one hand wasn't getting much easier. If the Wiseacre were back with them, Addison knew he'd have a nickname by then.

*Lefty* smiled and walked back toward town fifteen paces, turned, and faced his target. He wore his two-holster gun belt with the gun butts forward. Drawing the right sidearm, he thumb-cocked it, aimed, and fired. *Right between the eyes.*

Ten more paces, another practice round, and another good hit.

Another ten paces, another round fired. All three bullets hit within the space between a man's eyes.

Since the Holy Crusade, he'd been able to fire accurately with his left hand. He wondered if he could still draw fast. When he'd reached for the pistol before, his left hand had brushed against his right elbow. Mariah had his right hand snugged into place over his heart. That elbow dangling just above the holster could slow his draw by a second or so. A man had to think about these things. Sometimes a second was the difference between living and dying. Zig was right about that.

He gripped the gun belt and tugged to slip it around his waist. Before the belt moved any at all, a spike of pain shot through Addison's right shoulder. Like a bolt of lightning on a black, stormy night. One instant there, ripping a jagged tear in the fabric of darkness, and blinked out in the next.

"Be careful!" Mariah's constant caution. He hated having to be so careful. He hated being so dependent on his wife. She dressed him. As she did JR and Hope. She cut up his meat at the supper table.

Addison sucked in a big breath and huffed it out. "Be careful," he mumbled, and placed his hand on the gun belt. He began to pull on the belt to shift it left, away from that elbow. A twinge sparked in the right shoulder, and he eased off. Cautiously, he again tugged on the belt. He felt the twinge but kept pulling, and the belt moved. Just enough.

Prior to trying a fast draw, he moved ten paces closer to the target, did a couple of slow draws to teach Lefty where the gun was located, assumed the stance, and had Lefty hang loose.

"Now!"

Lefty reached. Pain erupted in his right shoulder. Inside his brain, all he saw was fire. As if he were in hell.

Thinking he might fall, he dropped a knee to the ground. And opened his eyes. And saw his target looking back at him. The hellfire in his head had gone out. His shoulder, the ache had dulled but persisted. Carefully, he got both feet under him.

*Mariah! Have to find Mariah.*

He turned to find her running from Ma's house toward him. It seemed like a good idea to wait for her to get to him.

She stopped and grabbed his left arm. Worry and concern were etched on her face and poured from her eyes. "What's wrong? What happened?" She held onto his left arm and started him toward their house.

"Hurt my shoulder."

"How?"

He explained.

She stopped, which stopped him. "I told you to be careful. I told you a thousand times." Now her countenance radiated anger.

"I … I thought I was being careful. I fired three rounds at my target. Everything was fine. Then I tried a quick draw. That's when I hurt my shoulder."

A sudden gust of emotional wind swept the anger from Mariah's face and left behind a look of shame and belly-of-the-soul-deep remorse. "Oh, Addison. It's my fault. I should have warned you about this kind of situation."

"It's not your fault. I didn't tell you I was going to practice shooting. I was afraid you'd tell me not to."

She told him she had seen a very similar thing when she'd worked for the doctor in Prairietown two years ago. The doctor had treated a man for a broken collar bone, and told him to take it easy, to be very careful, and that he'd check on him in a week. Six days later, the man had been feeling good, and went to practice with his pistol, and everything was fine until **he** tried a quick draw and re-fractured his break.

The doctor had told her that in life-or-death situations, like when how quick you draw your gun will determine if you live or die, it's like the brain sends a frantic message to every muscle in the body: "Do something. Now. Or we're going to die." In that situation, when the patient tried to pull his gun fast, some of his muscles pulled against the binding meant to hold his bones together so they could mend.

Addison insisted that reinjuring himself was his own fault. He was stupid. He hadn't been careful. He should have told her what he intended to do. Now, he had to go home and see if Mariah the Healer could put Humpy Dumpy—as Hope called the character—together again. When they arrived at their house, Mariah sent for Hermann Vogelsang. While waiting, she redid Addison's cloth bindings. Then Mariah drew a picture of a man's upper torso viewed from the rear and another with a frontal view. She penciled straps running across the figure's back and chest.

When Hermann arrived, she showed him the drawings. "Can you make a leather harness like this for Addison? I would need buckles here, here, and here."

"*Nicht schwer*," he said. "Not hard. You vill have before *abend essen*."

Mariah was pleased with the harness. The buckles enabled her to adjust the snugness of the fit just so. "But, Marshal Addison J. Freeman, this harness will hold you together better than the cloth bindings, but it will **not** heal your shoulder. You need to heal it. You need to **be careful!**"

The healer laid down further rules. He was to spend his next two days in bed, but he could eat his meals at the table. First, though, she'd made him practice getting out of bed under her watchful eye. If he promised to be more careful than he'd been before. Last, Lucy Abramson had to be in the house when Mariah was away. Addison sighed.

That night, Addison's maw cooked supper. Maybell and her baby ate with the Freemans often, but not that night. She had duty at the west lookout post, looking out into the setting sun. Girls in the Meeting House tended to Glory. Lucy Abramson ate with them every night and stayed with Hope in one of the bedrooms.

The mayor and Eunice were also at the table with the Freemans. After they had finished desert, coffee was poured. Addison lifted his cup, stopped, and placed it back on the saucer. "Mariah. It just occurred to me. Today, when I was out firing my firing my pistol—and being stupid—you came to help me pretty quickly. Were you watching me shoot?"

"No. One of the sentries in the watch tower hollered that you were hurt."

Addison frowned and looked at Eunice. "The sentries were watching me shoot, not looking for bushwhackers!"

Eunice turned away from his glower and sipped from her cup.

The marshal found his deputy's behavior maddening. Then, a shaft of sanity sunlight sliced through the dark storm clouds brewing in his head: *Be more careful than you were before.*

Addison took a shallow breath and huffed it out. A deep breath was not being careful.

Eunice looked back at him.

He could see she was holding something back.

She said, "I talked to them. Asked them the same thing you said. One sentry was always scanning the horizon. They took turns watching you shoot that pitchfork right between the eyes. If one a them was down shooting, and you were in the tower, you'd have done the same they did. Spend almost all your time doing your job, and, every once in a while, sneak a peek to check on the shooter."

"Daddy, you say, Eunice, I *sawwee.*"

"Sorry, Eunice. I should have known you'd be on top of the situation."

As he said the apology, he wondered if his wife, his healer, his prison warden would tack on an extra day to his sentence of days in bed.

Which she did.

Which he hated. Mostly because twelve-year-old Lucy had to empty his chamber pot for him. But also, because he felt a sense of impending danger looming outside the town and about to descend upon them.

And he was confined to bed.

The three days of bed sentence passed with nothing happening in and around Martinsville, except a lot of farm work getting done.

That night, they said their now-I-lay-me prayers together. Mariah leaned over and kissed him good night, settled back onto her pillow, and in less than ten seconds, her even breathing announced she was asleep.

She worked long days. At least—*and Thank You, God*—JR now sleeps at night and is awake during the day.

For Addison, sleep did not take him. He hoped he hadn't gotten his days and nights mixed up, what with all the time he'd been spending in bed.

# 30.

The bell in the Meeting House tower clanged.

Mariah shouted, "Lie still! Lie still! Lie still!

Inside Addison's head, another voice demanded, "Get up! Get up! Get up!" His heart pounded, but the rest of him lay still.

In the other bedroom, Hope cried, and JR howled. Lucy Abramson tried to calm them.

Mariah threw back the covers and hurried around the bed. She'd insisted Addison not try to get out of bed on his own. Taking his good arm, she pulled up, and he swung his legs over the side. He looked at the wall clock. Lamplight from the living room illuminated it. *Two a.m.*

The clanging stopped. The children hushed.

*Bong. Bong. Bong.*

"North, east, **South**," Mariah said. Then she dressed him. Drawers, socks, pants, boots, shirt.

At the front door, she strapped his gun belt around him and adjusted it, so the pistols hung where he wanted them.

Lucy walked out of the bedroom with a child in each arm. "Hope wants to say bye-bye."

After bye-byes and a prayer and kisses, Addison left the house and, reining in his pace, walked to the Meeting House. Inside, he found Eunice sitting at a table with the O'Reilly brothers.

Eunice said, "Start over and tell the marshal."

Sean: "We was making our rounds and got to the south lookout post when Hound started growling."

Timothy: "We drew our pistols and rode ahead real slow. Didn't get far before Hound stopped and growled again."

Sean: "We was riding into an ambush. That's what Hound was telling us. So, we turned around and started hightailing it back to town. I fired three warning shots into the air to signal the sentries in the tower."

Timothy: "When they started ringing the bell, we stopped. Folks come busting out of their homes dressed in night shirts and carrying guns. When the bells stopped, we came on, hollering loud as we could."

Eunice: "None of our people shot at them, Marshal."

Addison and Eunice had often spoken to the people about just that situation. Scouts encountering bushwhackers and having to flee back to town, and riding through people mustering to defend the town. Still, it was a worry.

Addison: "Sean, Timothy, did you check any of the other lookout posts before you went to the southern one?"

Sean: "Yes. We went by the northern and western posts."

Which left the eastern post. Addison asked them to check there and for Eunice to accompany them.

As the three departed, Abigail Reedley entered the Meeting House. She reported the reserve force was mustered behind Cannon House and that one of the cannons had been deployed to south edge of town.

Abigail departed, and Addison followed her out into the vestibule, where he hollered up to the lookout tower, identifying himself and asking for a report.

"It's Maybell. South. Cannon's set up. Wagons are in place to shoot from behind. Nothin' happnin' west and north. O'Reillys and—"

*Boom!*

Addison: "Buffalo gun. Which direction?"

Maybell: "One O'Reilly is down."

Addison considered moving outside and observing from the top step of the Meeting House, but he did not have a spy glass, and Maybell would see a lot more from the tower.

*Boom!*

Maybell: "Eunice is down.

"The other O'Reilly just dismounted where his brother fell.

"Eunice is up. She runnin' back here. She be ziggin' an zaggin'.

"Now that other O'Reilly, he running toward that stand a trees, and he firing a pistol in each hand.

"Don't see Eunice no mo. No O'Reilly neether."

*Save us, Lord!*

Abigail Reedley tore open the door into the Meeting House.

Addison: "Mrs. Reedley, post our reserve force to defend the east side of town. Then take ten from those defending the south and make them our reserve. Put two lookouts in the hayloft of the barn. Put two more at the north end of Second Street. And get a crew to man the cannon in Cannon House. Make sure all our people have saddled horses nearby."

She left again.

Addison: "Maybell. See anything?"

Maybell: "The two O'Reilly horses standing, ground hitched."

*Lost Eunice and the O'Reillys. And we haven't **really** started fighting yet!*

Addison: "Did you check all around us?"

Maybell: "All around, and Theodore, he be checking now."

Addison dragged a table and chair into the vestibule and set a lamp on it. He spread a map of Martinsville before him. Somewhere to the south, there were bushwhackers. Almost for sure. To the east, bushwhackers hid in the stand of trees. *That we use for a lookout post. Were these bushwhackers going to attack from all sides at once?*

Addison walked to the stairs leading up to the bell tower. "Maybell, see anything?"

"No, Mistuh Addison. Don't see nuthin', and we be lookin'." Pause. "It be three o'clock. How about I report ever half hour?"

"Report every fifteen minutes."

"Yes Suh, Mistah Marshal. Ever fifteen."

Addison's face heated. He knew what she had done. She'd figured he'd ask her to report every five minutes—which had entered his mind—and figured out how to get him to agree to a larger interval. *Maybell!*

He shook his head and returned to his table and the number one question: *Were Eunice and the O'Reillys dead, or were they lying in the prairie grass wounded?*

Addison wanted the answer to that question before they fired the Cannon House cannon. To find out, he'd have to send someone on foot. Maybell came to mind. As did Ansel Fishbock. He trusted Maybell's courage and ability. Addison trusted Ansel's courage, but he was still learning how to be a fighter of bushwhackers.

*Maybell.* He had to send her.

Just then a young women, one of those tending infants and children, opened the door into the vestibule. "Mr. Ruben is banging on the door of the corner office. Says let him out, and he'll help."

Addison checked his watch. Still ten minutes before he could ask for a report from the tower. He walked back to the corner office, and said through the door, "You dressed?"

"I am."

Addison unlocked the door.

Shirt, pants, boots. Hat in hand. "If I'da said, 'Not yet,' you'd have left me locked up?"

Addison didn't have time for questions like that. He turned, marched through where the children were sleeping, through the curtain, through the tables, and into the vestibule.

"I'd like you do something, Ruben.'

"I will."

"Listen first, then decide if you'll do it."

He explained about Eunice and the O'Reilly brothers being shot, that he had to know if they were dead or wounded, and that they had been shot by a bushwhacker with a buffalo gun. "I want you to know what you'd be getting yourself into if you decide to do it. I suggest you walk hunkered over for two hundred paces, then crawl the rest of the way. There's a half-moon this morning, so the dark won't hide you. The prairie grass will, though. So, will you—"

"I'll do it."

Addison hollered up to Maybell and told her what Ruben was about to do.

"Marshal Addison," Maybell said, "me and Theodore been talkin' bout the bushwhacker muzzle flashes we saw. We figure there's two of'em just this side of those trees. One's got a buffalo gun, the other a reglar long gun. We figure they had to be clear a the trees so's they could see their gunsights.

And we jus checked all around. Seen nothin'."

Good thing Maybell was in the tower that morning.

Addison told Ruben to wait to leave the vestibule until he took the lamp back inside the main hall. Which he did and waited until he heard the main door click shut. Then he returned with his lamp to his table. And waited. And checked his pocket watch. He'd check with the tower in twelve minutes. No! He'd not wait fifteen minutes between reports. Not with Ruben crawling through the grass. He'd give it five minutes. But Maybell would probably report in four.

Addison's mother entered the vestibule with a ham sandwich and a cup of coffee for him.

Twelve-year-old Missy Hemseth entered the vestibule with a strap bag across her shoulder and carrying a small bucket of coffee. She headed for the stairs leading up to the bell tower.

The bushwhackers won't attack until dawn, until they can see better than they can with moonlight. *Probably won't attack till then,* Addison corrected his thinking. Ma had figured that out and used the time to take care of those manning fighting stations.

*I should have. Well, now you are thinking about it. Stop wallowing in self-pity and do something!*

The voice in his head had sounded like Pa. Except Pa wouldn't have said anything. He'd just have taken a switch to his son. Just then, Addison wished his Pa was there to beat him.

"Ma, how about feeding … well, everybody?"

"I've got a crew together. We're serving your reserves as we speak. Next, we'll take care of the folks guarding this side of town. And then we'll work on how to take care of the others."

"Send Sylvester Dinwiddie and Mrs. Reedley to see me, Ma." Sylvester was in charge of the reserves.

Maybell hollered, "Ruben's crawling now. Hard to see him."

Addison instructed Sylvester to send members of the reserve force to relieve those on the north and west edge-of-town lookout posts so they had a chance to eat, too. Then Mrs. Reedley was to ride to the group defending the south of town and instruct them to feed themselves from the larders of the houses nearby. And everyone should take turns sleeping, until four thirty. Then everyone should be awake.

Maybell hollered, "Cain't see Ruben no more."

Then, there was nothing left for Addison to do but to sit at his table in the Meeting House and wait, worry, and wonder.

And to ponder which of those three W words ate the biggest hole in his stomach.

# 31.

"Addison," Maybell called from the tower. "Somebody riding toward us from the east lookout. He waving a white flag. See it good in the moonlight."

Addison hollered from his table, "The other directions?"

"Theodore checking now." Maybell paused. "All clear, he say."

Addison: "That white flag. He riding at us fast or slow?"

"At a trot, I be thinkin'. An he leading another horse."

Addison blew out his lamp, felt his way to the front door, then stepped outside onto the boardwalk, and hollered to the defenders of the town's east side: "Rider coming waving a white flag. Hold your fire."

The warning was repeated in both directions down Main Street.

Addison saw the white flag, but not the horse and rider. They blended in with the dark stand of trees at the east lookout post.

*More waiting! I should be good at it by now.*

The rider was still far out, but Addison pulled his pistol. Carefully.

"Maybell. Can you tell if it's Ruben?"

"Nope. Hat brim make his face dark. He still waving that flag, though. An' O'Reillys' hound following that second horse."

The rider and his mount became a shadow, then a black silhouette against the gray backdrop. He reined up a couple hundred yards short of the Meeting House and hollered, "It's Ruben."

Addison: "Come on."

When Ruben stopped again in the middle of Main Street, Addison saw two bodies draped across the second horse.

"Sean and Timothy. Both dead."

Addison thought his voice sounded dead, too, and the tone of it dumped a bucket of icy remorse over him, which washed away the tiny vestige of hope he'd held onto. He shook his head. "Eunice?"

"She's fine. Had her horse shot out from under her."

Sometimes it seemed as if hope were a virtue the devil planted on earth just so he could disappoint a person. But one out of three hopes fulfilled was definitely a gift from the Almighty. *Thank You, Lord, and please, rest the souls of Sean and Timothy with You in heaven.*

Addison: "Where is Eunice?"

"The east lookout post. Only had the two O'Reilly horses. She says she'll stay there but to send someone to help her. And to bring her a horse."

Sylvester Dinwiddie crossed B Street from Cannon House and stood by Addison on the boardwalk. He said, "I heard, Marshal. I'll take the horse with Sean and Timothy. We'll put them in Cannon House. Then I'll send someone out to help Eunice. She can have this bronc."

Addison: "Send two people out to man that post, with an extra horse. Have them tell Eunice to hustle back here."

Addison, Mrs. Reedley, and Ruben sat around the table in the vestibule in the lobby of the Meeting House.

While they waited for Eunice, Ruben told them about his trip through the prairie grass toward the east lookout post. He'd run hunkered over for a while; then crawled on his hands and knees. After a time, from in front of him, Eunice kind of hollered and kind of whispered at the same time, "Who's there?"

Ruben identified himself, and Eunice invited him to join her.

She, too, was on her hands and knees. She told him that by the gun flashes she had seen from the east lookout post, there were two bushwhackers. One of them had a buffalo gun. She intended to sneak up on the bushwhackers and asked Ruben to help. He did.

Eunice sent Ruben veering off to the right of the lookout post. She went left.

When he got close, he heard the two bushwhackers arguing.

"One said, 'The whole damn plan's busted to hell. We should go join the others.'

"The other one said, 'Hell no! After the warning bell and us shootin', our boys'll know the Abolitionists are onto us. And if we go riding up on them in the dark, our boys'll cut loose at us. We're staying right here.'

"Then the first one again, 'They wouldn't have pulled out on us, would they?'"

"'No!'"

"But the whole plan depended on surprise."

"Shut up!"

"That's when Eunice's pistol popped twice," Ruben said.

And that's when Eunice entered the Meeting House.

Mrs. Reedley poured a cup of coffee from the pot at the end of the table and offered it to the newcomer.

Eunice sat, sipped, and smiled, and sipped again.

Addison: "What do we know about the bushwhackers? Where are they? How many?"

Eunice: "To the east. There were the two of them at the lookout post. Musta walked hunkered over and crawled all night to get into those trees without our bell tower lookouts spotting them. Don't know if any more are farther east."

Addison: "South. You and the O'Reillys—"

Eunice: "And Hound."

"And Hound. You all figured there were bushwhackers to the south, but you don't know how many. Could it have been just one? Orson drygulched me all by himself."

Eunice: "Sean and Timothy were sure there were a number of men out in the grass. They didn't offer a number."

Ruben: "Remember I told you I heard one of the two at east lookout say they should join the others. I think that means a goodly bunch, like twenty, say. Like when … we was gonna ambush y'all on the road to Atchison."

Addison: "We have to assume there's at least twenty, maybe even forty. Could be all of them are to the south. Could be half to the south and the rest to the east."

Eunice: "I think it's clear the secesh are going to attack us. But it could be from any direction or even all at once."

Ruben: "I think there could be as many as forty. But they wouldn't split themselves into four separate squads. At most, they'd split into two attack groups. They'd want overwhelming force on their side. They'd think twenty shooting, screaming demons just cut loose from hell would have us wet … would have us scared to death."

Addison: "I've been thinking about their original plan. I figure the bushwhackers must have known about us putting lookouts in that post just before the sun came up. I think they put two secesh in the post to ambush our lookouts when they rode out to man the post. That would draw our attention to the east, and we'd have posted our people to protect us from a threat coming out of the sun. But they would have their force bunched to the south. Then once our attention was focused on the wrong direction, they'd attack at first light."

Eunice: "I think you're right about the original plan. But we gotta' think they're working on a new one. Or maybe they already got a new plan."

Addison looked at Ruben, who shrugged. The marshal stood up, walked behind his chair. Then he remembered he couldn't rest both hands on the chairback and sat back down again. "This is what we know. Bushwhackers are out there in the dark They want to kill us, every man, woman, and child. And they want to burn Martinsville to the ground."

Addison looked at Ruben. He nodded.

"We think," the marshal raised a finger, "there's twenty to forty of them."

A second finger elevated. "Some are to the south of town. Some **may** be to the east."

Eunice: "I would have checked in that direction if I could have gotten Hound to go with me, but he wouldn't leave Sean and Timothy."

Mrs. Reedley: "They're going to attack us, but we don't know where they'll be coming from."

Eunice: "That's right. They may come at us from two directions at once. One thing we have to do. That is, be ready to move in any direction to head them off. Take the cannon out of Cannon House and park it in the middle of Main Street pointing east. But have horses and the powder wagon positioned behind it, ready to roll to wherever we need it."

Though he wasn't wearing one, the marshal tipped his hat to his deputy.

# 32.

To the east, a faint glow heralded the daily visitation of the sun to the free state of Kansas. Eunice, Addison, and Mariah sat on chairs on the boardwalk in front of the Meeting House.

"Marshal," Eunice said, "still think we've got the bushwhackers' original plan figured right?"

Addison: "I do. They snuck two men to our east lookout post in the middle of the night, while they moved their main gang up on the south side of town. They expected us to send out our lookouts to man that east post, at the usual time, just before sunrise. Then the bushwhackers there would ambush our lookouts. We'd ring the alarm and position our defenses facing the sunrise. They'd expect us to think: *Yeah! Attack with the sun blinding us. That makes sense.* But then all hell would break loose from the south.

"Yes. I think we had that figured right. But another question is: How'd they know we posted lookouts just before sunrise?"

Mariah said, "What do you think they'll do now?"

Eunice: "They'll have heard their men shoot the O'Reillys, and us shoot their men and ring our warning bell. And I'd be willing to bet they know we have our forces set to meet an assault from the south. They know their original plan got flummoxed."

Addison: "They wouldn't have had time to move all the way around to attack from the north. They could come from any other direction, though. It's still possible they'll attack shortly. From there." He waved his good arm from southeast to southwest. "Eunice, your idea to pull the cannon from Cannon House was good. But they've unhitched the team and have it facing east. Have them hook the team up again, so if they come at us from the west, the team can charge down B Street and be there in minutes."

Eunice chuckled. "I can hear Charlie Ainsworth. 'Hook up the cannon. Haul it to Main Street. Unhitch the team. Now, five minutes later, you want us to hitch the team again?'"

Addison: "Tell Charlie, I'm sorry, but to hitch the team, and to be ready to move the gun to the other end of B Street. And also to be ready to unhitch it where it is and fire from there."

Eunice stood and walked left to give Charlie Ainsworth his new orders. Mariah headed back to Addison's Ma's house.

The marshal settled back in his chair, and mumbled, "Rat snot." Growing up, he'd thought being told what to do all the time by Pa was **the** worst thing in the whole wide world. Not now, though. Now the worst thing was telling other people what to do while he sat on his duff.

Fred Farrell, now the lead tower lookout, hollered down, "Clear all around."

Waiting for the bushwhacker attack, or the every-five-minute "Clear all around," stretched minutes into eternity

The next "Clear all around" took so long to arrive, Addison thought his hair had probably turned gray in the interim.

The eyeball of fire peeked above the band of haze rimming the end of the world.

*Any minute now!*

It was light enough then to read the face of his watch. But looking at it seemed to make time pass even slower. The space between a tick and tock wasn't time. It was agony.

*Agony. Jesus' agony in the garden. That was real agony.*

"Please, Lord Jesus," he whispered, "help me with this waiting. Help me keep from hurting myself again. Help me be careful."

Eunice stepped up onto the boardwalk. "You say something, Marshal?"

"I was praying."

"Praying! Marshal Addison J. Freeman. Long as I've known you, you still surprise me. Bloodthirsty bushwhackers are out there. We don't know when they'll attack, only that they will. We've done everything we can think of to get ready for them, but now we have some time on our hands. I've been thinking about a lot of things but not about praying."

"Eunice, there's something I have to do. Wait here till I get back."

He walked to Ma's house and asked Mariah to help him visit the outhouse.

When he was seated, he prayed that the bushwhackers wouldn't attack just then.

They didn't.

When Addison returned to the boardwalk in front of the Meeting House, the sun was above the trees by the east lookout post. "Eunice, go see Preacher Cromwell. Ask him to visit each of our units posted around town. Ask him to conduct a brief prayer service and then to have the people take turns eating and sleeping. I think the bushwhackers figured their early morning surprise attack wouldn't work, and maybe they'll wait until just before dark to attack. And they'll be hoping we'll be worn out."

"So, today our plan is to pray, eat, and sleep."

"Today our plan is to stay ready, pray, eat, and sleep. And for me to spend a lot more time praying and a lot less feeling sorry for myself for having to be so dadburned careful."

That morning, Addison got a fair amount of praying done. After the five past ten a.m. "Clear all around" report, he sent one of the young girls working in the kitchen to find Eunice.

It took three more "Clear all arounds" before she showed up. "Eunice, I been thinking."

"And prayin'?"

Addison scowled. "When I sent you and the O'Reillys toward the east lookout post—"

"Wasn't your fault, Addison. The notion that we needed to be guarding that direction—"

Addison held up his hand, and she shushed. "When I sent you, the wind was from the west, behind you, like it most always is. That's why Hound didn't smell those bushwhackers. I'd like to send a pair of scouts to try to find the main gang, but I don't want anyone to go unless Hound goes with them. Do you think he'll go with you?"

"I'll see."

Two bell tower reports later, Eunice returned. Hound wouldn't go with her. The dog just lay on the ground with its head on its paws, staring at the rear of Cannon House where the O'Reilly brothers' bodies lay inside. "But," she said, "I have an idea."

At quarter past eleven, Preacher Cromwell conducted a burial service for the brothers. Their graves were placed next to the mayor's family. Half the adults in Martinsville attended, including Eunice and Hound; the other half remained on guard duty. Following the service, communal dinner was served to the funeral attendees. After they ate, they relieved those on guard duty, who then paid their respects to the brothers before they ate in the Meeting House.

At one that afternoon, Eunice, Hound, and Ansel Fishboch met Marshal Freeman on the boardwalk in front of Cannon House. Hound sat on his haunches next to Eunice.

Addison hollered up to the tower lookout. "Which way's the wind coming from?"

"Out of the west, Marshal. Steady. Brisk. Not kicking up dust though."

Addison: "All right. Eunice, Ansel, Hound—"

At his name, the dog stood and looked at the marshal.

"From here, ride north for two miles, then turn right. Go another two miles and turn right again. On this leg, ride three miles before turning."

Ansel: "So we'll be going west then, right?"

Eunice nodded. "Why do you think the marshal wants us to ride as he said?"

Ansel shrugged.

Eunice: "Wind's from the west. It'll be behind us when we turn east, so Hound's nose won't do us much good on that leg of our scout."

Hound whined and pranced about a bit, as if eager to set out.

"Now, there is some possibility a gang of bushwhackers has hunkered down to the east of us, but the marshal thinks the odds of that are lower than them being to the south. When we turn so the wind's behind us, how far behind me you think you should ride?"

"Forty yards? Maybe fifty?"

"Three hundred and fifty yards behind me. You know why so far?"

"If they shoot you, they won't be able to get me, too."

"What do you do if they shoot me?"

"Well, I help you—"

Ansel seemed to read **wrong answer** on Eunice's face.

"No," Eunice said, "You hightail it back here and report what you've seen."

Addison: "When I sent the O'Reilly's out to the east lookout post this morning, Sean was in the lead, and he was shot. Timothy went to see if he could help him, and he was killed, too. Eunice was a hundred yards back and her horse was shot. Now, we do not want to lose either one of you, but losing both of you would be so much worse than twice as bad losing one.

"The important thing, though, is we have to know if the bushwhackers are still out there."

Addison then handed Eunice his ma's hand mirror. "Signal the tower every ten minutes."

Then, Addison waited. At his table. In the Meeting House vestibule. And he prayed: *Please, God, watch over Eunice and Ansel. And Hound. Keep them safe from harm.* Then he just waited.

Finally, "Clear all around!"

While he waited for the next tower report, he said a longer prayer. He raised the names of Jibway and Joshua Reedley to the Almighty.

And Maurice Reedley and those serving with the Kansas militia. And those serving with the Colored Regiment.

*And in Brotherton, Preacher Larrimer, Mayor Argyl, Mashal McTav—*

"Clear all around! And we got a mirror flash."

That meant the scouts had turned east.

Two hours, and a lot of prayers, later, the scouts—now well to the south of town—turned west.

The rest of the afternoon snail-ed along that same way. Until Addison watched the minute hand tick up to twelve at five p.m. That's when Eunice was to turn back toward town.

A tower sentry hollered, "We got five flashes from the southwest. They're coming back.

"Oh! And, otherwise, clear all around."

"Sentry, do you see Mrs. Freeman?"

"Yes. She's behind the Cannon House."

"Tell her to let the people guarding the south side of town know that Eunice and Ansel will be coming back from the southwest."

"Our people know they'll be coming in now it's five."

"We told them that four hours ago. Tell Mrs. Freeman to tell them again."

The other sentry hollered the message to her.

*So where are we Marshal Addison J. Freeman? What do we know?*

*One. We don't **know** anything. We are pretty sure bushwhackers are out there. Sure enough to have everyone in town old enough to be armed and posted to protect the town.*

*Two. We don't think they are east or south of town or Hound would have sniffed them. They could be north, but we ... I think the odds of that are small. Most likely they are somewhere between southwest and northwest.*

*Three. When will they attack? Maybe they'll come at dusk instead of dawn ... maybe.*

*I do know one thing. Fighting bushwhackers with buffalo guns is nasty business. And I need to talk to Eunice. Oh! And Ruben.*

# 33.

Eunice entered the vestibule of the Meeting House and removed her hat. "Marshal."

Addison, at his table, faced the door. He knew she and Ansel were both … alive from the tower lookout reports. Still, seeing her standing on her own two feet, and not draped across a horse and needing burial next to the O'Reillys, stuck a potato where his Adam's apple used to be. He cleared his throat and said her name; then he beckoned for her to sit opposite him.

"Rather stand for a bit, Marshal."

He shrugged. "Where's Ansel?"

"He'll be along shortly. We were riding down Second Street. When we passed the cemetery behind the mayor's house, Hound went and plopped next to the O'Reillys' graves. I told Ansel to go to Sean and Timothy's house and to take water and food to the dog."

Mrs. Reedley entered the vestibule through the front door and took a seat next to where Eunice stood.

Addison's ma walked in from the main hall carrying a coffee pot. A young girl with her had a tray of mugs. Both set their offerings on the end of the table, and Ruben poured for Eunice and Mrs. Reedley.

Eunice sipped, then sat. "On the second leg, didn't see much sign at all, but we did find a couple of places Hound sniffed at. Faint sign of someone crawling through the grass heading for our east lookout post. Then nothing else until we got due south of town.

"There we found a large circle of flattened prairie grass decorated with horse droppings. Took a big bunch of broncs to tromp down that much grass. The bushwhackers must have hunkered down for a spell, then the beaten grass pointed west. We followed that until it got to be five, and we came back here."

Addison: "They're going to attack. You agree?"

Eunice agreed.

Ruben: "They didn't bunch up and ride all the way here and then turn tail just because their plan got spoiled."

Addison: "At sunset?"

Eunice: "Could be any minute now. Or the middle of the night. Or sunup."

Ruben agreed with *any minute now* or *sunup*. "I think they'll wanna' know what they're ridin' into. Specially after we ruined their initial plan."

Addison: "They arrived south of town middle of the night, most likely. They've been repositioning all day. Maybe they think we expect them to attack at sunset, and that we've been ready for that all day. And then, if they don't attack at sunset, we'll still have to be on watch for them through the night. Maybe they're resting now and plan to hit us at sunup. When we're tired, and they're rested."

Eunice: "Lot of maybes."

Addison: "And we have to be ready for all of them.

"Mrs. Reedley, pull the people from the south side of town, except for two sentries, and redeploy them to behind the outbuildings of the houses on Third Street. Tell them the bushwhackers might show up at any time, but maybe not until tomorrow morning. If there is no attack by nine tonight, tell them to take turns sleeping. Also, no lanterns or even smoking pipes or cigarettes."

Mrs. Reedley got up to leave, but Addison stopped her. "If the bell tower sentries spot the bushwhackers coming, they won't ring the bell to warn us. Half of the town will be awake through the night. We'll pass word by messenger. I don't want that bell to warn the bushwhackers we're ready for them."

Then the marshal told Eunice to take Ansel and Ruben, along with Hound, to the barn on the far side of Third Street. Just then, Hound's nose was worth more than the extra tall sentry tower.

The sun set.

A few minutes later, lamps blinked on around town, as the marshal had ordered. At nine p.m., the lamps, one by one, blinked off. Again, as Addison had ordered. Also at that time, Mariah ordered her husband to use Ruben's cot to get some sleep. He went with her to the room and agreed to lie down.

She'd been about to unbuckle his gun belt when he insisted on wearing his pants, boots, and guns to bed. Mariah stepped back and stared at him.

He knew what she was thinking. Weighing whether to say this or say that.

She took his left arm and said, "Sit," which he did; then she swung his boots so they hung over the end of the cot, grabbed his left arm again, eased him back to prone, and said, "Now sleep." Mariah spread Ruben's bedroll on the floor and settled onto it. After removing her shoes. The sound of slumber's easy breathing reached him.

He chided himself for thinking of everyone's need to sleep, but he hadn't thought to make sure his own wife got rest. A horse had stepped on a young woman's foot. A man had injured a hand while moving the cannon out of Cannon House. She'd tended both and heaven only knew how many other patients.

*Marshall Addison J. Freeman! The bushwhackers! Remember?*

The bushwhackers. From which direction would they attack? He'd been over it, over what they knew and what they supposed, so many times. And he kept coming back to the wedge southwest to northwest of town. And he'd had Mrs. Reedley concentrate most of the Martinsville's defenses to protect against an attack from that wedge.

Only one thing to do. Go over it all again. He groaned and

sucked in a large breath, straining the straps across his chest. As he exhaled, he realized he was tired. Tired as all get out.

The next thing he realized was Mariah calling his name, but it was as if he was at the bottom of a deep well and she was calling from far above. "Addison. Addison." In that soft, slow, devoid of emotion, *be careful* tone of voice.

"What is it?"

"Let me help you up. And be careful."

*That soft, sloooooooow voice.* When his every sense tingled with **urgency.**

He closed his eyes, forced a handful of seconds of calm into his being, opened his eyes, and extended his left hand.

Mariah helped him up.

Addison: "What?"

"Eunice sent word," Mrs. Reedley said through the open door, "Hound is growling and looking to the northwest."

He reached for his hat on the chair next to the cot.

Mariah: "Use the chamber pot first."

Mrs. Reedley: "Listen to your wife. Or I'll sic your ma on you. We're not going to have time to change soiled britches for you."

*Judas priest! Does everyone know how helpless I am?* Followed by: *Women! They can be annoying. Especially when they're right.*

Addison: "Mrs. Reedley, tell them to move the cannon from Main Street to inside the barn, but not to unhitch the team. And tell everyone not to show any lights and to stay hidden. And be ready."

Mrs. Reedley left and closed the door.

Mariah unbuckled his gun, then pants belt, and Addison said, "Mariah—"

"Shush! It is a blessing to have you here, with us, alive. And if this is the price that needs to be paid for that to be, I'll gladly pay it till you're as old as Methuselah."

There were times when his love for his wife sprang up and flooded over him, much as the Red Sea must have crashed over the Egyptians when they chased Moses between the walls of water. That tidal wave of affection had sprung up and surprised him any number of times since they were married, but never like this. When he was as helpless as JT. And she'd said she'd gladly pay the price.

*Thank You, God of heaven and earth, for putting Mariah and me together.*

*Ad!* The voice of Zig spurred his mind onto bushwhackers.

When Mariah had his loins girt, she donned a Eunice skirt and a belt gun, slung the strap of her medical bag over a shoulder, and they departed the Ruben room.

Instead of heading toward the front of the Meeting House, Addison crossed to the far side of the room, where young girls watched the children. All the attendants slept, except one, who smiled as the Freemans walked quietly to look at their daughter and son.

"Sleep peacefully, Little Ones," Mariah whispered.

"While you can," her husband appended. And to the young woman, "You should wake your friends. It's liable to get real noisy soon."

Then, the marshal and the healer tiptoed to the curtain separating the Meeting House into two chambers. Once through it, they strode to the vestibule.

There, they found Ruben and Mrs. Reedley looking at the map of Martinsville. Ruben pointed at something. "Northwest is where the cornfields are."

"Corn's tall enough to hide a horse. Should've thought of that," Mrs. Reedley said.

"**I** should have thought of that," Addison said.

Mrs. Reedley: "We should move everyone stationed along Third Street to the right side of the barn."

The marshal: "No. Leave everyone where they are. We have our people posted in good positions. And I don't want anyone moving. The bushwhackers could see them." He rubbed his chin. "And Mrs. Reedley, find Hermann Vogelsang and have him meet me in the barn."

Mariah: "Addison!"

"I'm going to the barn, and I'll be careful."

"Yes, you will be. Because I'm going with you."

Addison: "Mariah!"

"I'm going with you!"

# 34.

Addison and Mariah arrived at the barn. Inside, it was can't-see-your-hand-in front-of-your-face dark. A lantern hung from a nail in the doorpost. He dug a match from his shirt pocket and asked Mariah to light it.

Ruben and Ansel came running from the opposite side to see who had violated the marshal's "No lights" order.

Ruben: "Marshal?"

"Lantern inside the barn is okay. They'll think we're tending livestock."

Addison led the others past saddled horses, the cannon trolley, and the powder and shot wagon. On the way, he directed Ruben and Ansel to bring an empty water barrel and two buckets. The last two stalls on the right were empty and clean. "Barrel in the second stall, here." He pointed. The lantern was to go atop the barrel.

"Die laterne!" Hermann Vogelsang stomped up to the group. "Marshal say no light. Put it out!"

Addison: "In here, the light is okay, and Hermann, those snow plows you built last winter, did you get them in place?"

"Ya. Like you said. One on each side of the cannon at the end of Third Street, but the plows are laying flat on ground. Vat good are dey like dat?"

Instead of answering, the marshal turned to Ansel. "Fetch Eunice and tell her to put Hound on a leash and bring him, too."

Ansel stepped toward the door and whispered. "Eunice. Bring Hound." He returned to the marshal. "Hound's been on a leash. Otherwise, he'd have gone off into the corn looking for a bushwhacker to have for breakfast."

Addison: "Hermann, get the cannon crew to help. Tear out the wall between these two stalls and remove enough siding to poke the cannon through. Then put up heavy, bullet-stopping lumber to protect this cannon crew, like your snowplows're gonna protect the other one. And, Hermann, work quick and quiet as you can."

Addison looked down the length of the barn and out the door. Houses, the church, the Meeting House all stood silhouetted against the starry backdrop. And a first faint hint of dawn. Then, he, and Mariah, walked toward the door where Eunice was trying to pull Hound to come along with her, but the dog was eager to tear off toward the corn field.

Eunice hissed, "Hound!" The dog stopped pulling against his rope leash and whined.

"Eunice, take Hound and hustle down Third Street to the cannon crew. There you'll find bullet shields lying on the ground. If we had those barriers up, I was worried it would alert the bushwhackers we were onto their new plan. But it's time to get them up now. I'm thinking the secesh sent a man with a buffalo gun to shoot the crew. If Hound starts acting like someone is out there, have them load the cannon with grape and point it where the dog indicates. But tell them not to fire unless the bushwhacker shoots or you hear shooting at the cornfield. Have them aim the cannon low enough to mow prairie grass. Questions?"

"Nope."

Hound followed Eunice as she wended her way through the cannoneers working under Hermann's supervision.

From above Addison, one of the hayloft lookouts said, "I can make out something at the far end of the cornfield. Looks to be horses. A lot of them."

"Ruben," Addison said, "go find the first person hiding behind the outbuildings opposite the cornfields—"

The crack of a buffalo gun followed by the boom of a cannon came from the south edge of town.

From the stalls, Hermann said, "Now verk qvick, not qvick und quiet!"

Ruben: "Do I still need to warn—"

Addison: "Yes. And hurry."

In the stall, a man kicked boards free from the side of the barn. The cannon crew drove their big gun cart to the barn door. The driver whoa-ed the team as a man and a woman untied the fetters securing the gun, and the crew muscled the gun off the cart and wheeled it into the widened stall with the end of the barrel a few feet short of the barn wall.

"Marshal," Harvey Montag, cannon crew chief, said, "ball or grape?"

Addison: "Lookout. What do you see?"

"Bushwhackers. Must be twenty of 'em. Mounted now. Heading right for us."

Addison: "Load grape." Then: "Lookout. See anything to the south?"

Seconds ticked away. Precious seconds.

"Don't see nothin' moving to the south."

A man ran into the barn from Third Street and to where Addison and Mariah stood. It was Ruben.

Addison: "Ride to the Meeting House. Have the sentries scan all around. Then hustle back here and tell me—."

A hayloft sentry yelled: "Thirty riders. Close!"

The bushwhackers cut loose with godawful yelling and their pistols popped. There was a sound, like grains of sand pelting the side of the barn during a windstorm. A bullet thwipped past Addison. He grabbed Mariah's arm and led her behind the cannon stall, where Hermann Vogelsang's bullet-stopping planks had been added to protect the cannoneers. Rifles banged from along Third Street. The cannon bucked and roared, and cannoneers swarmed the weapon to reload it.

And Ruben was still next to him.

Addison: "The Meeting House tower sentries. Go. Make sure they check all around."

Ruben ran through the barn, stopped, untied the reins of a saddled bronc, got one foot in a stirrup and one hand on the horn when the cannon fired again.

The bronc reared, knocking Ruben onto his back. The horse galloped out the door. Gazing after it, Addison saw Martinsville bathed in gray from dawn's early light.

Mariah ran toward Ruben. She stopped when he hopped to his feet and tore off after the bronc, down C Street, toward the Meeting House. She returned to the marshal and said, "Listen."

He listened, but all he heard was inside-the-head ringing from the roar of the cannon.

"No shooting," Mariah said.

All quiet on the western edge of town. Was that it? Could it be over already?

The Meeting House bell clanged, stopped ringing for two tick-tocks. Then: Clang. Clang. Clang.

Addison: "In the hayloft, see anything?"

"Some of our folks along third street are running toward the south end of town."

From that direction, pistols popped, rifles talked back, and the Third Street cannon roared.

A few more pistols popped, several rifles banged replies, and the cannon roared again.

A tentative silence hovered over Martinsville.

Addison called Hermann Vogelsang. "Fit two wagons with bullet shields, front and back of the beds. Make them tall enough to cover a standing rifleman. How long will it take?"

"We have wagons, lumber, und nails. We have verkers. Ten minutes."

"Get started."

Hermann gathered the cannoneers and explained their new task, and that they'd build the additions to the wagons next to the big gun, so if they needed to make it boom, they could do so "Qvick."

Addison and Mariah walked toward Third Street. As they exited the barn, hammering sounded behind them.

As they arrived at third Street, Ruben reined up. "Clear all around, the sentries say."

Addison thanked him and said, "New job. Hermann is building a set of bullet shields on a wagon. As soon as it's finished, get four riflemen from along Third Street to go with you in the wagon out into the smashed down corn. Go among the downed bushwhackers and gather up all their weapons. All of the weapons. Look for hidden guns and knives. Pull their boots off. Once you have gathered up all the weapons, take them to Cannon House and store them there. Then go back to the cornfield and pick up the wounded secesh and take them to the barn. Bunch them together on bedrolls in clean stalls. Leave a half dozen to guard them."

At the other end of the barn, hammering ceased.

Addison: "Hermann just finished your chariot, Ruben."

Ruben trotted through the barn.

To the east, the sun had raised the edge of its eye above the Missouri border.

To Addison's right, Mrs. Reedley ran her horse down Third Street toward him. She pulled up and dismounted. "Mariah, we need you back there." She handed the reins to the healer.

Mariah galloped off.

Addison wished he could go with her. He wished he had Ruben or Ansel to send. He thought of sending Mrs. Reedley, but he had something else he needed her to do.

Addison explained to Mrs. Reedley the purpose for the wagons with the bullet shields. Hammering came from the far end of the barn. Hermann was still working on the bullet shields for the second wagon. "Mrs. Reedley, let's go see what Hermann is doing. On the way tell me what happened at the south edge of town."

# 35.

Mrs. Reedley stepped away from Third Street. Addison fell in beside her as they entered the barn. She began rolling out her story.

Eunice arrived at the cannon. Hound began straining at the leash. He growled with his nose pointed southwest.

Eunice told us to get the snowplows set up to protect us.

We set them up the with just enough space between them for the cannon to poke through. Mayor Winifred was behind the cannon, getting it pointed exactly in the direction Hound fixed on. She'd been hunkered over, looking down the barrel. When she was satisfied with how it was aimed, she stood.

A buffalo gun boomed and knocked the mayor onto her back."

*God no! Not Winifred.*

Mrs. Reedley took a breath and continued her story.

The chief of the cannon crew touched his firestick to the powder hole and fired the weapon.

Hound tore the leash from Eunice's hand and raced off through the prairie grass. From out on the prairie, a man hollered, "I can't see. I can't see."

Eunice and a man and a woman from the cannon crew rushed to the mayor. Winifred had her jaws clenched. Easy to see her wound hurt something fierce. She'd been hit in her left upper arm. A stub of white bone poked through the torn, bloody flesh. Blood spurted with each heartbeat.

Eunice tore off her neckerchief and tied it around her arm. She stuck a stick through the bandana and twisted it tight. The spurting stopped. "Get the healer," Eunice barked.

"I jumped on my horse and raced here," Mrs. Reedley said.

Addison: "Please, God, let Mariah get there in time."

Mrs. Reedley: "Amen."

They reached the wagon, and Mrs. Reedley stared up at the bullet shields at the front and rear of the wagon as Hermann's crew hammered two-by-fours into place bracing the front shield firmly to the one in the rear. "Why all that?" She waved a hand at the addition to the wagon structure.

"This bunch of secesh. They have some pretty savvy characters amongst them. Might be some of them hunkered down in the grass waiting for us to come check on the wounded. They came here to kill us all. That didn't work, so they'll want to get as many of us as they can."

From the direction of the cornfield, a pistol popped. A horse screamed. A rifle, two rifles fired.

Addison hollered up to the loft, "Lookout?"

"A bushwhacker shot one the horses pulling the wagon. The other horse reared and jerked the wagon around some. The men walking behind the wagon shot the skulker."

Addison: "I told Ruben to put four riflemen **in** the wagon with the driver. Mrs. Reedley, when you return to the south side of town, seems like a good idea to use the wagon the Ruben way. Two riflemen riding, two walking behind."

A boy ran through the barn to where the marshal and Mrs. Reedley stood. Caleb Fishbock, Ansel's brother.

"Marshal ... your ma said to tell you ... tower sentry says ... clear all around."

Addison put his hand on the boy's shoulder. "You can walk back to the Meeting House."

Caleb said, "Yes, sir," and took off running.

Mrs. Reedley watched the boy race away.

Addison was sure he saw a hint of a wistful smile on her face.

She looked at him. "Even in the middle of all this, Caleb reminds me of you and Maurice at that age."

Pistols *pop popped* from the cornfield. Rifles banged.

The loft lookout hollered, "Two skulkers fired at the wagon. I think they was wounded. I don't think they's wounded no more."

Addison: "Mrs. Reedley, before, you said Hound ran after a bushwhacker. Did he come back?"

"Not by the time I left to fetch Mariah. Maybe he's there now."

"Mrs. Reedley, take the Hermann wagon to the south of town. Drive out to where the secesh are lying and gather up all their weapons. Guns, knives, even pocketknives. Deliver the weapons to the Cannon House; then load the wounded into the wagon and bring them to the Meeting House. If they give you trouble, shoot them.

"And send Eunice to see me."

Again, the Fishbock boy ran through the barn and up to Addison. "Marshal, lookout says clear all around except south. Long ways out, two riders hightailing it away from us." He ran toward the Meeting House again.

Addison: "New plan. Hurry to the south side of town. Tell Eunice to pick two others and go after those bushwhackers heading south. And each of them should take a spare horse and push hard. When they catch up, tell them to bring the secesh back here, sitting their saddles or across them.

"Then, you take the wagon and gather up the weapons like I said."

As Mrs. Reedley drove away through the barn, rifles again barked from the direction of the cornfield.

The loft lookout hollered: "It's our guys shooting downed bushwhacker horses. It's light enough now, and I can see near a half-acre of trampled down corn and all of it covered with bodies of men and horses."

The marshal walked through the barn and turned right onto Third Street. He desperately wanted to run as fast as the Fishboch boy. If he did, though, he'd likely render himself totally useless, instead of mostly useless. As he neared the last house, a woman screamed from inside. Addison stopped. His heart beat fast. He tried hard to keep the rest of himself calm.

The front door of the end house opened. Fred Farrell walked out of his house onto the porch, closed the door behind him, and shook his head.

Addison: "Fred, what happened?"

Fred looked up. His mouth was hanging open. "The healer. She's sawing off the arm of the mayor. I … I."

"Is anyone helping Mariah?"

"My wife. I … ."

"Fred. Fred!"

Farrel closed his mouth. His eyes were big and staring.

"Go find a couple of people. From out there." Addison pointed out onto the prairie where the Hermann wagon was moving past a Conestoga wagon on its side with ten people, all holding rifles, behind it. "Send them here to help Mariah. Tell them to hurry. And you hurry, too."

Fred ran.

Addison stared at the front door, sucked in a breath, huffed it out, and entered the Farrel home. He found them in a bedroom. Winifred lay on the bed. She lay still and quiet. The white sheets under her were red with blood. At the head of the bed, Mrs. Farrell stood on one side and Lucy Abramson stood on the other. Addison figured they'd held Winifred down. Until she passed out.

Mariah stood next to the bed. She held her bone saw in a bloody hand. Her eyes moved from her patient to her husband. For a moment, the husband thought his wife would come to him. In her eyes, on her face, he could see the enormity of what she had done weighed on her. She'd never amputated a limb before. But the moment passed. In her eyes, resolve replaced vulnerability.

Addison nodded toward pale Winifred. "Is she … ."

"She's alive," the healer said. "She lost some blood, but the tourniquet saved her life."

The front door banged open and the youngest Fishboch boy said, "The Healer's needed at the barn. My pa's been shot." And the boy turned and ran.

Mariah explained to Mrs. Abramson and Mrs. Farrell how to care for the mayor.

It turned out there were two more wounded Martinsville people in another bedroom, and the healer went to check on them.

There was a knock, and the door opened. Sal Martin and his wife Tish stood on the porch. Addison waved them in. "You here to help with the wounded?"

Mr. Martin stared at Winifred.

Mrs. Martin answered, "Yes."

Mrs. Farrell glanced down at her patient. Still unconscious. She said, "The healers back here. I'll show you."

Addison left the house and headed toward the activity beyond the south edge of town.

Fred Farrell was with the group behind the on-its-side wagon, as was Hound. A man held the dog's rope leash while it strained to get away. To head after Eunice, Addison figured. The light gray fur under Hound's snout was red.

Rifles banged out on the prairie by the Hermann wagon.

Addison drew his pistol and walked down the trail trampled through the knee-high prairie grass by Mrs. Reedley. His eyes were busy. One instant, they scanned the ground for ruts or things that would trip him. Then they searched ahead and to the sides for ambushers.

When he arrived at the Hermann wagon, Mrs. Reedley was talking to her crew, two men and two women.

Addison looked to his left, gasped in a breath, holstered his pistol, and removed his hat. Bodies of men and horses carpeted a large area. "Dear God in heaven!"

"You say something, Marshal?" Mrs. Reedley asked.

He could only wave his hat at the landscape of death.

"We've got the wagon loaded with weapons and saddles," Mrs. Reedley said. "I planned to send James and Kate here—she half nodded to her left—with the wagon to the cannon house and get it unloaded, then return here. That okay with you?"

Addison nodded. "Any wounded secesh?"

"Three were, but they tried to shoot us."

"When the wagon returns, load the bodies and take them to the field across from the mayor's house. And Mrs. Reedley, don't let up on your guard. We might still have bushwhackers hiding in the prairie grass."

"The dead horses," Mrs. Reedley said. "I'll butcher two for supper tonight and bury the others where they lay."

Addison agreed. "I'm going to the barn. Dealing with the dead men and horses in the cornfield will be more complicated. Don't want to destroy any more of the crop. And there's a lot more dead men and animals. Sometime this afternoon, I want to get together in the Meeting House to take stock of things. I'll send a messenger once I pick a time."

At the on-its-side wagon, Addison sent those assembled there out to help Mrs. Reedley. Except for Bert Bailey. He struggled to keep Hound from charging off onto the prairie.

Addison said, "Hound!"

The dog stopped pulling against the leash.

Addison said, "Hound, come," and started walking toward the edge of town.

Hound whined, then followed. As did Bert.

# 36.

At three in the afternoon on the last Friday of September, the marshal met with Mrs. Reedley, Ruben, Ansel Fishboch, and Preacher Cromwell around a table in the Meeting House. Addison had not invited Ansel because his pa had been killed by the cornfield bushwhackers, but the young man had heard about the meeting and asked to come. Eunice had not yet returned from her mission.

The preacher led them in a prayer.

The marshal announced that Ansel would take notes in his journal on what transpired during their meeting. Young Fishbock sat next to the marshal so he could see what was being written.

The marshal led them through a review of the events that had led up to and occurred during Thursday. "I want to mention here my decision to rely on the extra tall belltower rather than on manned compass point lookout posts a quarter mile from town. I worried about it being harvest time and keeping eight of our people tied up with sentry duties around the clock when there was so much work to do in the fields, and this being our first harvest—"

"I know what you're doing," Mrs. Reedley butted in, "you're going to say you made a mistake by stopping the manning of the lookout posts. Have you forgotten that Orson Seiling snuck up on you at the southern post? The secesh knew about our sentry posts, and they even knew how we handled the eastern one, manning it before sunup. Keeping our compass point posts manned wouldn't have made a lick of difference. But through these two days, you camped out here in the vestibule, and then in the barn, and kept in touch with what was going on through the sentries in the tower and reports from—"

"You, Mrs. Reedley." Addison had not intended to use the harsh tone of voice he'd heard himself employ.

"I'm sorry for snapping at you. However, we don't have a lot of time. The preacher is conducting a burial service for the fifteen secesh killed south of town—he glanced at the wall clock—in fifty-five minutes. Tomorrow will be busy as well. Since I got snuck up on, I started keeping a journal of the lessons I've learned being marshal. It is my hope it will help the person who follows me make fewer mistakes than I have."

Mrs. Reedley gave the marshal a tiny smile. "Apology accepted."

Addison felt his cheeks grow warm. Then he shook his head as if mosquitoes buzzed around his ears. He cleared his throat. "Mrs. Reedley, will you give us a rundown on what happened south of town?"

"First, though," the preacher cut in. "We should take note of what Mrs. Reedley said. 'The secessionists knew about our sentry posts and how we handled the eastern one.'"

Ansel scribbled on his pad of paper.

Mrs. Reedley didn't wait for Ansel to finish writing. "When the warning bell rang at two a.m., everyone responded well. A defensive position was established just beyond the south edge of town. And all of us knew the O'Reilly brothers and their dog would be visiting the compass point lookout posts. So, nobody shot at them when they rode back to town. Letting everyone know our plans was important. If the people hadn't known, we'd have killed the brothers as they rode back.

"Sending the O'Reillys with Hound to scout the sentry posts:

Good decision. It, more than anything else, upset the bushwhackers plan and saved us."

A spike of annoyance fired in the marshal's head. *She keeps grabbing control—*

Preacher Cromwell said, "So, the lesson here is never stop worrying about your enemy's intentions."

Addison: "Thanks, Preacher. One more thing, Mrs. Reedley. When we pulled our people off the southside defensive position and deployed them along Third Street—"

"Seemed like the best thing to do," said Abigail Reedley. "By that time, you'd had information from Eunice, and Hound, about signs they'd seen, and we talked about where they could be, and settled on that southwest to northwest wedge as the most likely area they'd attack from."

Addison nodded. "But then they came at us from the south, after we'd pulled our defenders from that side of town."

Ruben: "Marshal, several times I heard you say this bunch of bushwhackers had some savvy fighters among them."

Marshal Freeman: "Yes, and it was fortunate we had Maybell in the tower. She rang the bell to warn of an attack from the south, even though I'd left word to not ring the bell but to pass the word by messenger."

Mrs. Reedley: "Immediately after the bell stopped ringing, Ezra Gundecker, he was in charge of those along that half of Third Street, ordered everyone to return to the on-its-side wagon. The last to move were Lorelei Seiling and Ezra. They were both wounded before they reached the wagon."

"Are Lorelei and Ezra, and the mayor, still in the Farrel home?" the preacher asked.

Mrs. Reedley: "No. Ezra is in his house. His wife is taking care of him. Lorelei is here in the Meeting House. In Ruben's room. He's been assigned the O'Reilly house to live in. And the mayor was carried on a stretcher to Mrs. Freeman's house, where the healer has her office."

Addison: "Mrs. Reedley, I heard Hound killed the bushwhacker who shot the mayor. That right?"

"Yes. Hound killed him." She paused, then, "He's one of those to be buried at four."

The marshal: "Ruben, tell us about the Third Street defenders on the other side of the barn."

Ruben: "The bushwhackers didn't start shooting until they were almost clear of the corn. Albert Fishboch was in charge, and he'd told our people to not fire until after the bushwhackers started shooting. When the secesh did start shooting, they were aiming their pistols at the barn. Then, Albert ordered, "Fire," and we knocked a number of men from their saddles. The cannon roared, and the corn field was filled with men falling off horses, horses bucking and screaming and running back through the corn. Albert fired his rifle a couple of times, then he noticed how much corn the bushwhackers had flattened, and he hollered, 'My corn,' and he walked out from behind a shed, firing, screaming, firing again. Till he went down. Killed. Marcel Neidermeier went to help him, and he was killed, too. Then the cannon fired a second time, and the secesh were done. Nothing was left of them but dead and wounded. And horses, some dead, some struggling to stand, but unable." Ruben stopped talking.

Addison allowed a moment of silence to tick by.

Then the marshal said, "Ansel, would you go into the vestibule and holler up to the tower. Ask them if they see anything coming from the south. Like Eunice, maybe."

Ansel pushed back from the table, strode to the door, pulled it open, and hollered, "Lookouts, see anything to the south?"

A pause, then: "Clear south."

As Ansel shut the door, "Clear all around."

Addison invited Ruben to talk about gathering up the weapons of the bushwhackers in the cornfield.

"When I drove the Hermann wagon onto the cornfield, it was rough going. We got jostled around something fierce. I put two riflemen afoot behind us, so they'd be better able to protect us. And we needed their protection. In all thirty-two secesh attacked through the corn. All of them were killed by rifle bullets and grape except for eight who were wounded. Five of them shot at us, and they died. The other three bushwhackers are still in the barn with the healer."

Marshal Freeman: "Mariah said she expects all three to recover. And I asked Hermann to build a cell for them on the back of the Cannon House." Then, he looked at Ruben. He had planned to ask him to relate plans for the dead secesh and their horses, but Ruben sat with his shoulders slumped and staring at the tabletop.

Addison decided to tell that story. "In the corn, like to the south, once their riders had been shot, half of the horses managed to run away. Tomorrow, after we have the funerals for Albert Fishboch and Marcel Niedermeier, we'll bury the thirty-two cornfield bushwhackers next to where the south-of-town ones will be laid this afternoon. Any questions?"

No questions, but Mrs. Reedley had one more observation. "Last night, Marshal, when you had people go around town and light lamps, and then later put them all out, I think it fooled the secesh into thinking we had at least half our people in their houses. Put that down as a good idea, Ansel."

"A more important point," Addison said, "is that every man, woman, and child of this town did their jobs, and did them well. Now, I think we should adjourn and get to—"

Ruben interrupted. "I got something to say."

Addison looked at Preacher Cromwell. He said, "Go ahead, Ruben."

Ruben stared at the preacher. "When I was with the gang that wanted to stop you from getting here, we intended to kill all of you. Children included. We wanted all the adults dead, and then it would have been cruel to leave the children untended. That's what we told ourselves. And, we would not have buried you. We'd have left you for the buzzards.

"But this morning, Marshal Freeman asked me to search the pockets of the dead raiders from the south of town. To see if they carried anything that might identify them. Only four of the fifteen had letters. He entered those names in his journal. Then he said he wanted some way to list the others as well. The first of the other eleven went into his journal as—I remember the first one—Less than thirty. Brown hair. Skinny. Average Height. While he was doing that, I thought he was turning these blood thirsty killers back into men before we buried them.

"And for the first time, I saw what I had been before you all took me in."

Addison searched for something to say.

After a moment, Preacher Cromwell closed the meeting with a short prayer.

The prayer he said at the burial that afternoon was not so short.

Preacher began with, "Brothers and sisters, we are gathered here this afternoon to bury our enemies. Men who came hoping to slay us. And Thank You, Lord God Almighty. You saved us and laid them low. But brothers and sisters, these are not just enemies. They are also creatures created by God, just as we, all of us, were created out of His holy mercy and love. At the time of our death, when a soul takes leave of mortal flesh, we do not know if there is time for that soul to repent of evil doings, even those being committed at the time of death.

"So, brothers and sisters, join me in praying that our loving God created us that way, with a last-minute, just after life on earth ends, to grasp salvation. And that one day, we will join these men in heaven praising God forever."

Addison thought: *Praise God standing next to a murdering secesh?*

In the next instant, though, the potato that liked to shove his Adam's apple aside from time to time was back.

Mariah, next to him, whispered, "You're hurting my hand."

He raised the hand to his lips and kissed it as a tear dropped onto it.

Preacher then read the four names and eleven sets of descriptives and concluded the service.

Next was a communal supper in the Meeting House.

Waiting for them there were Joshua Reedley and Jibway Jim.

# 37.

Preacher Cromwell led everyone to the Meeting Hall.

Addison worried about Martha Fishboch and Frannie Niedermeier, the two new widows, and how they would take the preacher's words. Martha and Frannie stayed by the fresh graves. The marshal remained as well, though he couldn't think of a thing to say them. Mariah would know what to do, but she was tending the mayor.

The last of the crowd filed away, leaving Addison's ma and Mrs. Reedley behind. Abigail Reedley approached Frannie Niedermeier with open arms, and Frannie walked into them and sobbed on Abigail's shoulder.

Martha Fishboch glared at Addison's Ma, and snarled, "Why did Preacher Cromwell say that? Stand beside those—she pointed toward the mounds of freshly turned dirt—heathen, murdering, baby killers and praise God with them in heaven? If they go to heaven, I don't want to go there!"

Mrs. Freeman grabbed Mrs. Fishboch by the shoulders and shook her. "Martha! Martha! Listen to me!"

Addison was surprised. He'd never seen his ma behave so forcefully with anyone.

"Harden not your heart, Martha. If you keep that hate inside, you cannot go to heaven. You will go to hell and be with the ones who did not grasp the last-minute chance for salvation."

Martha raised a hand to her cheek. As if she'd been slapped. Her hard-hearted-Martha mask shattered. She sucked in a couple of breaths that were part sobs; then Addison's ma embraced her.

The two widows needed help bearing their burdens. Two very different approaches had been required for them to accept it. *Thank You, Lord God, Ma and Mrs. Reedley were here!*

Mrs. Reedley stepped back. "We don't have to go to the Meeting House. Come home with me. I'll fix us some supper."

Frannie shook her head. "All day, the people here have been so supportive. I may not be able to eat anything, but I need to go there and thank them."

"I'm going, too," Martha said. "Martinsville is more a family name than a town name. I need to be with my family."

The two widows hugged. And cried for a time. Then they separated and used their hankies.

Addison watched the four women link arms and set off for the Meeting House. He tagged along behind.

Preacher Cromwell waited for them in the vestibule. "Ladies, I wanted to warn you before we go in. Joshua Reedley and Jibway Jim returned while we were all at the graveyard."

Martha extracted her arm from under Abigail's. "Go to your husband."

Abigail tucked her arm under Martha's. "I'm going in with you. Then, I'll go to him."

Preacher Cromwell opened the double doors.

Peering over the ladies, everyone from Martinsville, except for the sentries, appeared to be standing by tables and staring out into the vestibule. It was quiet in the hall. A child fussed. A mother shushed. The silence settled again, a quiet of anticipation tinged with trepidation.

The four women entered the hall and stopped behind the first row of tables, and in the center aisle. Addison noticed Joshua and Jibway, with Maybell beside him, standing in front of the curtain. Preacher Cromwell stepped to the left of the ladies. Addison thought he intended to speak.

Before the preacher opened his mouth, Martha said, in a Preacher Cromwell voice, "My brothers and sisters, I want to thank you for the support—she glanced at Frannie, who nodded—you've given to Frannie and me all through this difficult day." She turned to her left. "And thank you, preacher, for your words back at the graveyard. My soul needed those words. They reminded me of another thing you told us. 'Hate the sin but love and forgive the sinner.'

"So, thank you, Preacher. Thank you, Mrs. Freeman. And thank you all for your example. And now, Preacher, perhaps you'd like to offer a word of welcome to Joshua and Jibway, and then lead us in prayer. My son Caleb is looking at me with *Ma, it's way past supper time* written all over his face."

After the welcome and grace, the parade of platters and bowls from the kitchen began. Addison marveled at the kitchen crew his ma had trained. At sunrise, many of the women had been along Third Street firing a repeating rifle. He shook his head, then made his way to Joshua and Jibway.

Joshua said, "Marshal."

Jibway touched the scar on his blood brother's forehead. Addison knew he was taking some of the wound to himself.

Addison: "Sure happy to see the two of you. I was getting worried."

Jibway: "We had to be careful. All the way through and down to the southeast corner of Missouri, we were surrounded by pro-south people."

Joshua: "We couldn't risk a letter falling into the wrong hands."

Addison: "Too bad you didn't get here coupla' days sooner. Could'a used your help."

Jibway: "You all handled things, from what we've heard. Forty-four secesh killed and three prisoners; and Eunice is chasing down two others."

Joshua: "Four dead and three wounded. A heavy price to pay. Coulda' been a lot worse."

Addison sought solace in those last words and found a measure of it. Then, "Anything we need to talk about right away?"

Joshua: "It'll wait. Tomorrow's more burying. Then Sunday. Monday will do."

Maybell: "Mariah is with the mayor. They've already had supper. Eat with us."

Addison did. He, Maybell, and Abigail Reedley filled Joshua and Jibway in on all that had happened over the last few days. Over coffee, Addison told the table about Maybell disobeying one of his orders. To not ring the bell if an attack came from an unexpected direction, but to send word by messenger. But Maybell had seen the secesh bunch coming from the south, appreciated the urgency of the situation, and rang the bell. "If she hadn't rung that bell, we'd have had more Martinsville people to bury."

Maybell: "I's blushin'—"

Jibway finished his wife's explanation. "Being colored, I gots to tell yuh when I be blushin','"

Saturday morning, Preacher Cromwell conducted a funeral service for Albert Fishboch and Marcel Niedermeier in the church. Following the service, the two men were buried next to the O'Reilly brothers.

At ten, the preacher conducted a graveside service for the cornfield secesh.

At eleven, Eunice and her partners arrived back in town. They'd shot and killed the two bushwhackers fleeing south. Neither carried anything to identify them. Both were buried out on the prairie.

"You need something to eat?" a woman asked.

Eunice shook her head. "Ain't closed my eyes in two days. Just wanna' sleep."

The wives of the two men who'd ridden with Eunice took charge of them. Mrs. Freeman left with Eunice. Others took care of the horses, the three the trio had ridden, their spares, and the two bushwhacker mounts. All had been pushed hard.

That afternoon, Addison sent six men to round up secesh mounts that had fled the cornfield heading west. Most of the rest of town set to burying the dead secesh horses to the northwest of the cornfield.

That evening, the roundup men returned, each leading two broncs on ropes.

Through Saturday night and into Sunday morning, the marshal did not post sentries at the compass point lookout posts. Every three hours, though, Ruben and Hound visited all four posts. Joshua Reedley rode with him on the first, Jibway on the second, and Ansel Fishboch on the third.

On Sunday, Preacher Cromwell declared a day of thanksgiving for Martinsville. Thanks for deliverance from the hands of their enemies, for the lives and service of Sean, Timothy, Albert, and Marcel, and for the wounded: Lorelei, Ezra, and Mayor Winifred.

Preacher Cromwell concluded the extra-long service with, "And thank You, Lord, for assembling this band of holy warriors to do Your will here, in Martinsville. This extraordinary band of holy warriors whose hearts are fierce in battle while at the same time able to love our enemies ... as soon as they stop trying to kill us."

Following the service a communal dinner was held in the Meeting House.

That night, the people of Martinsville all seemed to prefer supper in their own homes. Addison thought pretty much all of them hankered for a return to normalcy. His Ma, however, was concerned with those who'd had their picture of what was normal shattered. She commandeered a couple of tables in the Meeting House, and with two helpers, prepared a meal for widows Martha and Frannie, and wounded Winifred and Lorelei. The Reedleys, Jibway, and Maybell came too.

After supper, as the Reedleys were leaving, Joshua said to Addison, "First thing tomorrow morning. Your office. That all right with you?"

The marshal replied, "Yes, sir."

# 38.

The Monday morning meeting convened in Mrs. Freeman's house. The mayor wanted to attend. The healer, however, did not want her patient to move farther than from the bedroom to a stuffed chair in the living room.

Mariah arranged for wounded Lorelei Seiling to move in with Frannie Niedermeier; then she reestablished her healer's office in what had been the Ruben room.

Contrary to Joshua Reedley's opinion that the meeting should get together "First thing, Monday morning," the attendees were not all in place until just before nine. Assembled were the marshal, the mayor, Joshua, Jibway, Maybell, Preacher Cromwell, Eunice, Mrs. Reedley, Mrs. Freeman, and Ruben.

Preacher Cromwell said a prayer. One not too long. Nor too short. They all amen-ed.

Joshua: "Abigail told me the secesh knew about our lookout posts and how we handle them. You think she's right, Marshal?"

"I do. Through two days of dealing with them, it was clear. They knew a lot about us, and they were a wily bunch."

Jibway: "Many travelers pass through here now? When we left, there weren't."

Abigail Reedley: "A few more. David Isaacson comes through once a month. With his wagon train to supply us and the militia down south. Should be through here tomorrow or the next day."

Eunice: "David and his crew always spend the night here. Used to be I knew most of his wagon drivers and outriders. Last coupla' months, though, I didn't know any of them."

Abigail: "Last month, I asked Isaacson about the new people with him. One of them had asked if he and his friends could join the wagon train, as they wanted to enlist in the militia down by the Indian Territory. They could drive wagons and serve as outriders, and David wouldn't have to pay them. He didn't have a regular crew. Just hired what he needed for each trip." She looked at Addison. "Shoulda' told you, Marshal."

Addison: "How would Isaacson get his wagons back to Atchison if his whole crew was going to join the militia?"

Abigail: "David asked the young man that very question. He replied, 'There's men down there whose enlistment expired. They'll drive your wagons back to Atchison.'"

Addison: "That's how the secesh knew about our lookout posts. They spent the night here last month with the wagon train."

Eunice: "Isaacson always uses the road farther east to return to Atchison. So, we never see him on his return trip."

They discussed what to do about the impending visit from Isaacson's wagon train. Should they try to divert it to the eastern road, or should they allow the train to enter Martinsville as usual? They decided on *as usual* and developed a plan:

The new plan:

Eunice, Ruben, and Hound would go to meet Isaacson and his wagons. David knew Eunice and Ruben.

Eunice was to tell David that Martinsville had been attacked by a large band of secesh. The town had suffered losses but fought off the raid. She'd say the marshal sent her and Ruben to scout toward Atchison to make sure no band of secesh hid beside the road to waylay the supply wagons.

As soon as the tower sentries spotted wagons, they'd ring the bell, signaling a designated half of the adult population of Martinsville to assemble behind the houses on Main Street. Isaacson would be allowed to lead his train into town and stop, as he always did, at the Meeting House, his wagons strung out behind him.

Addison, as he always did, would meet the wagon train from the boardwalk. When he raised his hand in greeting, those behind the houses would swarm out and disarm the drivers and outriders.

After Eunice and Ruben rode off in accordance with the plan, Addison, Joshua, and Jibway interrogated the three wounded secesh. They spent half an hour with each, trying to get them to respond to questions, but all three sat silent and staring at the floor. It was explained that if they did not respond to questioning, they would be executed by firing squad. The warning did not dent their armor of sullen silence.

The recommendation to execute the three was presented to the council and approved. A firing squad was selected by drawing straws, and the sentence was carried out. Addison watched, and, as it always did when he witnessed unarmed men being mowed down, it hollowed the inside of him from his Adam's apple to his belly button. The deceased were buried. Preacher Cromwell prayed for all those in Martinsville who'd been forced to kill other men to protect their town and its people. He prayed for the hard-hearted secesh who would not give up their hatred.

Following the service, the people returned to their homes for their midday meal.

At one, Martha Fishboch, who'd taken over her husband's role as manager of the town's farms, ordered all able-bodied workers into the fields. Everyone was to be armed. When the tower bell rang, those designated were to drop their tools and hustle to assemble behind Main Street.

The bell didn't ring that day. But it did the next. At ten in the morning.

The new plan worked well. For the people of Martinsville. Seven drivers and four outriders were secessionists. Each of the four outriders drew a pistol when the Martinsville people swarmed the wagons. All four were blown out of their saddles.

The seven secesh drivers were herded into the cannon house and guarded there. Addison, Joshua, and Jibway questioned them one by one. Five were executed by firing squad. The other two confessed they expected to find Martinsville burned to the ground and no one left alive. But if part of the town still stood, they were to gather as much information as they could about the people who remained and report to their leader in the Indian Territory.

Jibway: "These last two, they should be shot also. They talked to us because they're scared of dying. We can't trust them to become like Ruben."

Addison: "It took a long time before Ruben started to come around, to see us as human beings and not just hated abolitionists. It may not happen, but perhaps one, or even both, will see the good in the people living here, and see, as Ruben did, that what he'd been told about us was wrong. I'm going to recommend to the council that we lock them in the cell Hermann added onto the rear of the Cannon House."

Jibway and Joshua said nothing.

With the town council's approval, Addison picked five men and two women to drive Isaacson's wagons south to resupply the militia.

Joshua and Jibway would serve as outriders. They'd depart first thing in the morning.

That afternoon, the group reassembled in Addison's ma's living room. Joshua and Jibway reported on their foray through Missouri. They thought the people of the state were predominantly pro-south, and more for states' rights than for slavery. A few towns had a Union Army contingent assigned to them. "Like an island of north in a big sea of south," Jibway said.

Joshua said, "I think the Blue Bellies around Independence serve as a buffer between Missouri secessionists and us here in Kansas. That includes the Colored Regiment."

Jibway: "Throughout the state, southern sympathizers are not shy about spouting their allegiance to anyone who will listen. You can pretty much tell a northerner by how quiet he is, like he wouldn't even say 'Ow!' if you stomped on his toe."

Joshua: "There are bands of … outlaws, I'll call them, scattered about the state, some about the size of the bunch that attacked you all here, but I do think the forces around Independence can handle those. Confederate army units could come out of Arkansas and slash across the state and south of Independence and get to us, but I wouldn't expect anything like that until summer next year."

Jibway: "The outlaws we heard about attack from ambush. Let their enemies get close without suspecting they're in danger. Then they bust out of hiding, screaming and shooting, and all bunched up. Them being bunched and us with repeating rifles saved us last year, and again when they attacked you last week. Of course, you also had cannon and grapeshot."

Joshua: "So far, we've been able to handle the outlaw bushwhackers, but if a Confederate Army unit comes up out of Arkansas, cuts across Missouri with hundreds of men, and cannon of their own, that'll be altogether something else for us to contend with. Something for us to ponder over the winter."

Jibway: "In the meantime, when we deliver the supplies to the militia, maybe we can figure out what other devilment the Indian Territory secesh are planning for us."

Joshua: "Any questions, Madam Mayor? Or anyone else."

Winifred had listened attentively to the discussion, but she was looking tired now.

Mayor Winifred: "Thank you for going on and completing your mission and for sharing what you learned. Perhaps you and Jibway should go home to your families now. See if your wives even remember what you like for supper. Preacher. Adjournment prayer please."

After that, the mayor asked Addison to help her back to her bed. "You know," she said, "a one-armed person helping another."

# 39.

Mid-October, mid-afternoon, Addison and Eunice sat across from each other at the table in the marshal's office, discussing the two secesh prisoners from Isaacson's wagon train, Charlie Maxwell and Warren Simpson.

Eunice: "When we captured them, Maxwell and Simpson were just scared kids. This morning, when Ruben and I visited where Charlie Maxwell was working, we found our young men working with him acting too friendly. I had Ruben watch Charlie while I talked to our people, reminding them that Charlie was our enemy. That two weeks ago, Charlie Maxwell wanted to see all of us in Martinsville dead and our town burned down.

"Talking to Ruben afterward, he said he thought Charlie had never been as all-fired anti-abolitionist as he, himself, had been. That maybe Maxwell and Simpson had been told they'd be shot if they didn't follow orders. To ride with the others to Atchison and then volunteer to drive Isaacson's wagons."

Addison: "I saw the same thing with Warren Simpson. I also spoke with Ruben about him. He thinks Warren and Charlie are both good at fitting in. That they had to become that way to survive."

Eunice: "Do we go to the town council and recommend they be executed?"

Addison: "Not yet. I'm going to ask Preacher Cromwell and Ruben to work together with each of them. It took a long time with Ruben."

Joshua and Jibway entered the marshal's office.

Jibway sniffed. "Ah! White man coffee."

Addison rose and stepped toward Jibway. The two pressed their blood-brother-scarred left thumbs together.

Then the marshal said, "Welcome home. Have a seat. And some coffee."

Eunice had placed cups and saucers on the table, and she filled them as the men took their places.

Jibway: "Wagon train's about an hour behind us."

Eunice: "Isaacson always arrives in time for supper."

Jibway took the chair next to Addison, Joshua the one next to Eunice. He sipped, and as always, his face betrayed nothing about what he was thinking. Next to him, however, Addison could feel his blood brother's anxiety to say something. But they all waited on Joshua.

Reedley finished his coffee, carefully placed the cup on the saucer, and stood. He said, "I need to see Abigail. Eunice, come along. I'll tell you both together."

Alarm flashed over Eunice's face. "Maurice?!"

Jibway: "He's not hurt. He's with the wagons."

Joshua took Eunice by the elbow and urged her to stand, urged her toward the door, and out.

Addison turned away from the door and faced his blood brother.

"Maurice," Jibway said. "He is not a wiseacre anymore." He sucked in a breath and huffed it out. "His enlistment expired. He'd planned to sign up again. Before he could, a band of Confederates—that's what they call them down there—attacked. The Kansas militia prevailed. After the fighting stopped, his captain handed his sword to Maurice and told him to finish off nine wounded grey coats. 'Ain't wasting no bullets on them,' the captain said.

"Maurice told the captain his enlistment was up, and he was not going to hack wounded men to death. The captain pulled his pistol and threatened to shoot Maurice on the spot if he did not carry out the orders he'd been given.

"Other Kansas militiamen were there, watching this all unfold, but according to the men from here, everybody was afraid to say or do anything for fear the captain would shoot Maurice.

"After Maurice stabbed the last Confederate, the captain holstered his pistol and said, 'Sergeant Reedley, clean my sword and bring it to my tent.' Then the captain turned and walked away. Maurice ran after him and smashed his shoulder into the officer's back. Sprawled him face down on the dirt. Maurice laid the sword on the ground, placed a boot across the blade, and jerked up on the handle, snapping the blade.

"One of the other men around the fallen officer said, 'Was I you, **cap'n,** I wouldn't say nothin' 'bout this.' Another: 'Was I you, **cap'n,** I'd desert."

Addison: "Maurice tell you that?"

"No. One of those from Brotherton Orson talked into signing up. Nielson."

The blood brothers thought about Orson for a moment.

Jibway: "That all happened in the morning. We arrived in the afternoon and set up a camp separate from the militia. Maurice and the others who joined the militia from Brotherton and here stayed with us until David concluded his business with the supply major. On the way back here, Maurice said he was not going back to the militia in the spring, and neither were his friends." After a pause. "He isn't a wiseacre anymore."

Addison: "Because of that captain?"

"Yes. Maurice said he wasn't fighting for anyone who had an officer like him on their side."

David Isaacson, his empty wagons, and the ex-militiamen returned to Martinsville in time for supper. Before the meal, however, there was a church service of Thanksgiving for their sons returning from military service alive and well.

Addison had looked forward to welcoming Maurice home. Eunice had ridden out to meet him. They had gone directly to their home. Which Addison found annoying on one hand and understandable on the other. *As if I had two good hands,* he chided himself. Then he remembered what Jibway had said about Maurice. During the service, Addison prayed for all the returnees and for Joshua and Abigail's son. Both of them attended the service. Neither came to the supper.

In the morning, Addison's ma and her kitchen crew prepared breakfast for the ex-militiamen from Brotherton and the men and women from Martinsville who'd drive Isaacson's wagons back to Atchison.

Maurice showed up for breakfast sporting a black eye. Everyone used the tables closest to the kitchen. Reedleys' son sat by himself. Addison took his plate and sat across from his friend. His friend rose and moved to another empty table. There he shoveled in his food and left the hall.

After the meal, those from Brotherton, including Maurice, struck out for home across the prairie. Isaacson and his crew departed.

Addison walked to his office. Eunice was there. She'd made coffee and poured a cup for the marshal at the table.

Eunice's lower lip was split and swollen. Her jaw sported a purple bruise.

"Maurice?"

She nodded and raised her cup to her lips, winced, and replaced the cup on the saucer.

"When I rode out to meet the wagons, Maurice didn't act like he was happy to see me at all. I asked him what happened. 'Nuthin', he said.' I said it sure looked like something happened, but he wouldn't say anything. The other men from here told me about the sword.

"We arrived back here, and he wanted to go home. So, we went there."

Eunice's cheek, the one that wasn't bruised purple, turned pink. "He was rough with me. Mean."

She sighed. "He said, come morning, he and I were leaving. Heading back to Brotherton. There we'd wait for a wagon train heading west to stop at Dobb's Trading Post, and we'd join it. I told him I wasn't leaving Martinsville. He slapped me, and I punched him. Knocked him flat on his butt. And I told him again I was not leaving this town. And that he was not sleeping in **my** house, and that he could sleep in the shed with the horses. Which he did."

# 40.

The rest of October slipped away. Peacefully. Vigilance, however, never slacked. Sentries manned the tower round the clock. At night, Eunice, Jibway, Ruben, and Ansel Fishboch took turns visiting the compass point posts with Hound.

In late November, word from Brotherton reported Maurice had hitched himself to a wagon train bound for Sante Fe. The mayor announced the news at a communal dinner following Sunday services. Addison and Mariah sat with Eunice, Joshua, and Abigail. Not one of the three reacted. However, the revelation did raise a chilly bank of invisible fog over the table. The fog contained a message: *Don't talk about Maurice!*

Abigail complimented Mariah on Hope's outfit. "Did you make it."

"No. Mrs. Freeman made it."

Then the food started arriving, and there were the children to tend. Eunice fed JR,

Abigail spoke with Hope as they both ate dainty bites, then resumed talking. Joshua also took dainty bites from his plate. Addison was pretty sure it was to keep food in his mouth as long as possible.

It was the most uncomfortable dinner Addison had ever attended.

After the meal, Addison and Mariah walked toward their house. Hope sat on Addison's shoulders saying "Giddup, Giddup." Mariah carried their son.

Mariah: "When Winnie mentioned Maurice, none of the Reedleys so much as blinked an eye. Did they already know?"

"It's possible. But Eunice has not wanted to talk about Maurice. Joshua doesn't say much, period. Has Abigail said anything?"

"Not that I've heard. And Eunice, maybe she needs some time to understand what happened to her husband and to their marriage."

Addison: "Well, all we can do is to pray for them."

The next day, Eunice arrived at the marshal's office. His deputy sat at the table across from him. Addison poured coffee for her. She sipped, grimaced, shook her head, and looked him right in the eye.

"You need to take Jibway, or Maybell, or Ruben as your deputy."

"What? Why?"

"I'm going to have a baby. Mariah says since I lost my first one, I have to rest, take it easy. 'Stay off of horses' she said."

The next day, a foot of snow fell. After Hermann and his bullet-shield snowplows cleared the streets, Addison and Jibway met in the marshal's office.

"Kansas," Jibway said. "A land where only winter can stop the bullets flying and the blood flowing."

"Blood Brother, I think you should be Martinsville's marshal."

"No, Addison J. Freeman. Even with one arm, you **are** this town's marshal. Take Ruben as your deputy. And please, God, let it be spring before Martinsville really needs the two of you."

# PRINCIPAL CHARACTERS

Addison J. Freeman, spouse Mariah, daughter Hope, son Jonathon Ruben (JR)

Joshua Reedley, spouse Abigail, son Maurice, daughter-in-law Eunice

Jibway Jim, spouse Maybell, daughter Glory

Preacher Larrimer

Preacher Rufus Cromwell

Otto Vogelsang, son Hermann

Ziggy Hostetler

Orson Seiling, spouse Lorelei

Winifred Martin

Albert Fishbock, spouse Martha, son Ansel, son Caleb

Ruben Fleming